Eric Wilder

New Orleans Dangerous

Gondwana Press

Edmond, Oklahoma

Other books by Eric Wilder

Ghost of a Chance
Murder Etouffee
Name of the Game
A Gathering of Diamonds
Over the Rainbow
Big Easy
Just East of Eden
Lily's Little Cajun Cookbook
Of Love and Magic
Bones of Skeleton Creek
City of Spirits
Primal Creatures
Black Magic Woman
River Road
Blink of an Eye
Sisters of the Mist
Garden of Forbidden Secrets

Gondwana Press
1802 Canyon Park Cir. Ste C
Edmond, OK 73013

For information on books by Eric Wilder
www.ericwilder.com

ISBN: 978-1-946576-09-5

Acknowledgments

I wish to thank Donald Yaw and Linda Hartle Bergeron for beta reading, editing, and providing valuable input involving timeline and character development. I'd also like to thank Andrea Annis and her daughter Brooke for their research that inspired me to write *New Orleans Dangerous*.

For Marilyn

New Orleans Dangerous

A novel by
Eric Wilder

Chapter 1

Murders rarely go as planned. Though Darth Heaney reflected on the thought as he field-stripped a cigarette before tossing it overboard, he wasn't worried about it.

A deckhand on the towboat Emma Lou, Darth was the lowest man on the totem pole. Though he'd worked onboard for more than a year, the rest of the crew hadn't let him forget it. Garbage duty, kitchen patrol, and all the extra early-morning watches didn't bother him as much as the names he'd heard the crewmembers call him: stupid, slow, dumb. None of the slurs bothered him as much as the torment heaped on him by one crewmember in particular.

Sammy Ray Nations was a huge man, his broad shoulders and muscular body covered in tattoos. He was the strongest person aboard the Emma Lou. At least that's what everyone thought. Everyone except Darth. Though Darth was only five-foot-six, he had the strength of a champion powerlifter. The strenuous labor he did on the boat only served to make him even stronger.

Sammy Ray had taken it upon himself to torment Darth since the day he signed on the Emma Lou. Spitting in Darth's eggs and then rubbing his face in the sticky mess was the least of Sammy Ray's transgressions against him. When the huge man cornered Darth in the shower and tried to bully him into performing oral sex on him, Darth's disgust had turned into burning hatred. Though years had passed since he'd killed anyone, he intended to change all that and to do it that very night.

Emma Lou was one of the biggest towboats on the lower Mississippi River. Its twelve-thousand horsepower engines pushed forty barges laden with thousands of pounds of cargo to St. Louis, and even more on the return trip to New Orleans. Twenty-eight days on and fourteen days off was the normal working schedule. The often-dangerous river journeys had never bothered Darth. He had no friends either on the boat or in New Orleans, the city he called home.

Now, the Emma Lou was less than five miles from New Orleans. Two in the morning, Darth puffed on the cigarette he'd lit from the last one he'd smoked. Sammy Ray was a light sleeper. He awoke around this time every morning to smoke, drink his cheap whiskey, and walk the deck. This particular morning, Darth had a plan for him. When Sammy Ray came into view, Darth stepped out of the shadows.

"What the hell!" Sammy Ray said as he took a backward step.

"Didn't mean to scare you," Darth said.

"You couldn't scare shit, you little shrimp. You come to suck my dick?"

"I got something to show you," Darth said, moving toward the much larger man.

Sammy Ray glanced down at Darth's cupped hands. "What the hell is it?"

"This," Darth said.

Darth opened his hands long enough to show the big man there was nothing in them, and then came up under Sammy Ray's chin with his right fist.

Sammy Ray's eyes blinked once as his knees collapsed and he sank to the deck. Darth looked around to see if anyone had witnessed the incident. Thick clouds covered the moon and stars leaving only darkness, Darth the only person awake except for the morning pilot in the wheelhouse on the far end of the large boat.

Darth used his switchblade to slit Sammy Ray's wrist and then began lapping the blood as it poured from the vein. Darth had a silver flask with a special engraving. It was the only thing his father had ever given him. After filling the flask with blood, he removed his shirt, using it to tie Sammy Ray's wrists.

He'd found an old anchor on the St. Louis docks. After hooking the barb through the shirt, he pushed Sammy Ray's body overboard. Even if the man's blood loss weren't enough to kill him, he would drown when the anchor dragged him to the bottom of the river.

Because of the strong currents in the middle of the Mississippi, Sammy Ray's body might not surface until it reached the Gulf of Mexico. If anyone ever found it, the anchor would be long gone. With no marks of violence except for the slit on Sammy Ray's wrist, the authorities would likely rule his death accidental.

There was little time to worry about it as

tugboats would soon arrive to break the barges loose to complete their river journey. It would still be dark when the Emma Lou docked, and the crew departed. No one would notice Sammy Ray was missing until he failed to pick up his paycheck at the company headquarters. Even then, days might pass before anyone went to check on the alcoholic seaman.

Darth Heaney left the Emma Lou, walking down the gangplank with a duffel bag over his shoulder. It wasn't far to the Riverwalk. Heavy fog was rolling in from the river when he reached the scenic New Orleans' walkway. Having decided to quit smoking, he tossed his pack of cigarettes into the bushes. A couple in the act of lovemaking didn't stop what they were doing as he walked past. Darth didn't notice, smiling when he saw the lights of Café du Monde.

Darth and his mother Mona Marie had lived in the Old Ursuline Convent on Chartres Street most of his life. She'd been the live-in caretaker there, dusting the statuary and mopping the corridors. She didn't make much money, but their lodging was free, and the nuns brought them food almost every day. When they didn't, Darth would buy fruits, vegetables and po'boy sandwiches at the nearby Farmer's Market.

He often visited Café du Monde. All the waiters and waitresses there knew him and always gave him free coffee and beignets when he showed up at the backdoor. Though he now made lots of money as a deckhand on the Emma Lou, he still went to the backdoor, drinking coffee and eating beignets with the people who worked there. He continued to smile, dusting powdered sugar off of his shirt as he headed back into the darkness.

Darth knew every alleyway in the French Quarter. After leaving Café du Monde, he took his own route to the Old Ursuline Convent. Colorful masonry walls hid the garden courtyards of the residences from the people passing on the streets. As they had for the past three hundred years, citizens of the Big Easy guarded above all else their privacy.

It was spring, flowers in full bloom. High walls couldn't mask the climbing roses cascading over them. Darth loved springtime better than any other season and used his switchblade to cut a rose from the bush. Before walking away, he inhaled the blossom's fragrant aroma.

The old Ursuline Convent of New Orleans wasn't far away. It lay deserted at night, all the doors, and windows locked, the courtyard surrounded by an eight-foot-high masonry fence to keep winos and homeless people from camping out inside. It didn't matter to Darth. He had a master key that could unlock every door in the building.

A cat screeched in a nearby alleyway, garbage cans rattling as Darth opened a service entrance in the back of the building and slipped inside. Utility lights lit the hallway as he hurried past the main chapel, careful to avoid the security cameras.

Though the stairway was dark, Darth didn't miss a step as he hurried up the stairs to the second story. He knew every creaky board on the floor because he'd traversed it more times than he cared to count. Darth's head had begun to pound and he stopped a moment to massage his throbbing temples. When the pain subsided, he shook his head to regain his senses.

The convent was now a museum during the day and unoccupied at night. Except for the girl. She was as elusive as a gust of wind. He knew she lived alone in the convent though he didn't know where. He would sometimes feel her stare and maybe even catch a fleeting glimpse of her when he wheeled around. He could feel her now.

The second floor once had cells where the nuns lived. Now they were empty, much of the second floor a research library for scholars and visiting dignitaries. Not all the cells were vacant. His mother still occupied the one where he'd lived for much of his younger life. It wasn't where anyone could find it.

Forgotten by most, secret passageways laced the old building. Darth knew where they all were. Growing up, he'd had not a single friend and spent his days playing in the passageways and creating a fantasy world that sometimes crossed over into reality. When he tapped at a special spot on the wall, a sliding panel opened. Not needing a light to know where he was going, he entered the Stygian darkness of a hidden passageway.

His mother's room was behind a door at the end of the darkened hallway. Darth could find it in his sleep. After locating a candle in a cranny in the wall, he lit it. The convent was one of the oldest surviving buildings in the United States. It smelled like it when Darth opened the door.

The reek of must and mildew burned his eyes, causing him to sneeze as he went around the room lighting candles with a match from the souvenir box advertising the towboat Emma Lou. A single bed occupied the room, a washbasin with a mirror, two old chairs and little else. His head began to ache again.

"Hi, Mona Marie. You miss me?"

Darth got no answer to his question from the woman, or remains of the woman, lying in bed beneath a faded quilt. Long gray hair capped the eyeless skull, its teeth smiling in a perpetual grin. Something about the room was causing him to change into someone he wasn't. He bent down and kissed the skull, unmindful of the spider crawling out of the empty eye socket.

"Got something for you."

Darth slipped the red rose into the bony remains of his mother's hand.

"I'm in town for a while and happy to be home."

Darth climbed on the bed, lying beside his mother's skeletal remains. Flickering candlelight cast dancing shadows on the windowless walls of the cell. Only the sound of a mouse gnawing on something inside one of the walls, and bats stirring in the attic disturbed the room's silence.

"You're looking good. How you been?"

Darth rolled off the bed, not waiting for an answer. Before he'd taken a step, he grabbed his head with both hands, moaning as he sank to his knees. He rubbed his temples, trying to will the pain away. Long moments passed before he stood again, his grimace gone.

Darth's transformation was complete when he opened the door of a closet. Stripping off his clothes, he began donning the vestments of a Catholic priest. With an alb over his clothes and preaching scarf around his neck, he took the rose from the grasp of the skeletal hand.

"I see Darth is back in town. Tell him I'm looking for him. Right now, I have a service to perform."

Taking the rose with him, the person who had become Father Luc left the room, heading down the stairs to the first floor. The Old Ursuline Convent had many ornate altars. The altar to where Father Luc was headed was not one of them. He continued past the main altar to a door at the end of a dark hallway. Using his passkey, he entered a room that wasn't much bigger than a closet.

A small shrine occupied a wall in the little room, a silver chalice sitting on the communion table. Father Luc lit a votive candle atop the ancient altar painted in white enamel. He wasn't done. After placing the rose in a crystal vase and a hundred-dollar bill in the silver chalice, he grasped the stole around his neck, bowed his head and closed his eyes.

"With the blood of hogs on the altar of the King of Hell, I pray the god of all the minions below ratify my offering. Make me your strong right arm and give me the strength to destroy the Roof of Lucifer so that I may set you, the supreme master, once again free. In Nomine Satanas, sic faciam illud."

Father Luc left the altar to return to the hidden room on the second floor. Once he'd disappeared up the stairs, someone else entered the little room. Taking the blood-red rose from the vase, she replaced it with one that was white.

Chapter 2

Spring had arrived in the French Quarter. I realized it the moment I stepped out on my balcony overlooking Chartres Street. Tourists were stirring on the sidewalk below, a mule-drawn carriage plodding toward Jackson Square. Sounds of produce trucks unloading over by the French Market filled the air with the sweet fragrance of fresh fruits and vegetables, along with the perfume of magnolia trees and flowers in bloom around St. Louis Cathedral.

As I got dressed, Kisses, my cat lay in the sun, watching the sparrows and pigeons grousing for scraps of food dropped by tourists on the street. I lived in a small apartment over Bertram Picou's Chartres Street bar. Even though it was still early, I could hear Bertram's distinctive baritone voice as he held court for some lucky visitors to his establishment.

When I descended the stairs, I saw the place was empty except for two women sitting at the bar drinking martinis and talking to Bertram. One of the women was someone I knew and whom I hadn't seen in quite some time: Lilly Bliss, a writer I'd met during an assignment on a resort island south of New Orleans.

Like the last time I'd seen her, Lilly's hair was

short and black, and the same color as the frames of the thick glasses she almost always kept perched on her head. Though not a drop-dead beauty queen, her expressive green eyes could cast a spell on you if you weren't careful. Lilly smiled when she glanced up and saw me coming down the stairs.

"Wyatt," she said, getting off the barstool to give me a hug. "How are you?"

"A whole lot better after seeing your pretty face."

"Keep your eyes on this one, Avory. He'll have your panties off before you realize he's touching you," Lilly said.

Ignoring her catty remark, I said, "What brings you to New Orleans, Miss Lilly?"

"Couldn't quit thinking about that damn Cajun behind the bar," she said. "He has a better line of bullshit than you do, and I kind of like his coonass accent. Wyatt Thomas, meet my best friend, Avory."

Lilly's friend was laughing and shaking her head at Lilly's remark.

"Glad to meet you, Avory. Don't believe the stories Lilly tells you about me," I said. "She's a fiction writer, and that's pretty much synonymous with a paid liar."

Avory had blond curly hair, a glorious smile, and big blue eyes.

"Have we met?" she asked.

"Only in my wildest dreams," I said.

Avory glanced at Lilly and said, "I think you're right about this one."

"Miss Avory is a movie writer," Bertram said.

I gave her a closer look. "Of course, you're Avory Dorean."

"You have to be kidding," Avory said. "I'm not exactly a celebrity. How did you know who I am?"

"I never forget a face," I said. "While waiting

in a checkout line, I saw your picture in a movie magazine, and a little blurb about some of the scripts you've written."

"Avory and I are developing the script for the movie Quinlan is currently working on," Lilly said.

A Hollywood producer, Quinlan Moore, had hired me to investigate a gruesome murder at a resort island for artists and actors. It was on that assignment where I'd met Lilly. Quinlan had put me on retainer when he'd returned to New Orleans to film a movie.

Bertram and Lilly had become a number during the making of the movie. Even though Bertram had courted many women, none had meant quite as much to him as had Lilly. He'd pouted for weeks after her abrupt departure. Lilly must have noticed my expression of concern when she caught me giving him a glance.

"If you're worried about Bertram and me, just stop it. I spent the night with him last night. In fact, I may never leave again," she said. "Isn't that right, Bert?"

"Baby doll, ain't a minute gone by since you walked out the door that I haven't missed you," he said.

Lilly joined him on the other side of the bar, putting her arms around him.

"You're a bigger liar than Wyatt. I still love hearing it. I also missed you, more than you'll ever know."

"Enough to spend all your time here in New Orleans with me?"

"Sweetie, I was hoping you'd ask because when we arrived in town, I didn't bother checking into a hotel," Lilly said. "Take my stool, Wyatt. I'm going to help my wonderful man behind the bar."

Lady, Bertram's collie, must have missed Lilly as much as Bertram had because her tail was wagging when Lillie knelt down and gave her a hug.

"Can you and Lady watch the place for a while, Cowboy?" Bertram asked. "Me and Miss Lilly got some important business in back to attend to."

"Why not?" I said. "Won't be the first or the last time Lady and I held down the fort for you. With no customers, it'll be a piece of cake."

Before leaving, Bertram mixed Avory another martini and poured me a glass of lemonade.

"Mind if I try it?" Avory said. I handed her my glass and watched as she took a sip. "There's no liquor in here."

"I'm an alcoholic," I said. "Though I fall off the wagon every now and then, I've remained mostly sober for several years now."

Someone came in the door. It was Quinlan Moore. "Wyatt, my man," he said. "Just the person I was looking for. I see you've already met Avory."

"Bertram and Lilly are in the back," I said, stepping behind the bar. "What are you drinking?"

"Vodka, with a splash, and only a cube or two of ice."

"Gotcha. Lilly said you were in town doing some leg work for a new movie."

Quinlan hugged Avory and gave her a kiss. As I mixed his drink, he stood behind her and draped his arms over her shoulders.

"I'm scouting locations."

"What's your movie about?" I asked.

"Don't know yet. It's still in pre-production. Got any ideas?"

"You can barely wake up in the morning in New Orleans without tripping over a new mystery," I said.

Once an actor, Quinlan Moore was a

handsome man with dark eyes and blond hair beginning to gray around his temples. The nerdy pencil mustache he'd sported when we'd first met was gone. Quin was dressed in dark slacks, his expensive sports coat highlighting his broad shoulders. The buttons of his silk shirt were opened enough to reveal his hairy chest. He gave Avory another kiss on the neck.

"How you doing?" he asked.

"Taking it all in," she said.

"When I'm in the Big Easy, Wyatt's my man from Havana. He's helped me a bunch in the past. Wyatt's always on retainer when I make a movie here."

"What do you do?" Avory asked.

"Investigations," I said.

"Avory and Lilly are developing the script for my movie," Quinlan said.

"Thought you didn't know what the movie's about yet."

"I soon will. Like you said, there's a story around every corner. Lilly already knows New Orleans. While I'm off developing locations, Avory needs someone to escort her around town. Have anything else going?"

"You know I'm happy to help out any way I can. You don't have to pay me to do that," I said.

"Nonsense," he said. "You're already written into the budget. How's Tony doing?"

"Good," I said.

"Who's Tony?" Avory asked.

"Tony Nicosia, a former homicide detective with the N.O.P.D.," I said. "Tough as nails and knows the underbelly of New Orleans like no one else in town. He's now a private investigator, and we occasionally hook up on projects."

"Tony's a sweetheart," Quinlan said. "He has buddies on the force who are always happy to assist. Though he doesn't know it yet, he's also on retainer."

"That'll make him happy," I said.

Quinlan glanced at his Rolex Commander. "Gotta run," he said. "Can you tell Tony I'm in town and that he's on the clock?"

"You got it, boss," I said, saluting.

"And Wyatt, please make sure you keep Avory happy while I'm off doing the dirty work of Hollywood producing."

Quinlan downed his drink before disappearing through the door. I locked it behind him.

"May as well shut the place down," I said. "No customers, anyway."

"Quin is maddening," Avory said. "If he weren't such a genius, I'd be happy to never see him again."

"He pays so well, I won't have to work for six months."

"Boring," she said. "I like staying busy. If I had a project, I'd work every day."

"You and Lilly are here on a project, or did I hear Quinlan wrong?"

"The script might not get written for months. The reason I'm here is Quinlan is my boyfriend. He doesn't like traveling alone."

"But. . ."

"I know," she said. "He's married."

"Does his wife know about your arrangement?"

"She could care less," Avory said. "Quinlan's rich and powerful and buys her anything she wants. She has her own boyfriend."

"Then why bother staying married?"

"They're a power couple. Quinlan's a producer, Penelope, an actress. They have two great children and all the money in the world."

"But. . ."

"Neither of them wants to take a chance on

losing even a whit of their power and influence by undergoing a messy divorce," Avory said.

"I see," I said. "And you?"

"I like being in the sphere of Quinlan's power and influence. I've written lots of movies because of him, even if I've had to occasionally twiddle my thumbs."

"My guess is you've never twiddled your thumbs."

Avory tapped her glass against mine. "I think I'm going to like you, Wyatt. Are you sure you're a private investigator and not an actor?"

"Closest I ever came to acting was a part in the Mikado in the fifth grade. I had one line, and I muffed it. Why would you think I was an actor?"

"You're good-looking enough to be a leading man. I wouldn't put it past Quinlan to hire someone to report back to him on what I'm doing."

"He wouldn't do that," I said.

"Oh, yes, he would. He's a control freak, or haven't you noticed?"

"I'm not an actor."

"And you're not married?"

"Nope."

"Where do you live?"

I pointed. "The top of that flight of stairs."

"A suite?"

"Just a small room and bath. I do have a balcony overlooking Chartres Street, and there aren't many places in the world as relaxing."

"I'd like to see it," she said. "Can you mix me another martini?"

"My pleasure." Lady was taking a nap behind the bar when I joined her. "Even if my martinis aren't as good as Bertram's, I've never had any complaints."

"I'll bet you haven't," she said.

Avory couldn't believe her eyes when we went

upstairs, and I opened my apartment door.

"I told you it was small," I said.

"I like it," she said. "It has the ambiance of Antebellum New Orleans. I'll bet this is how it felt two hundred years ago."

"You can say that about any place in the Quarter. My little apartment is comfortable. I wouldn't live anywhere else," I said.

Avory and I were soon sitting on the balcony in my deck chairs. Kisses jumped into her lap the moment she sat down.

"You don't seem to me like a man who likes cats," she said.

"Have you ever had one?"

"Several," she said. "I love cats."

She smiled when I said, "You don't seem like a woman who would like cats."

"Touché," she said. "Do you have a girlfriend?"

"Just Miss Kisses."

"I'd like to be your girlfriend while I'm in New Orleans."

"What about Quinlan?"

"Quinlan has the morals of an alley cat. He's probably in his hotel room right now screwing some waitress he picked up in a bar."

"He's not afraid you might return and catch him?"

Avory grinned. "Quin's too smart for that. We have separate rooms. Hell, we're not even staying in the same hotel. He knows how to play the game. It's likely I won't see him the entire time I'm here."

"Amazing," I said.

"Quin is paying you handsomely to keep me happy while I'm in town. Can you handle it?"

"Depends," I said. "What's the name of the game we're playing?"

"House," she said.

"I'm an investigator, not an escort service."

"Don't get your panties in a wad," she said. "I'm like Quin and hate being alone. Nobody said anything about sex, though it's not out of the question. I want to soak up the local culture. I think you're the one to help me do it and you told Quin you'd be happy to show me around."

"No problem," I said.

"I want to check out of my hotel and move in with you."

"That little bed is all I have. I love the wood floor, but it isn't very comfortable."

"We'll work something out," she said. "You may have a problem with my rules."

"Rules?"

"No permanent attachments. Once I leave town, I don't intend to ever see you again. No calls, no forlorn letters, nothing. Understand?"

"I thought all I was doing was to show you around town."

"I don't want to get started in this relationship if it's going to turn messy," Avory said.

"Since you're setting the rules, what does our relationship entail?"

"Like I told you, we're playing house. Why are you smiling?"

"Because you're so full of bullshit, I can't believe a word you say. Are you setting me up for some bad joke?"

"You want me to strip off my clothes, climb in your little bed and show you? Damn you, why don't you stop smiling?"

"Because this is like a teenager's fantasy, being asked by a gorgeous woman less than an hour after meeting her to have a no-holds-barred relationship with no permanent ties."

"You may not be serious. I am," she said.

Avory began unbuttoning her blouse. I was

still shaking my head in disbelief after she'd removed it and sat staring at me in her black, push-up bra.

"Getting cold feet?" I asked.

"Screw you. Every other man I've pulled this act on would have pretty much creamed his pants by now."

Her confident smile returned when I said, "How do you know I haven't?"

As Avory buttoned her blouse, she said, "We're going to have some fun together. I want to return to the hotel and get my bags. Will you take me?"

"Are you still acting?"

"The moment I saw you walking down the stairs, I knew I was going to like you. I don't know how this movie is going to turn out because I've yet to write the final scene."

Chapter 3

We took a cab to the hotel, Avory remaining silent during the ride. Though I didn't worry about it for long, I was wondering what I'd gotten myself into. I watched her disappear into the front door of the twelve-story Canal Street hotel.

Since the weather was delightful, I decided to walk back to Bertram's. I found Bertram and Lilly behind the bar, talking with a Catholic nun who was sitting on a stool and enjoying one of the Cajun bartender's martinis. Bertram flashed me a dirty look when he saw me.

"Where you been?" he asked. "We been looking for you."

"I took Avory back to her hotel."

"Well, someone's here to see you."

Since no one else was in the bar except for the nun, I introduced myself.

"I'm Wyatt Thomas."

The woman shook my hand. "I'm Sister Lydia. My diocese requires the services of a private investigator. Your name was suggested. I'm here to talk to you about it."

"Of course. How can I help?"

"What I have to say is confidential. Can we discuss the matter in private?"

"There's a booth in the back where we can have some privacy."

Sister Lydia smiled for the first time as she slid off the stool and gave Bertram a glance.

"Your martinis are very good, maybe the best I've ever tasted," she said.

"I'll bring you another," Bertram said. "And Sister Lydia, you're drinking on the house."

"Thank you," Sister Lydia said.

The tall nun was at least thirty years older than me, and maybe more. Because of her infectious smile and sparkling brown eyes, she was still quite attractive. When I needed to talk to a client in private, I always did so in my favorite booth in the back of Bertram's bar. Sister Lydia followed me there, craning her neck to make sure we were far enough away from Bertram and Lilly's ears before situating herself in the booth.

"Now, how can I be of service?" I asked.

"Are you familiar with the Old Ursuline Convent?"

"My mother took me there once when I was younger," I said.

"The fact that you are Catholic is part of the reason we are considering you for the job."

I didn't ask how Sister Lydia knew my religious preference.

"Maybe you'd better explain," I said.

"The Old Ursuline Convent is now a museum. As you probably already know, the convent is one of the oldest buildings in the United States."

"And?"

"We have a problem that requires attention," she said.

"Please explain."

Before Sister Lydia could answer, Bertram arrived with a fresh martini for her and another glass of lemonade for me. Sister Lydia waited until he'd returned to the bar before continuing with her story.

"The convent is closed at five. Last night, an illicit ceremony was performed there."

"Someone broke into the convent?"

"There's no indication anyone forcibly entered the building. Still, some unauthorized person was there last night."

"How do you know an illicit ceremony was performed?" I asked.

"You'll understand when I show you. Please take my word for it until then," she said.

"Have you reported this incident to the authorities?"

"The Old Ursuline Convent is part of the Greater Archdiocese of New Orleans. We prefer to handle as many problems internally as possible without involving the city. The Archdiocese wants our own person to investigate, and not the local police."

"Are you an Ursuline Nun?" I asked.

"I'm not. The Ursulines moved to a new convent long ago. The Old Ursuline Convent is part of the Greater New Orleans Archdiocese which includes the St. Louis Cathedral and St. Mary's Church. I work for the Archdiocese."

"I see," I said.

"The Archdiocese has already checked your qualifications. If you are amenable to helping us, then we need to discuss your fee."

"Like you said, Sister Lydia, I'm Catholic. I'll do anything I can to help you. No charge. When do we start?"

As if she'd expected nothing less, Sister Lydia nodded. After draining her martini, she slid out of the booth.

"Now, if you have no other plans."

Jackson Square lay between the Old Ursuline Convent and Bertram's. I stopped outside the door to hail a cab.

"It's an absolutely marvelous day," Sister Lydia said. "Let's walk."

The nun started up the sidewalk at such a fast clip I had to hurry to keep up with her.

"Isn't that habit a bit warm to expend so much energy?" I asked.

"I've grown accustomed to the tools of my occupation during my seventy years."

"You're not seventy, are you?"

"Nuns don't tell lies, Mr. Thomas."

Without commenting on her claim, I said, "Please call me Wyatt. Mister Thomas was my father's name."

As Sister Lydia had said, the day was marvelous. We weren't the only people on the sidewalk. Throngs of tourists and locals reveled in the beautiful weather and the sights and sounds of the French Quarter. When we reached Jackson Square, we found it alive with activity. Artists were painting portraits. In the plaza in front of Andy Jackson's statue, a jazz combo was holding court to an appreciative crowd.

Palm trees wafted in a gentle breeze, their fronds a vivid green usually seen only on the sandy beaches of some tropical isle. Sister Lydia clasped her rosary beads and closed her eyes when we strolled past the open doors of St. Louis Cathedral. It prompted me to reach for my St. Christopher's Medal before remembering I had lost it years ago.

Sister Lydia wasn't even breathing hard when we reached the Old Ursuline Convent farther up Chartres Street. Distant memories flooded my thoughts as we entered the gate. Sister Lydia introduced me to the person collecting admission from the visitors.

"This is Mr. Thomas. He's working for the Archdiocese and has free rein to the convent.

Please allow him to come and go as he pleases."

"Yes, ma'am," the young woman with curly hair and a single earring said.

I followed Sister Lydia down the sidewalk through the sculptured hedgerows decorating the expansive front lawn of the convent. When she pushed through the front doorway, I could almost smell the antiquity. Inside, everything was polish, lacquers, and vivid colors. Sister Lydia led us to the magnificent altar in the main chapel where she knelt, bowed her head, and said a prayer.

"I'd forgotten what a splendid example of French Colonial architecture this building is," I said.

"It's the oldest building in the Mississippi Valley; almost three-hundred-years old. Two floors and an attic level with three dormers. The building itself has twelve bays."

Sister Lydia frowned when I said, "Lots of threes there."

"I assure you, there is no numerological meaning intended."

Sensing my offhanded remark had annoyed the nun, I quickly changed the subject.

"Please show me where the ceremony took place," I said.

"Of course," she said.

I followed her to an unmarked door, which she opened with an antique key. The dark little room wasn't much bigger than a large closet. Sister Lydia pointed a flashlight at the small altar residing on a shelf on the wall.

"This closet has no light fixture," she said. "We'll have to make do with my flashlight."

"Has anything been moved?" I asked.

"We left everything as it was when we discovered the disturbance."

I inched past her for a closer look. A white rose occupied a small vase. Despite the darkness and the lack of water in the vase, the rose looked as fresh as the moment it had been cut from the vine. A patina of age coated a silver chalice resting in the middle of the lacquered altar. There were words engraved on the chalice.

"Can you translate the inscription for me?" I asked.

"Latin isn't an easy language to translate," Sister Lydia said.

"What do you think it says?" I asked.

"Pig's blood."

I gave her a glance, thinking maybe I'd heard her wrong. "Pig's blood? What does that mean?"

"You'll have to get the answer to that question from someone other than me," she said. "I've told you all I know about the inscription."

"You said there was a ceremony here last night. How do you know?"

"Look in the chalice."

Not wanting to desecrate the relic, I used my ball-point to tilt the silver chalice toward me. I fished out a fresh hundred-dollar-bill with the pen.

"What's the significance of the money?" I asked.

"Look on the back," Sister Lydia said.

When I flipped the bill over, I could clearly see the number 66 someone had written on it. The color was oxidized red. My best guess was the number was written in blood. Sister Lydia's reaction to my earlier comment about numerology became apparent.

"You think someone performed a satanic ritual here last night?" I asked.

"That's what I think happened," she said.

"Mind if I take a few pictures with my cell phone?"

"Go right ahead."

After taking multiple pictures of the altar, the

bill and the chalice, I said, "Since there was no forcible entry, is there anyone on your staff with access to the convent who might be responsible?"

"No," she said.

"Sure about that?"

"I'm sure."

"What about a caretaker, or perhaps someone on the janitorial staff?"

"We no longer have a full-time caretaker. The Archdiocese employs a contract janitorial service. The janitors have no keys to the building and only work when someone from our staff is close by."

"Does anyone other than your staff have a key to the building?"

Sister Lydia shook her head. "You now know as much as I do. Can you help us?"

"Maybe. Please show me around the museum."

After watching Sister Lydia relock the closet, I listened to her running commentary as I followed her through the museum.

"The convent has been a school for boys and girls, an orphanage, and even the residence of the Archbishop. It had fallen into a state of disrepair until we restored it to its former glory. It's now a wonderful museum chronicling much of the religious history of New Orleans."

The building was divided into various brightly painted rooms with polished wood floors, colorful statuary depicting nuns, priests and saints, and an almost overwhelming sense of antiquity. Exhibits and displays were marked to facilitate the visitor's self-guided tour of the museum. After leading me through the first floor, Sister Lydia removed the rope barrier blocking the stairs and started up them.

"The nuns who once occupied the convent lived in cells on the second floor. No one lives here now. The cells are empty. A portion of the second floor is a research library for visiting scholars."

After Sister Lydia had given me a tour of the library, I said, "What's in the attic?"

"It's empty," she said.

"I'd like to see it," I said.

"We have an alarm I'll need to disarm first."

I watched as Sister Lydia punched in a series of numbers on a keypad mounted on the wall.

"Why do you have an alarm if there's nothing up there?"

"You're from New Orleans. I'm sure you've heard about the Casket Girls."

"Please refresh my memory," I said.

Sister Lydia explained as I followed her to the top of the stairs. "Most of the early settlers to the colony were men. Women were needed to sustain its growth. France sent a group of young women to New Orleans for that reason. They brought all their earthly belongings with them in crates resembling caskets."

"And these women stayed in the convent with the Ursuline Nuns until they were married?" I said.

"Yes, and it led to rumors that the convent was occupied by vampires brought over from France by the Casket Girls. The young women were the supposed hosts of the vampires who lived in their caskets in the attic. It's an old wives' tale that won't go away."

Sister Lydia didn't smile when I said, "Maybe because there's a certain amount of truth in every old wives' tale."

"I understand why the rumors were propagated. After having spent months on a ship, mostly below deck, there's little wonder the women were pale and ashen."

"So there are no vampires in the attic?" I said.

We'd reached the alcove at the top of the stairs. Sister Lydia used her key to open the door. "You're about to see for yourself," she said.

Chapter 4

I almost expected to see bats fly out of the attic door when Sister Lydia opened it. That didn't happen. Unlike the floors below, the attic wasn't paneled, ceiling beams and braces unpainted, the walls unfinished. Unpolished wood creaked when I stepped through the door.

"You aren't coming with me?" I asked.

"I'll wait here for you."

"Then may I borrow your flashlight?"

Sister Lydia handed me the light. I quickly used it to illuminate the attic. The ceiling wasn't as high as on the lower floors. When I walked closer to the walls, I had to stoop to keep from hitting my head. The attic was pitch-black except for my beam of light. Had the dormers been open instead of tightly shut, they would have provided an excellent view of the surrounding area.

A squeaking mouse startled me when I almost stepped on it. I watched it scurry away across the floor. Far away from the open attic doorway, the darkness seemed to engulf me, making me glad it was morning and not midnight. After carefully surveying most of the attic, I was almost convinced of Sister Lydia's assessment that it was empty. What I found in a cranny near the far end of the attic made me realize otherwise. I bumped into a large crate which, upon second glance, could possibly be a wooden coffin. I turned around when Sister Lydia's voice echoed through the attic's hollow expanse.

"Find anything?"

"Nothing in here, just like you said."

Before returning to the beckoning light of the open attic doorway, I touched the casket-like crate to make sure I hadn't imagined it.

"What now?" Sister Lydia asked.

"I'll need a master key to the building. I'd like to return after dark when everyone has gone home. I also want access to security codes, the film from the security cameras. I'll also need convent employment records for as far back as you have them. And Sister, that includes members of the clergy as well as lay workers."

Sister Lydia reacted to my thinly-veiled suggestion that a member of the cloth could have been responsible for the desecration.

"Am I a suspect in your investigation?"

"Everyone's a suspect until I prove otherwise," I said. "Is that a problem?"

"I wouldn't have it any other way," she said, glancing at her watch. "I have another meeting after lunch. Here is a passkey that will open every door in the building. The third floor is the only place in the convent with an alarm system. You won't need the code because you've already seen what's in the attic." She handed me a card with her contact information. "Keep me updated on your progress."

After slipping her card into my shirt pocket, I followed her down the stairs to the second floor.

"I'm going to check out some of these cells," I said. "I'll call you tomorrow with an update."

I watched the stately nun descend the stairs, her sparkling smile replaced with a solemn frown. I knew she'd already contemplated what I was thinking: the satanic ritual was quite possibly conducted by someone who worked for the Greater Archdiocese of New Orleans; perhaps even a member of the clergy.

I'm not sure why I hadn't told Sister Lydia about the coffin I'd found in the attic. I had a hunch about the nun, though my hunches didn't always prove accurate. As I opened the door to one of the cells, I forced myself not to draw conclusions before I'd gathered all the facts.

The tiny second-floor room was empty, though the window and shutter were open. A bit of movement caught my eye as I gazed out the window at a patch of greenery situated between the parking lot and one of the smaller convent buildings. When I saw what it was, my mind did a double-take.

Lying amid the vegetation was a smiling young woman, an animated sparrow resting on her outstretched hand. More birds were flying around her head, and several others alit on her shoulders. Her skin was ghostly white, her dark hair braided, a black feather protruding from her braids.

The little-bit-of-nothing white chemise she was wearing highlighted every muscle and feminine curve of her body. When I banged my knee against a shutter trying to get a better view, the striking young woman glanced up at me. I blinked. When I opened my eyes, she was gone.

Without bothering to shut the door behind me, I hurried down the stairs. As I exited the building, I encountered a couple with a baby swaddled in a blue blanket entering their car.

"Did you see a young woman just now?" I asked.

The couple shook their heads, staring at me as if I were a crazy person. I watched them drive away and then found the spot where I'd seen the girl. Situated between concrete and stucco, the plot of vegetation was like an oasis in a desert. Thick grass grew in the shade of a large palm tree. Pink hibiscus blossoms sated the air with perfume. The birds were gone, and so was the mysterious young woman. Returning to the entrance, I queried the attendant.

"There was a woman in the back of the convent. She was lying in the grass and playing with the birds. Did you see her?"

I got the exact expression from the woman as I had from the couple with the baby. Her answer was the same as theirs. At least a dozen visitors were taking the self-guided tour of the Old Ursuline Convent. None of them had seen the young woman.

The coffin in the attic and the appearance of the bird girl left me with questions. Grabbing my cell phone, I dialed someone who might be able to answer them for me.

I was out of breath when I reached Bertram's. Though not yet noon, the bar, filled with tourists and locals looking for a respite from a hard day of fun in the Big Easy, was buzzing. The person I'd called before leaving the Old Ursuline Convent was waiting for me. In need of a glass of Bertram's lemonade, I quickly joined him.

Rafael Romanov was the man who had married my ex-wife, Mimsy. When she'd died, we'd met at her funeral. We'd since become close friends. Rafael was tall and slender, his long nose and strange gray eyes imparting him with mysterious good looks. Rafael was a defrocked priest. He now made a good living working for a cruise ship company sailing out of New Orleans, performing weddings, comforting passengers and performing the duties of a priest.

Rafael was the perfect person to answer some

of my questions about the Old Ursuline Convent. He was drinking scotch. When I sat on the stool beside him, he pushed a chilled glass of lemonade toward me.

"I had Bertram make you something. How you doing?"

"I'm good. Yourself?"

"Couldn't be better. I'm between cruises and have a few days off before I return to work. What's up?"

"A problem at the Old Ursuline Convent last night. A nun from the Greater Archdiocese of New Orleans has hired me to help."

"What sort of problem?" Rafael asked.

"Seems someone performed a satanic ritual there last night."

"At the main altar?"

"In a dark little room not much larger than a closet," I said.

"A makeshift altar?"

"That's what's so strange. Even though the altar is small, I have the distinct feeling it was part of the convent and not something placed there by someone other than the clergy."

I pulled out my cell phone and showed Rafael the pictures of the tiny altar. He studied them with great interest.

"You're right," he said. "The carvings on the lacquered cabinet comport with the colors and style of the main altar. Was there an inscription on the chalice?"

"It said 'sanguis sues terrestres.' When I asked Sister Lydia what it meant, she said, pig's blood."

Rafael gave me a glance. "Did she now?"

"She also said Latin was a hard language to translate. How would you translate it?"

"The blood of hogs," Rafael answered without hesitation.

"What the hell does that mean?"

"It's from a passage written by the 14th Century Italian poet Petrarch in which a character meant to represent Pope Clement the 6th makes a pro-satanic statement."

"Such as?" I asked.

"I'm not sure I remember the passage verbatim."

"Then tell me what you do remember."

Rafael grew silent, sipping his scotch before beginning the recitation.

"*I have entered into a compact with robbers, and it has been ratified with the blood of hogs on the altar of the King of Hell. It may be odious to the Gods above, but it is sacred to those below, and accepted as lawful by them, to whom it is offered up as a sacrifice with money.*"

"But that's just fiction, right? No pope would have ever said that, would he?"

"Petrarch moved in the highest circles. Before the Renaissance, early religion was a mixture of magic, mysticism, and folk religion. People believed in witches, wizards, and especially the devil. Petrarch's writings were partly responsible for bringing about the advent of the Renaissance."

After thinking about Rafael's quote, I said, "Maybe the alleged beliefs of a 14th-century pope are still prevalent today. Could that little altar be a permanent fixture of the convent?"

Before answering me, Rafael motioned for Bertram to bring us another drink. Bertram was busy, so Lilly brought them to us.

"Hi, handsome," she said. "Long time no see."

"Lilly Bliss," Raphael said. "Come around this bar and give me a hug."

"I thought you'd never ask," she said.

When they pulled apart from their embrace, Rafael said, "You haven't gone back to that bounder, Bertram, have you?"

"Yes, I have. Bert is my baby."

"You're not in town just to see Bertram, are you?"

"Quinlan Moore's in New Orleans scouting locations for a new movie. I'll help write the script soon as Quin makes his final decisions about where the plot is going."

"Good," Raphael said. "Then I still have a chance with you?"

"You're a doll, Raphael, and a bald-faced liar. If I pulled off all my clothes and sat in your lap, you'd probably reject me."

"Why don't you try it and see?" he said.

Lilly was smiling when she pushed him away. "Sugar wouldn't melt in your mouth. Right now, customers are streaming in, and I have to help Bertram."

As she disappeared behind the bar, he said, "My lap is always available."

When Rafael returned to his stool, he had a big grin on his face.

"Did you forget our conversation?" I asked.

"Momentarily," he said. "Now, where were we?"

"Discussing Satanism in the 14th Century. It's interesting your quote spoke of sacrifice with money because this was in the chalice."

I handed him the hundred-dollar-bill I'd put in my shirt pocket when Sister Lydia wasn't looking.

"Interesting. The number 66 looks as if it's drawn in. . ."

"Blood? That's exactly what it is. Fresh blood, I'd say. I know 666 is the mark of the beast. What does the number 66 mean?"

"It has many meanings."

"Then give me a quick and dirty," I said.

"Most notably, Freemasons think it's a powerful number. Titans of industry and commerce have used it to help their business causes. Route 66 and Phillips 66 come to mind, though there are other examples."

"Sister Lydia mentioned the Old Ursuline Convent has two floors and an attic level with three dormers and that the building has twelve bays. She grew defensive when I said, that's a lot of threes. The convent has nothing to do with Freemasonry, does it?"

"Don't be too sure," Rafael said. "The Catholic Church banned Freemasonry in 1738. If you were Catholic, you couldn't be a Freemason. Seems to me 1738 was about the time the convent was built."

"Catholics believe Freemasonry is linked to Satanism?"

"Enough so that Catholics were banned from being members of the Masons, or any other secret society until Pope John Paul issued a dispensation," Rafael said. "Did you notice the hedgerows at the entrance to the convent?"

"How could you miss it?"

"Study its triangular design. It has deep symbolic meaning to some people."

"Freemasons?"

"Maybe."

"Then is my culprit a Mason?"

Raphael held up a palm. "Whoa! You're moving way too fast. The Ursuline Nuns moved from the convent in 1824, ceding the property to the Greater Archdiocese of New Orleans. It was used for various purposes. During the seventies, the property was all but abandoned and in a horrible state of disrepair. After the Feds pegged the building as a National Historic Landmark, both the church and the city squabbled to gain control of it."

"So what you're telling me is we aren't dealing with a straight-line lineage."

"Correct," Rafael said. "Though there may have been Satanists at the convent in the past, they are dead and gone. Any connection with the past and what happened at the convent last night is probably coincidental."

Spring rain had begun falling outside on the sidewalk. It served to increase the number of customers filing inside for mid-day toddies. Someone I recognized was coming in the door. Realizing my private meeting with Rafael was near an end, I left him with one thought before Avory Dorean joined us.

"You've heard of the Casket Girls?"

"Who in New Orleans hasn't? What about them?"

"Local legend has it the Casket Girls brought vampires to New Orleans, and the coffins of the vampires are still in the attic of the Old Ursuline Convent."

"Most people believe it was just a misinterpretation of the name they were called, filles à la cassette," Rafael said. "Women with suitcases."

"Maybe. Strangely enough, though, the attic is the only part of the convent protected by a burglar alarm. When I pressed Sister Lydia, she allowed me to explore it. She didn't, however, share the passcode with me."

"What's up there?" Rafael asked.

"A few bats and mice and absolutely nothing else, except. . ."

"Except for what?" he asked.

"I found an old coffin in the back of the attic."

Chapter 5

vory smiled when she saw Rafael and me sitting at the bar. Rafael slid off the stool and shook Avory's hand.

"I'm Avory. Who are you?"

Rafael kissed her hand and said, "Right now, the most awestruck man on earth."

"Then maybe you'll buy me a drink," Avory said.

Avory gave me a peck on the cheek before sitting on Rafael's vacated stool. Rafael pulled up the one next to it, sandwiching her between us.

"I'm Rafael Romanov. Wyatt never told me about you."

"How rude of him," she said.

Having spotted Avory entering the bar, Lilly arrived with a martini for her. She also brought another scotch for the always thirsty priest and more lemonade for me.

"You're in real trouble now, honey, sitting between two of the most eligible bachelors in the Big Easy," Lilly said.

"The kind of trouble I like," Avory said. "Put my martinis on Rafael's tab."

"I told cheapskate Bertram you were drinking on the house. He'll be more than happy to find out he can charge them to Rafael," Lilly said. "If these two try to double team you, just get my attention."

"Hope they do. Sounds like fun," Avory said.

Lilly gave her a wink and then hurried away to help Bertram with the busy bar. Avory tapped her glass against Rafael's.

"What's your claim to fame?" she asked.

"No fame here," he said. "I'm just a humble priest."

"Does that mean . . . ?"

I answered Avory's question for Rafael. "Though still technically a priest, Rafael's been defrocked. Celibacy is no longer a condition of his job."

"Why were you defrocked?" Avory asked.

"My mother is a witch," he said.

"Are you serious?"

"As a heart attack," Rafael said.

"Even if she is a witch, what does that have to do with you?" she asked.

"The mother church has no tolerance for witches, and that includes their offspring."

Avory gave me a glance. "Is he lying?"

"I've had the pleasure of knowing Rafael's mom Madeline for several years. I can assure you he's telling the truth," I said. "Rafael works as a rent-a-priest on a cruise ship sailing out of the Port of New Orleans."

Avory gave Rafael an assessing look. "And what the hell does a rent-a-priest do?"

"Provide comfort, perform marriages, and be available to the passengers as their onboard spiritual guide," Rafael said. "It's easy work, pays well, and I get to visit beautiful island resorts for free."

"Nice," she said. "How did you two meet?"

"After their divorce, I married Wyatt's ex-wife. Mimsy, unfortunately, contracted a terminal disease and passed away at a much-too-early age.

Wyatt and I met at Mimsy's funeral. We've been friends ever since."

"Oh," she said, giving me another glance. "You didn't tell me you were divorced."

"You didn't ask," I said.

"What else haven't you told me?"

"Almost everything," I said. "We just met a few hours ago."

"Then I take it you two aren't dating?" Rafael said.

Avory gave me a dirty look when I said, "We're playing house."

"Interesting," Rafael said.

"I'm beginning to see why Mimsy divorced you," Avory said.

"I like playing house," Rafael said.

Avory grinned. "You're a priest."

"Defrocked priest. Like Wyatt said, celibacy is not required."

"I think you are both full of shit. Doesn't matter. I like weird people," Avory said.

Rafael and Avory tapped their drink glasses again. "What brings you to New Orleans?"

"I'm a screenwriter. Lilly and I are writing the script for Quinlan Moore's next movie."

"Oh? What's it about?"

"Don't know yet," Avory said. "Something mysterious and supernatural. Any ideas?"

"Maybe," he said.

"If you really have something, then don't keep me in suspense."

Avory grinned, when Rafael said, "What's it worth to you?"

"I can think of something," she said.

"Unfortunately, I'm not at liberty to discuss it. Perhaps Wyatt will tell you."

Avory gave me another glance. "Tell me what?"

"A case I'm working on. I can't talk about it," I

said.

"Why not?"

"It would be a violation of my employer's privacy."

"You told Rafael."

"That's different," I said.

"How is it different?" she asked.

"Rafael knows more about the Catholic religion than anyone I know. I needed his help to move forward with my case."

"Maybe I can help. Besides, you're not a lawyer. You're not bound by lawyer-client privilege."

"Actually, I am," I said.

"You told me you're a private investigator."

"I was disbarred. I've never been reinstated," I said.

"Then, like Rafael's celibacy, you are no longer bound by a lawyer's rules. Now, tell me what you're working on before I knock you off that stool."

"She's right, you know," Rafael said.

"You're no help," I said.

"My genre is paranormal mysteries," she said. "Believe me when I tell you I've done extensive research into all phases of the subject. If you let me, I'm sure I can help you."

"My client desires to have the matter kept quiet and out of the media. The last thing she would want is to have her problem made into a movie," I said.

"She?" Avory said.

"I've already told you too much."

Avory stared at me as she sipped her martini. "Names can always be changed."

"How are you going to change the name of a National Historic Landmark?" I asked.

"Nobody believes in the supernatural," she said. "You're a lawyer. A jury would never find you guilty of libel for writing a story about ghosts, goblins or aliens."

"There's still the matter of honoring my client's wish for privacy," I said.

"Tell me about your case," she said. "I promise I won't get you in trouble with your client."

"I hear what you're selling. I'm not sure I'm buying it."

Avory leaned forward and gave me a burning kiss on the lips.

"Tell me," she said.

"If you don't tell her, I will," Rafael said.

Avory smiled and kissed Rafael. Even before she'd kissed me, I'd decided she might actually be of help in the case.

"A nun from the Greater Archdiocese of New Orleans hired me this morning to investigate a satanic ceremony that occurred last night in the Old Ursuline Convent."

"Go on," she said.

"The ceremony took place at a tiny altar in a room the size of a closet."

"A makeshift altar?" Avory asked.

"Anything but," I said. "The altar looked as though it were put there by the original occupants of the convent."

"Then what makes you think it's a satanic altar?"

"There was a silver chalice with the inscription *sanguis sues terrestres*."

"Blood of hogs," Rafael said when Avory glanced at him for clarification.

"What the hell does that mean?" she said.

"It's part of a passage from a character in a fictional work by the 14th-century Italian poet Petrarch. The character seems to portray Clement the 6th and strongly suggests the good pope not only believed in the devil but also had dealings

41

with him."

"Is that possible?" Avory asked.

"The church today has evolved greatly since the 14th century," Rafael said.

"The satanic altar in the Old Ursuline Convent seems to indicate otherwise," I said.

"So you think it's possible some members of the clergy still worship the devil?" Avory asked.

"Even if it were true, and that's a big if, the lineage was broken decades ago," I said. "The altar is the same vintage as the rest of the convent—more than two and a half centuries old. The Ursulines no longer occupy the convent. It lay vacant and in disrepair for years."

"Then someone who knows about the altar's history is using it to practice an ancient segment of the Catholic religion," Avory said.

"That's a possibility," I said.

"What makes you think there was a ceremony performed?" she asked.

I handed Avory the hundred dollar bill marked in blood.

"There was a fresh white rose in a vase, and we found this in the chalice," I said.

"Oh my God!" she said. "Is the number 66 written in blood?"

"Yes," I said.

"66 isn't the Mark of the Beast," Avory said. "What do you think it means?"

Rafael's scotch glass rang when he tapped it with a long fingernail.

"It's a number believed by Freemasons and other secret societies to have great power," he said.

"Freemasons? What do they have to do with anything?" Avory asked.

"About the time the Ursulines arrived in New Orleans, the church banned Freemasons and members of secret societies from being Catholics.

Right or wrong, the pope linked their activities with the worship of the devil."

"The number 66 is a possible link to Freemasonry, and maybe to the person who performed the ceremony," I said.

"Interesting," Avory said. "Some people say there are vampires in the attic of the convent."

"Ask Wyatt," Rafael said. "He explored the attic earlier today."

"No way!" Avory said. "I've heard it's impossible to get in there."

"I was in the attic less than two hours ago," I said.

"You're lying," she said.

"I promise you I'm not."

"What did you find?"

"Absolutely nothing," I said. "Except. . ."

"Except for what?" she said.

"A wooden crate that looked like a coffin."

"You're still lying," she said.

"No, I'm not."

"What was in the coffin?" she asked.

"Don't know," I said. "It was nailed shut."

"Then let's get a crowbar, go there and see what's inside it," Avory said.

I signaled Lilly that our drinks needed refilling. "Not so fast," I said. "The old convent is a museum now. It'll be swarming with tourists and people who work for the museum. We would cause quite a stir if we showed up with a crowbar and proceeded to let a vampire out of his coffin."

Lilly was busy and left quickly after bringing us fresh drinks. Once she was gone, Avory sipped her drink.

"This is the best martini I've ever had," she said.

"Bertram Picou," Rafael said. "The man's a national treasure."

Avory put down the martini and stared at me

until I became uncomfortable.

"I want to see what's in that coffin," she said.

"So do I, though it'll have to wait until after dark when there's no tourists or employees around."

"How do we get in?" Rafael said.

"I have a passkey," I said.

"You said Sister Lydia didn't tell you the passcode. How are you going to get around that?"

"I watched her key in the code and memorized the sequence," I said.

"You have a photographic memory?" Avory asked.

"Pretty much," I said.

Rafael cocked his head. "You're a dog," he said.

"I had a feeling she wasn't going to share it with me. I made sure she didn't have to."

Avory tapped a nervous fingernail against her martini glass, causing it to ring like a bell.

"If Sister Lydia doesn't believe there's anything there, then why is she so protective of the code?" she asked.

"Indeed?" Rafael said. "Why would the Greater Archdiocese of New Orleans bother to put a burglar alarm on the third floor when there's nothing in the attic?"

"Doesn't make sense, does it?" I said.

"They're hiding something," Avory said.

"Or covering something up," Rafael said.

"Or both," I said. "That's why I memorized the passcode. I intend to visit the convent's attic again very soon and find out the significance of the seemingly unneeded security precautions."

"And when you do, I'm going with you," Avory said.

"I never agreed to that. This is something I have to do alone."

"Kiss my ass!" Avory said. "You aren't going

without me."

"Or me either," Rafael said. "If there's a vampire in the casket, you'll need a priest to perform the necessary ceremony."

"What the hell are you talking about?" I asked.

"The proper prayers of the dead," he said.

"What if it isn't dead?" I asked.

"Precisely," Rafael said. "Only a priest will know what to do."

"It won't be dark for hours," I said. "I'll think about it until then. There's something else about the convent I haven't told either of you."

"What?" Avory said.

"I was exploring the second floor of the convent after Sister Lydia had gone. I was in one of the cells in which the Ursuline sisters once lived. The window overlooking the back of the building was open, and there was a mysterious person in the courtyard."

"A possible suspect?" Avory asked.

"I don't think so. It was a woman, probably in her twenties, lying in a patch of greenery with birds flying around her. A sparrow had landed on her finger, and she looked as if she were talking to it. That wasn't everything strange about her."

"What else?" Avory said.

"She had dark hair with a black feather in it that made her look like an Indian. Her skin was pale, almost ghostly as if she'd rarely seen the light of day. She was wearing a white chemise which was all but transparent, and with nothing on underneath."

"Maybe she works there," Rafael said.

"A half-naked ghostly girl?" Avory said. "I don't think so. Did you talk to her?"

"I startled her when I banged my knee against a shutter. She was gone when I ran downstairs."

"You didn't see where she went?" Avory asked.

"She just disappeared. None of the employees or any of the visitors I quizzed knew anything about her. I apparently was the only person who saw her."

"That's so strange. What do you make of it?" Rafael asked.

"Don't know, though I have a feeling she's connected in some way to the mystery in the convent. I'm going to quiz Sister Lydia and find out what she knows about her."

"If I don't stop drinking these martinis, I'll be drunk long before dark," Avory said. "I missed lunch. I need to eat something."

"Me too," I said.

"There's a music festival at Louis Armstrong Park," Rafael said.

"Where is that?" Avory asked.

"Not far from here. There'll be plenty of food booths, and we can take in the sights and sounds of the festival until the concert begins," Rafael said.

"Then what?" Avory asked.

"The concert will last until well after dark. It isn't far from Louis Armstrong Park to the Old Ursuline Convent. When the concert ends, we'll go take a look inside Wyatt's coffin."

"You forget something," I said.

"What's that?" Rafael said.

"I'm pretty sure Bertram has a crowbar he'll lend us. Doesn't matter because we can't walk around the concert carrying a crowbar. We'll have to come back here to get it."

"No, we won't," Rafael said. "I'm parked nearby. We can put the crowbar in the backseat of my vehicle. At any rate, it'll be safer taking the car than walking around the French Quarter after dark."

Chapter 6

Father Luc felt like hell when he opened his eyes. All the candles had gone out, the little room as dark as the inside of a cave. Holding his head over the edge of the bed, he threw up on the floor. He was holding a bone from Mona Marie's skeleton when he rolled on his back. After gnawing on it a moment, he tossed it on the floor.

Father Luc fumbled to find a candle in the darkness and lit it. Though the little room had no windows, he sensed it was after dark. He didn't know how long he'd slept, but his hunger was powerful. Kicking the bone across the floor, he went to the broken mirror of the little vanity against the wall. His expression changed when he saw he was still wearing the vestments of a priest. He glanced at the skeleton on the bed.

"Has Darth been here?"

He didn't seem to notice that the skeleton failed to answer him. His vestment was rumpled from having slept in it since the previous night. He didn't care. The silver flask with the special inscription he'd given Darth was on the vanity. He opened it and took a drink. Sammy Ray's blood, some of it dripping on his white collar, had begun to clot. Father Luc made a disgusted face and dumped the clumps into the washbasin. Suddenly overcome by his hunger, he tried to smooth the wrinkles out of his vestment. With Sammy Ray's blood on his collar, he left the little room without bothering to shut the door behind him.

The little priest didn't need a light to find his way in the dark. The workers had left for the night, the air conditioning switched off. Now, the air was warm and stale. Father Luc didn't notice. He wasn't alone and could feel the cold stare of the girl. Her presence pissed him off. If he could catch her, he would kill her, but not before using her warm blood to satiate his hunger.

Father Luc exited the backdoor of the convent, careful to lock it behind him. The night was glorious, bright lights and the sound of music emanating from the French Quarter. Something was going on at a nearby venue. A celebration. It didn't surprise Father Luc. In New Orleans, the party never ended. Following the sound of the music, he decided to check it out.

⚜

Rafael signaled for Bertram to bring our tab. The friendly Cajun was all smiles when Rafael handed him a credit card without looking at the invoice.

"You're too trusting, Padre," Bertram said. "One of these days I'm gonna stick an extra hundred on your bill. You'd never know the difference."

"I'm confident you would never do such a thing," Rafael said.

"Got a crowbar in the back?" I asked.

"Plan to do a little breaking and entering?" Bertram asked.

"Something like that," I said. "And, while you're at it, wrap it in a towel."

"Speaking of while you're at it," Rafael said.

"You may as well make a couple of go cups for Miss Avory and me. Don't want to get thirsty between here and Armstrong Park."

"Got you covered, Padre. Wouldn't want to let that happen."

Bertram was shaking his head as he headed for the cash register. He had something long and heavy wrapped in a towel when he returned with Rafael's credit card. As he handed it across the bar to me, I knew it was the crowbar.

"If the police nab you," he said. "Don't tell them where you got that thing."

The go cups were in boxes with protruding straws. Rafael took a sip to see which drink was his before pushing the other toward Avory.

"We can leave here with these?" she asked.

"Perfectly legal," he said.

"You have strange laws in this state," Avory said.

"You can buy a frozen daiquiri from a drive-through bar, though it's illegal to drink and drive. Go figure!" I said.

"Does anyone ever sober up around here?" Avory asked.

"You have to learn to pace yourself," I said. "If you're like me, it's almost impossible."

"I love it," Avory said.

Rafael got off the stool and squeezed Avory's hand.

"Wait with Wyatt while I go for the car," he said. "Meet you out front in about fifteen minutes."

Rafael took the crowbar with him. Fifteen minutes later, Avory and I were waiting in front of Bertram's doorway when a flashy silver SUV pulled to the curb to pick us up. I climbed into the backseat as Rafael escorted Avory to the passenger seat.

"I love your vehicle. What is it?" Avory asked.

"Cadillac Escalade," Rafael said.

"Looks expensive," she said. "How much did you pay for it?"

Rafael waved off her comment. "Don't ask," he said. "It's still a while before dark. How about a scenic spin around the lake?"

"Why not?" Avory said.

Rafael turned the big vehicle onto Canal Street, heading toward the cemeteries.

"The widest street on earth," he said. "The buildings were devastated and Canal in shambles after Katrina. Like new vegetation every spring, the lights and activity have returned."

"It's really different," Avory said. "Most cities are so similar, it's hard to remember if you're in Dallas or Atlanta. If you woke up on Canal, you'd know instantly you were in New Orleans. Where are we going?"

"We'll turn up ahead and drive past cemetery after magical cemetery," Rafael said. "If you woke up and saw the above-ground crypts, you'd know you were in New Orleans."

We were soon on Lakeshore Drive, following the bank of Pontchartrain, the lake bordering the city. Rafael didn't stop until we got out to watch a delightful water display in a large fountain decorated with symbols of Carnival season.

"Mardi Gras Fountain," Rafael said. "Few tourists know it's here because they rarely come this far around the lake."

"Love it," Avory said.

We sat on a park bench, watching salty waves lap the shore of Lake Pontchartrain as the sun began to set over the giant waterway. Puffy clouds warned of rain as the noise of a passing flock of seagulls melded with the music of the fountain.

"What a beautiful sunset," Avory said. "Thanks for bringing me here."

"I knew you'd like it," he said. "Right now, I

could use a bowl of gumbo."

"They have gumbo at the festival?" Avory asked.

"You bet. Gumbo, etouffee, fried alligator along with icy pink Hurricanes to quench our thirst."

Avory finished the last sip of her martini from Bertram's go cup. "I still can't believe drinking in the open is legal here."

"So many different nationalities comprise the city's population, there's a complex mixture of customs and beliefs," I said. "You wouldn't like it here very much if you were a prude or a puritan."

"Sounds like Eden to me," Avory said.

Rafael took a different route back to the French Quarter. After finding a parking spot, we followed the music and the lights to the arch marking the entrance to Armstrong Park. Avory was tipsy, Rafael clutching her arm as we entered the festivities and made our way through the meandering masses of visitors already enjoying the celebration.

The festival at Armstrong Park was one of the many French Quarter events occurring throughout the year. The park, named for Louis Armstrong, one of the city's favorite sons, edged the Quarter and featured a statue of the jazz legend overlooking scenic walking trails, lagoons, and bridges. The evening was glorious, a gentle breeze wafting through the branches of the surrounding oaks. Avory was suddenly all smiles.

"I'm starting to love New Orleans," she said. "Does this many people show up for every event in the French Quarter?"

"You kidding," I said. "You should be here during Mardi Gras."

The festival was a maze of food and souvenir booths, a crowd dressed in shorts and tee-shirts taking in the sights, sounds and wonderful aromas emanating from the food booths.

"The city will intoxicate you if you let it," Rafael said. "Some visitors never want to leave."

As a jazz combo serenaded the masses on a make-shift stage, we strolled through the crowd of slow-moving visitors, and the booths selling everything from gumbo to voodoo dolls. Rafael bought Avory a souvenir tee-shirt with a red crawfish on the front. She was giggling when she pulled it over her blouse. After buying drinks and food, we sat on a bench overlooking a lagoon to eat our festival fare and take in the music.

Despite Avory's worry she might be too drunk to visit the convent, she and Rafael continued drinking. Both were sipping some icy concoction through red straws. I stuck to iced tea, enjoying the music when Rafael saw someone in the passing crowd he thought he recognized.

Pointing to a short man with crewcut hair and wearing the rumpled vestments of a Catholic priest, he said, "I think I know that man. Be right back."

Rafael wasn't gone long. "Who was it?" Avory asked.

"He looked like Father Luc, a priest I used to know. He disappeared into the crowd before I could catch up with him."

❧

Armstrong Park wasn't far from the Old Ursuline Convent, and Father Luc merged with the crowd streaming into the entrance. The man who'd sold him an oyster po'boy had eyed the bloodstain on his vestment. It spooked Father Luc enough that he hurried away without taking his drink.

The venue was crowded, everyone dressed casually and no one paying attention to the little priest. Out of the lights and in the darkness beneath a large oak, he finished his po'boy.

Though the sandwich tasted good, it didn't satisfy his real craving. He had other things on his mind and knew with all the alcohol being consumed and the dark surroundings away from the lights of the festival, he'd soon find what he was looking for. It wasn't long before he'd spotted a potential target.

A group of college girls was laughing as they sipped their sugary Hurricanes. Standing away from the crowd in the darkness of the many oak trees bordering the park, they were enjoying light jazz and the mild April evening. Father Luc moved closer for a better look, his dark vestment the perfect camouflage for his subterfuge.

Father Luc didn't want to attract attention though he knew he already had. He hadn't recognized the tall man who had chased after him through the crowd. A case of mistaken identity he assumed, though in the deadly game of assault, it was never safe to assume anything.

Before Father Luc could get close enough to the girls, the jazz combo stopped playing. As he watched from a distance, they began checking their watches, hugging each other, and dispersing through the crowd. Backing further into the shadows, he started looking for a secondary target. He soon found one.

A young woman with brown frizzy hair had drunk too many sugary drinks and had wandered away from her group to throw up in the bushes. She was passed out when he found her, her face buried in a pool of her own vomit. In the condition she was in, he knew she would put up no resistance. Wiping the vomit off her wrist, he proceeded to slice it with Darth's knife, careful not to cut too deeply.

The little priest lapped the woman's blood until his appetite was sated, and then began filling Darth's silver flask from her vein. Music had started up again when he slipped out of the shadows. The festival wouldn't end for another hour. Long before then, he'd be back in the security of the convent.

He was careful not to take too much blood, though he knew the inebriated woman wouldn't remember the dark priest lapping it from her wrist. When her party found her lying in the vomit, they'd take her home and put her to bed, never suspecting she'd been the victim of an assault.

Father Luc regretted one thing: he wished there was a way to take the woman with him to the dark room where he was staying. There were too many people around, and it was too far back to Old Ursulines to accomplish his desire. Satiated for the moment, he slunk into the shadows and made his way back to the convent.

Chapter 7

New Orleans will kiss your lips one minute, and kick your ass the next. Giggling drunk, Avory was the eccentric old lady's latest victim. The concert had ended, the lights going out in the concessions. Avory had her arms around Rafael's neck, drooling on his collar.

"I think I better take her home," he said.

"Good idea," I said. "I'll check out the coffin alone."

Though Avory was in no condition to go with me, she was coherent enough to protest, even if her words were slightly slurred.

"You're not going without me," she said.

"I need to visit the attic. I want to have a look tonight."

"Then wait until I sober up," she said.

"That'll take hours," I said. "By then, it'll be too late."

"Doesn't matter. Either take me with you now or else postpone your visit until later."

Realizing I'd hit a brick wall, I said, "Okay, we'll do it tomorrow night."

"You sure?" she said.

"I won't go without you. Right now, you need to let Rafael take you home."

Avory hiccupped before asking, "Are you lying

to me?"

"I'll wait until tomorrow night. Trust me on this one."

Avory glanced at Rafael. "Can I trust him?"

"Of course you can," Rafael said. "Let's go to the car."

I climbed into the backseat when we reached Rafael's parking spot.

"Can you drop me in front of Bertram's?" I asked.

"Yes," he said.

Avory was sprawled across the console and breathing softly as Rafael let me out of his Cadillac. Knowing Rafael wouldn't approve of my lie, I spirited the crowbar out of his car without him knowing it. I watched his big vehicle disappear down Chartres before starting up the street toward the Old Ursuline Convent.

It was getting late, the weather mild, and people still crowding the street. No one seemed to notice the towel-wrapped crowbar I was carrying. Once I'd passed Jackson Square, the foot traffic thinned out. I was alone, though feeling secure with the lethal weapon in my hands. At the front gate, I realized I had a problem.

Despite what Sister Lydia had told me, the passkey she'd given me wouldn't open the door. Following a moment of frustration, I walked around the compound until I found a side entrance. After trying the gate and finding the key still didn't work, I stepped away from the door. Aggravated, I took a deep breath and scratched my chin.

It struck me maybe there were two passkeys, one for the main building, and another to get into the compound. If this were the case, I could vault the fence and then enter the building using the key I had. Though the wall was only about eight feet high, I quickly learned that crawling over it was easier said than done. With the crowbar in my hands, it was all but impossible. After tossing the heavy bar of steel over the fence, I climbed over after it.

I didn't hear it hit the ground because it had landed in a row of shrubs growing against the wall. I found out as much when I dropped into the shrubbery. The spot where I'd scaled the fence was in a dark area of the compound. Without a light, I was reduced to blindly searching the foliage on my hands and knees. I was beginning to curse myself when I finally touched the cold steel of the crowbar.

I considered climbing back over the fence and returning to the compound when I was better prepared. Remembering the flashlight Sister Lydia had left at the top of the stairs, I decided to enter the building and hope for the best.

Sister Lydia's passkey opened the backdoor of the convent. Auxiliary lights, all I needed to find the stairs leading to the attic, cast dim shadows on the walls of the old building. It didn't matter if I was recorded on the surveillance cameras because I was on the payroll, and Sister Lydia knew I intended to visit the convent after dark. Out of habit, I skirted around them anyway.

Old wood creaked as I made my way to the top of the stairway. When I reached the attic level, I found Sister Lydia's flashlight waiting for me in a recess in the wall. The red light on the keypad went green when I entered the code, the heavy old door groaning as I pulled it open.

It's one thing to enter a dark attic in a creepy convent in broad daylight, and quite another stepping into total darkness when you're the only one in the building. The mice and bats that were mostly quiet the first time I visited the attic now contributed to a noisy chorus. Getting turned around, I bumped my head on the sloping rafters as I unexpectedly approached a wall. I had to stop and take a deep breath, and then think about what had just happened.

Something else, the sound of footsteps from behind, disturbed me. I waited in silence, trying to determine if I had heard things, or if there was someone in the attic with me. When I halted, the footsteps and noise of the bats and mice ceased.

There had to be an opening in the attic allowing the bats to enter and exit. I switched off the flashlight, letting my eyes grow accustomed to the darkness. When they did, I saw where the bats were coming in and out. A shuttered window was open, stars and a near-full moon clearly visible. As I watched, what must have been hundreds of bats began flying out the window. I waited until they were gone, flinching when a mouse ran across my foot.

I was beginning to think the footsteps I'd heard were just my imagination. Switching on the light again, I began walking toward the wall farthest from the door where I had entered the attic. Stepping into a spider web, I quickly realized that mice and bats weren't the only denizens living in the attic.

I tore at the elastic web clinging to my ears and eyelashes, frantically brushing my face and neck in case the spider had come along with its web. When I'd brushed away the last silky strand from my head, I was in a sweat from the warm and humid attic. A sudden breeze whistled through the open window, thankfully cooling the perspiration dripping down my neck.

I found the casket when I stumbled into it, banging my knee against a sharp edge. When my leg quit aching, I used the flashlight to get a good look at it for the first time.

If this was truly one of the original caskets brought over from France, it wasn't hard to understand why those who had seen them thought they were coffins. It was even shaped like a coffin, wider at one end than the other. I used the crowbar, wondering what I'd find when I got the wooden box open.

The top of the casket was nailed securely shut, and it took me a while to accomplish the task. When I finally pried the top off, I fumbled for the light on the floor. I was creeped out when I shined the light and saw what it contained.

A jumble of bones littered the inside of the wooden box. From the skulls I saw, I knew the bones were human. The box contained more than a single body. I wanted to see if there was something else beneath the top layer of bones. I first had to overcome my aversion to touching them. The sound of footsteps beginning again did nothing to suppress my aversion. My words echoed against the empty attic when I called out.

"Who's there?"

Though the footsteps ceased, no one answered me. Something inside the casket other than bone flashed when I shined the light into it. I had to place the light on the floor before I could begin digging in the pile. I soon found a strand of rosary beads. Caught up in the sudden zeal of discovery, I began tossing the bones on the floor.

Before the casket was empty, I'd found several objects other than bones: a nun's habit, a cross carved from a single piece of wood, and a couple of documents that seemed equally old. I had no idea about the age of the bones. They could have been in the casket for centuries, though the thought crossed my mind they might also be the recent remains of victims of a serial killer.

I listened for a moment, trying to hear the footsteps again. Fascinated by my search through the casket, I could have missed the approach of a killer. He might be standing directly behind me, waiting to make me his next victim. When I wheeled around and flashed the light, I saw something that scared the hell out of me.

Standing not ten feet away was the same young woman I'd seen in the courtyard. She was staring at me, her eyes flashing and her skin casting a pale white aura. The light went out, leaving me in almost total darkness. It came back on when I bumped it with the palm of my hand. The woman was gone.

I called out, "Hello. Who are you? Where did you go?"

As before, I got no answer.

Without bothering to return the bones to the casket, I scooped up the other items I'd found and started for the door. I'd lost track of time in the darkness and had no idea how long I'd been in the attic. The only thing I knew for sure was my shirt was soaked with sweat and plastered to my back.

As I exited the attic, it felt as though the weight of the world had been lifted from my shoulders. The air was warm and humid, though nothing like the attic's heat and humidity. My foray into darkness had produced more questions than answers. How old were the bones? Was I dealing with a serial killer? Who is the young woman who lives in the convent? Reaching for my cell phone, I decided to call someone who could help me. Former N.O.P.D. homicide detective Tony Nicosia answered on the third ring.

"It's three in the morning," a groggy voice said. "This better be good."

"Sorry, Tony, I didn't realize how late it was."

"I'm used to it," he said. "What's up?"

"I just left the attic of the Old Ursuline Convent. Among other things, I found several skeletons in a single coffin."

"Did you fall off the wagon again, Cowboy?"

"I'm sober. Sorry I called you so late. There's nothing either of us can do right now," I said. "I was wondering if I should report this to the authorities."

"If it were several bodies, I'd say yes. Skeletons can wait until tomorrow. Where'd you say you are?"

"The Old Ursuline Convent on Chartres Street."

Tony paused before replying, and I thought for a moment we'd become disconnected. We hadn't. I could hear his wife Lil in the background reprimanding him for talking on the phone at three in the morning. He finally came back on the line.

"Sorry about that," he said. "I'll meet you at Bertram's tomorrow at around ten."

Tony hung up the phone without saying goodbye. It didn't matter because I had two more calls to make. As if expecting to hear from me, Sister Lydia answered on the first ring.

"Hope you're not angry with me for calling you this hour of the morning," I said.

"You have something important to tell me?" Sister Lydia asked.

"Very important. I called an associate of mine, a former N.O.P.D. homicide detective because we need his help. His name is Tony Nicosia. I'm meeting him at Bertram's at ten. Can you make it?"

"Is there nothing you can tell me before then?" she asked.

"Please, allow me to explain the situation tomorrow," I said.

"Then I'll see you at Bertram's at ten," she said.

As an afterthought, I dialed Rafael. "Are you in jail?" he asked.

"I'm at the convent. I found some things."

"Like what?" he asked.

"I'm meeting Tony Nicosia and Sister Lydia at Bertram's around ten. Can you be there?"

"Wouldn't miss it," he said.

I'd forgotten to return the flashlight to the recess. Hurrying back up the stairs, I dropped it off and then exited the building. There was a back entrance to the convent. When I tried my key, I found it worked. At least something was going my way.

Back at my apartment, I found Miss Kisses gone, prowling the patio through the door I always left ajar. After stripping off my clothes, I began showering without waiting for the water to grow hot. Not bothering to put on pajamas, I climbed beneath the covers of my little bed, quickly realizing I wasn't alone. The possibility of getting any sleep that night flew out the window when someone screamed and sat up in bed.

Chapter 8

With nerves already jangled from my visit to the convent, the unexpected shriek sent me flying out of bed. The woman who had caused my near-heart attack sat straight up, turning on the lamp on the stand beside the bed. It was Avory, still wearing the crawfish tee shirt Rafael had bought for her at the music festival.

"What the hell do you think you're doing?" she asked.

"I live here," I said. "What are you doing?"

Without bothering to answer my question, she said, "You're naked."

Grabbing a pair of khakis from my closet, I quickly pulled them on and zipped them up. Avory was still dressed in the same frilly dress she was wearing at the festival. Though she didn't wear much makeup, her smudged mascara imparted her pretty face with a comic book appearance.

"Sorry," I said. "I was dogged out. When I got out of the shower, I didn't bother putting on pajamas. I wasn't expecting to find anyone in the bed. You scared me half to death."

"Where else would I go? I checked out of the hotel."

"I see."

"Where have you been?"

"Here and there," I said.

I'd left the items I'd retrieved from the convent on the floor against the wall. When Avory glanced around the room and saw them, her serious expression turned even graver.

"You lied to me. You went to the convent alone, didn't you?"

"What I told you wasn't a lie. I simply changed my mind after you and Rafael drove away.

Avory got out of bed and made a production of smoothing the wrinkles from her dress.

"I've misread relationships all my life, but you take the cake. You're a lying, no-good son-of-a-bitch!" Her words and the absolutely absurd situation I suddenly found myself in caused me to forget the convent's dark attic and made me grin. "Why are you smiling, you smug asshole?"

"What in the hell are you ranting about? We just met earlier today. We've never even held hands. We're not married, or even dating," I said. "We have no relationship."

"What's that on the floor?" she asked.

"Some of the things I found in the casket," I said.

"Some? What else was in it?"

"A bunch of human skeletons," I said.

"Vampire skeletons?"

"How would I know?" I asked.

"The canines. Did the skulls have vampire canines?"

"It was dark. I didn't get a good look at the bones," I said.

Avory frowned, folded her arms tightly across her chest and turned away from me.

"Shit!" she said. "You opened a coffin in the attic of the Old Ursuline Convent and didn't even bother to look at the skulls you found?"

"There were other distractions," I said.

"Such as?"

"The bird girl. She followed me into the attic and almost scared the hell out of me. I'm lucky I made it out of there with what I did."

"Get your clothes on," she said. "We're going back to the convent."

"You're crazy," I said. "The sun will be coming up soon. We can't be traipsing around in the attic when the museum employees start arriving. "

"If you get your butt in gear, we'll have plenty of time," she said.

"What difference does it make? There are no such things as vampires."

"How do you know?"

"I've never seen one, and I've never heard of anyone who has."

"Then you've obviously never lived in L.A."

"That's a fact," I said.

"If you're too frightened to go back to the convent, then give me the damn passkey and tell me the code," she said. "I'll go alone."

Not believing what a sorry state of affairs I'd found myself in, I finished dressing and tied my shoes.

"Let's go," I said, holding the door for Avory. "We need to get in and out of there before the sun comes up."

"You're working for the Archdiocese. What difference does it make?"

"I don't know," I said. "Maybe nothing."

"Then let's go," she said.

I followed her as she hurried out the door and down the stairs. Bertram's bar was dark and locked for the night. Chartres Street was also dark, all the hardcore partiers sucking down booze somewhere else in the Quarter. The tourists in town just to see the sights were still asleep in their hotel rooms. I glanced down the street, looking for a cab.

"Let's walk," she said. "It can't be that far."

"Far enough that we'd be cutting our window of opportunity too close. I see headlights coming our way."

I flagged down the passing taxi, the yawning cabbie dropping us off in front of the convent. Avory hurried to the main entrance.

"The key doesn't work on that gate," I said. "We need to go around back."

The streets were deserted as I fumbled in the darkness with the keys.

"Can't you hurry?" Avory said.

"I'm doing the best I can," I said.

The door opened with a humid whoosh. Even with nothing except auxiliary lights to illuminate the inside of the convent, the building's spectacular interior was enough to awe a first-time visitor.

"It's beautiful, in a creepy sort of way," she said.

"If you think this is creepy, wait'll you see the attic," I said.

I found the flashlight waiting in the recess in the wall. The light on the keypad was green, and I realized I'd forgotten to lock the attic door.

"Good thing we returned. I didn't rearm the alarm or relock the attic," I said.

"Hope that's all you forgot," Avory said.

The attic was warmer and more humid than the rest of the convent. As we entered the cloying darkness, I sensed Avory's resolve was waning. The floor groaned when she took a step. I shined the flashlight on her when she stiffened and refused to move.

"What's that sound?"

"Bats," I said. "They're returning to their perches through an open window."

"You didn't tell me there were bats up here."

"And mice, spiders and probably roaches. Want to wait for me at the door?"

"I'm fine," she said. "Lead on."

Avory had a firm grip on my arm as we negotiated the length of the musty attic. When we reached the spot where I'd seen the casket, I came to an abrupt halt and shined the light in a circle around the area. The casket was gone, as were all the human bones I'd left scattered on the floor beside it.

"It isn't here," I said.

"What isn't here?" she asked.

"The casket. It's gone. I emptied it of bones in this exact spot. I didn't bother returning them or nailing the top back on. Doesn't matter because it's not here. Someone moved it."

"There's no one here but us," she said.

"Except maybe the bird girl," I said.

"Could she have moved the casket by herself?" Avory asked.

"Not likely."

As we stood in the darkness wondering what had happened to the casket, blue flashing lights began shining through the open window. Just as quickly, the powerful beam of a spotlight illuminated the attic ceiling.

"Damn it!" I said. "It's the N.O.P.D."

"What'll we do?" Avory asked.

"Get the hell out of here," I said.

We started toward the light of the open attic door when Avory kicked something with her foot. Reaching down, she picked it up.

"What is it?" I asked.

"I know what I think it is. Shine the light on it," she said.

Avory had a skull in her hand. Even in the dim shadows of the attic, we could see the prominent fangs protruding from the jaw.

"Good God!" I said. "We have to hide it someplace. We don't want the cops to find us with this in our hands."

"Where?"

"The library on the second floor. We'll stash it there and come back for it later," I said.

By now, the sirens were screaming outside on the street. The police were at both the front and back and probably had keys to the museum. I opened the door of the library and fumbled on the wall, searching for a light switch. Before Avory could find a place to hide the skull, she tossed it to me.

"Hold it up and let me take a picture," she said. "And hurry."

With her cell phone, Avory snapped off several pictures of me holding the skull. We had little time as the police were already inside the convent. I tossed the skull back to her.

"Hide it behind those boxes," I said.

Avory found a spot for the skull behind a random row of boxes.

"Now what?" she asked.

I handed her a book I'd pulled from a shelf. "Open it and pretend your reading."

Avory found a chair and opened the book. I was doing the same when the police burst through the door with their pistols raised.

"Police," the lead cop said. "Get your hands up."

A half-dozen cops soon had us cuffed and surrounded. A man in blue whose nametag said Sergeant Weimer was doing the talking.

"What the hell are you doing here?"

"I work for the Archdiocese," I said. "We're researching something for them."

"At this hour?" he said.

"We're trying to get our work in before the tourists start arriving," I said.

"Can you prove it?" he asked.

"I have a card in my wallet of an administrator of the Archdiocese. You're welcome to give her a call. She'll verify we have permission to be here."

"We'll find out. Right now, we're taking you downtown," Sergeant Weimer said.

The sun was just beginning to come up over the eastern part of the city when the cops loaded us into the back of a patrol car. Having likely never been arrested, Avory had grown quiet, her complexion pale.

"Do something," she said beneath her breath.

"Relax," I said. "This will take a while. Sister Lydia will vouch for us once they call her."

"You sure about that?"

"She will," I said.

"And if she doesn't?"

"I have some other names to drop. Stop worrying. It'll do us no good," I said.

We were taken to the precinct and herded into a holding cell, the police stopping short of booking us. We stewed in the cell until they called Sister Lydia. They released us soon afterward. We'd been at the station for more than four hours, and it was almost ten as we waited for a cab to take us to Bertram's. Avory was incensed.

"I've never been so humiliated in my life. They treated us with no respect at all."

"Get over it," I said. "The police deal with criminals all day, every day. You'd act the same if you were doing their job."

"No, I wouldn't," she said. "Who are you calling?"

"Tony Nicosia. He's waiting for me at Bertram's."

"For what?" she said.

"Tony's an ex-homicide detective with the N.O.P.D. You remember. Quin put him on retainer.

I called him last night after leaving the convent. I need to tell him we're running late."

"Like I said, for what?" Avory asked.

"Several skeletons in a single casket. We could be dealing with a serial killer. No one knows more about murder investigations than Tony."

"If there really is a casket filled with skeletons in the attic, then where did it go? Are you sure you didn't imagine things?" Avory asked.

"Were we both imagining the vampire skull? Somebody picked the bones up off the attic floor, put them back into the casket, and then moved it somewhere," I said.

"Your bird girl?"

"The casket was too heavy for her to move, even a few feet," I said.

"Sure about that?" Avory asked.

"The blood on the hundred was human blood; fresh human blood," I said.

"Then why didn't you tell the police about your suspicions?"

"The Greater Archdiocese of New Orleans hired me, and Sister Lydia told me she wanted the investigation kept secret with no police involvement. She covered our butts when they called her. We're doing the same. She, Tony, and Rafael are waiting for us."

When we reached Bertram's, we found the nun, the ex-cop, and the priest sitting together at the bar. None of them looked happy. Sister Lydia was drinking one of Bertram's martinis, Rafael and Tony, scotch.

One of the toughest cops I'd ever known, Tony Nicosia was about five-nine and built like a fireplug. His hair and eyes were dark, his accent straight from the Irish Channel District of New Orleans where he'd grown up.

"Trouble with the cops again, Cowboy?" he

asked.

He grinned when I said, "A fairly normal consequence of my job. I see you and Rafael have met Sister Lydia."

"I know Sister Lydia from way back when," he said. "She grew up in the Channel and was friends with my Aunt Dot. She ain't speaking to Rafael, though."

"Oh? What's the problem, Sister Lydia?"

"This man has been defrocked," she said.

"Rafael's one of the best persons I know, and he's a god-fearing human being," I said. "He's helping with our problem. We need him. If you can't look past his transgressions, at least put up with him until we solve this case."

"Then maybe you should catch me up on exactly where we're at," she said. "Seems to me as if the Archdiocese's little problem has become much more complicated since I last saw you."

"You can't even imagine," I said. "Sister Lydia and Tony, this is Avory Dorian. She's also part of our team. Please grab your drinks and let's adjourn to my booth in the back. I'll join you after I fetch some things I left in my room upstairs.

Chapter 9

Bertram's liquor was working its usual magic, everyone all smiles when I returned to the booth, my hands loaded with the objects I'd found in the casket.

"Everything okay?" I asked.

"Father Rafael was reminding me of things which happened twenty years ago," she said.

"Father Rafael?" I said.

"Even though the Mother Church no longer recognizes him as such, Father Rafael is still a priest. Since his mother's a witch, he does have unique knowledge and perspective of the occult. I'm receptive to having him, and Detective Nicosia, help us."

"What about Avory?" I asked.

"Though the young lady is obviously very intelligent, I'm not sure what she brings to the table," Sister Lydia said.

"I know more about vampires than anyone sitting here," Avory said.

Because of Avory's comment, Sister Lydia's eyes had grown larger.

"To what are you referring?" she asked.

Avory passed the nun her cell phone with the picture of the fanged skull open for her to see.

"Wyatt and I found this thing in the attic of

the convent. You can see for yourself it's not a normal skull."

"Let me see," Tony said.

After taking a long look, he passed it to Rafael.

"It's a vampire's skull," Avory said.

Sister Lydia waved, catching Bertram's attention, and signaled for him to bring more drinks.

"I'll have to think about this vampire thing," she said. "Avory can continue as a part of our team until I decide what to do about it."

"You won't be sorry," Avory said. "You're going to need me before this is all over with."

"Maybe so. Right now, I need another martini. Then, Wyatt can tell us what has occurred since yesterday," she said.

I sipped my fresh lemonade, waiting for Bertram to return to the bar. Tony spoke before I could begin my story.

"Sister Lydia already told me about the satanic ceremony. Show me the hundred you found in the chalice."

I handed him the bill. "The number 66 is marked in blood. You think Tommy can have DNA run for us?"

"I didn't think you wanted the cops involved," he said.

"We don't," Sister Lydia said.

"Maybe he can help on the sly," Tony said. He gave Sister Lydia a glance. "Mind if I share some of the details with a cop I know?"

"Do you trust him?" she asked.

"With my life. Tommy O'Rear is my former partner. Though he's ten years younger than me, he also grew up in the Channel."

"Winnie O'Rear's grandson?" she asked.

"That's him," Tony said.

"He hasn't been to mass in quite a while," she

said.

"I'll talk to him about it," Tony said. "Should I get him involved."

"Winnie and I grew up together," Sister Lydia said. "If you say he's okay, then I'm not opposed."

Tony nodded and saluted Sister Lydia with his glass. "Okay then, Cowboy. Let's hear your wild tale."

I sipped my lemonade, waiting for everyone's full attention before beginning.

"I wasn't completely truthful with you yesterday when I told you I'd found nothing in the attic. I came across a large wooden casket shaped like a coffin. I couldn't open it because the top was nailed shut."

"That's quite impossible," Sister Lydia said. "I've been over every inch of the attic. I saw no coffin."

"When was that?" I asked.

"Some time ago," she said. "I can't remember when."

"Lots can happen in a short time," Tony said.

"Of course," Sister Lydia said. "Please continue with your story."

"After finding the casket, I checked out one of the cells on the second floor. A window and the shutters were open. A young woman, a bird on her finger and others flying around her head, was lying in the bushes in the courtyard. I ran downstairs to see who she was. When I reached the spot where I'd seen her, she was gone."

"What's so strange about seeing a young woman in the courtyard?" Tony asked.

"Her appearance," I said. "She had dark braided hair and skin so pale it almost looked as if she had an aura surrounding her. She was wearing a skimpy white chemise and had nothing on underneath."

"Interesting," Tony said.

"I asked several of the visitors, and the woman at the front desk, if they'd seen her. None of them had. Do you know anything about this person, Sister Lydia?"

"Visitors to the convent have reported seeing a young woman, as you describe," Sister Lydia said.

"Have you or anyone else on staff seen her?" I asked.

"New Orleans is more than three-hundred years old," she said. "There are sightings of ghosts almost every day."

"You think the person I saw was a ghost?" I said.

"Though spirits abound in New Orleans, there are no ghosts in the Old Ursuline Convent, at least as far as I know," she said.

"Then, the young woman I saw is real. "Maybe she performed the satanic ceremony."

"I don't think the person you saw, or think you saw is either real or a ghost," Sister Lydia said.

"Then, what was she?" I asked.

"A hallucination, or maybe a mirage. You'd just come from a stuffy attic. Perhaps the heat and the mold caused a reaction."

"I don't think so. I felt fine, and the young woman seemed very real to me."

"If she was in the courtyard, in plain sight, then why didn't anyone else see her?"

"Let's just say, hypothetically speaking, I did see either a ghost or a strange young woman. What would be your explanation?"

"Maybe she's a tragic victim of some evil that occurred within the walls of the convent," Sister Lydia said. "If that is so, her soul is trapped there forever, unless divine intervention releases her."

"Is there something you need to tell us?" I asked.

"Just saying," she said.

"Forever is a long time," I said.

"Or until the sin of her death is rectified."

Rafael clutched Sister Lydia's hand when he realized the nun was suddenly overcome with emotion. Tony and I exchanged a glance.

"Are you okay?" Rafael asked.

Sister Lydia took a deep breath, and then a long sip of her drink.

"Enough about the girl. Tell us what you found in the attic besides vampire's bones."

I handed her the nun's habit. "This looks very old to me," I said.

"The habit of an Ursuline nun," Sister Lydia said. "We have similar ones on display in the museum. It's at least two-hundred years old. What else do you have?"

I showed her the wooden cross. "Is this also old?" I asked.

A tear rolled down Sister Lydia's cheek when she said, "It's a religious relic with important meaning. It's been missing for many years."

"Is it the same age as the habit?" I asked.

"Much older," Sister Lydia said. "This was carved from the wood of the cross Christ was crucified on. It's the Cross of Gilead. It protects the good and punishes the bad. When I tell you it's priceless, I'm not exaggerating."

"I can't believe it," Rafael said. "The Cross of Gilead has been missing since. . . ."

"Stolen from the Vatican in 1738," Sister Lydia said.

"The same year as the Papal ban of Freemasonry. Is there a connection?" Rafael asked.

"Freemasons were suspected of the theft," Sister Lydia said.

"Oh, my God!" Avory said. "Can I touch it?"

"You may," Sister Lydia said. "But let me

warn you this relic is blessed. A single touch has the absolute power to change your life forever."

"For the good?" Avory said.

"I can't guarantee that," Sister Lydia said. "It depends on your actions and intentions."

Avory drew back her hand. "Guess I better not take a chance."

Wyatt has already touched it. That cannot be changed. Would either of you two gentlemen like to touch the cross?"

"Think I'll pass," Tony said.

"I'm defrocked, and not worthy in the church's eyes," Rafael said. "I can't touch it."

"Very well," Sister Lydia said.

"Should we accompany you to the Archdiocese to deliver the relic to them?" I asked.

"It's not going to the Archdiocese," she said.

"Oh?" I said.

"This is complicated. I can't explain just now," Sister Lydia said. "Does Bertram have a safe?"

"You're not going to leave it here, are you?" I asked.

"That's exactly what I intend to do," she said.

Sister Lydia waved to get Bertram's attention. Thinking she was ordering more drinks, he quickly appeared with another round.

"Sit with us a minute," I said. "Sister Lydia has something to tell you."

Bertram scooted in beside her. "Sister, I'm sorry I haven't been to church lately. I'll try to do better."

"I'm sure you will, though that isn't what I need to speak with you about. The wooden cross on the table is centuries old, carved from the same tree upon which Christ was crucified."

Bertram scooted backward in the booth. "No way!"

"It's a priceless holy relic. I need to leave it in your safe for a while."

"My safe ain't no bank. Sure you don't want to put it someplace safer?"

"It'll be just fine in your safe, though you must let me put it there. A touch of the cross has the power to transform your life, for good, or maybe for the bad. Do you want to touch it?"

"No, ma'am," Bertram said.

"One more thing," she said. "You must all take a solemn vow that you will never speak to anyone outside this group about this cross. Do you all agree?"

Sister Lydia got assents from everyone in the booth.

"Let's do it," I said.

The nun covered the cross with both of her hands.

"Bow your heads and put your hands on mine. Don't touch the cross." She waited until everyone had complied. "Repeat after me," she said. "I solemnly swear."

"I solemnly swear," we chorused.

"Upon penalty of eternal damnation, I will never speak of this religious relic, the Cross of Gilead, other than to those in this group until it is returned safely to its rightful place in the Vatican."

After we had repeated her words, Sister Lydia said, "Amen."

When she and Bertram left the booth to deposit the wooden cross into his safe, the rest of us exchanged uneasy glances across the table.

"You think we'll be damned to hell if we violate the oath?" Avory asked.

"Me, I ain't taking no chances," Tony said.

"Nor am I," Rafael said.

"I'm a lawyer," I said. "I wouldn't anyway."

"Shut the hell up, Cowboy," Tony said.

At least my irreverent comment caused everyone to relax. We were smiling and drinking when Sister Lydia returned.

"Did someone tell a joke?" she asked.

"A lame one," Rafael said. "At least it relieved the tension we were all feeling."

Sister Lydia sipped her martini. "Now, Wyatt, what else do you have?"

"Just this old document."

Sister Lydia took the document that looked as old as the Cross of Gilead. The foreign words on the old paper were handwritten in ink.

"May I see it?" Rafael said. "It's in Latin. I'm a Latin scholar. I can interpret it."

Sister Lydia handed it to him. "Of course you may. We should return it to the library at the museum," she said.

"I can tell you it's a priceless relic and I'll need some time to study it," he said. "Can I have access to the library? Maybe I can find an answer to our quandary in the archives."

"Of course," Sister Lydia said. "It's imperative we keep everything that has happened at this table to ourselves."

Rafael nodded. "Did you find anything else?" he asked.

I pulled out the drawing of a symbol. "What's it mean?"

"A hexagon within a circle," Rafael said. "Six nodes, six triangles, and six ellipses. Could be a Freemason symbol, though I've never seen this one before."

Tony was glancing around the booth. "I've heard the word Freemason more than once. Is there something to this Freemason connection?"

"Sister?" I said. "Do you have an answer?"

"Freemasonry and other secret societies were banned for a reason," she said. "Is there a connection between Freemasonry and Satanism? I don't know."

"What about the skeletons and the casket?"

Tony asked. "Where did they go?"

"I forgot to tell everyone I saw the bird girl in the attic. Avory suggested she might have moved the casket. She's so slight, I don't see how it's possible," I said.

"But she probably knows who did move it," Tony said. "I'd like to talk to her."

Sister Lydia was shaking her head. "As I said before, Wyatt was hallucinating. There is no girl in the convent. What else do you have?"

"One more thing," I said. "A set of plans, also very old, and an old map marked with an X."

"Plans for the Old Ursuline Convent," Rafael said. "I have no clue about the map. What do you think it means, Sister?"

Sister Lydia killed her martini before answering. "It marks the exact location of the entrance to hell."

Chapter 10

The first thing Darth Heaney saw when he opened his eyes was the girl. He couldn't remember the last time he'd seen her so close. She was staring at him with piercing eyes.

"Why do you keep haunting me?" he asked.

Darth didn't expect an answer, and he didn't get one. It didn't matter because he knew what she must be thinking. When she was alive, he could read her mind, and she could read his.

"I'm sorry I wasn't able to save you and Mom. You know that, don't you?"

Again, he got no answer.

Darth climbed out of bed and walked over to the washbasin. Though he was naked, the girl was his twin sister. They'd seen each other naked as far back as either of them could remember. He washed his face in the basin. When he turned around, the girl was gone. He had things to do and couldn't worry about it.

Darth needed to visit the home office of the shipping company that ran the Emma Lou and pick up his paycheck. Finding clean clothes in his duffel bag, he dressed in jeans and a blue denim work shirt before leaving his mother's dark little room.

Secret passages, though few remembered

their existence, laced the old convent. If Darth had wanted to, he could have taken one all the way to the back door. Instead, he followed a cramped passageway to the first floor. The museum was self-guided, no nuns or museum personnel usually present in the main building. The visitors wouldn't know he lived there, and that he wasn't a visitor. Since the museum was closed on the Sabbath, it didn't matter.

Although Darth had a passkey to the back gate, he always preferred to simply jump the fence. Young and athletic, the endeavor was easy for him. Trees, shrubbery and other vegetation, growing lushly in the sub-tropical climate of New Orleans masked his exit from the compound to the alleyway directly behind it.

Darth's twin sister had been a natural beauty. His own good looks always brought him appraising stares from the opposite sex. His diminutive size was his downfall, the victim of bullies his whole life until he'd grown strong enough to defend himself. The constant abuse he'd suffered at the hands of his father wasn't the reason he'd killed him; it was the abuse his sister had suffered that had finally pushed him over the edge.

Darth could no longer recall how he'd killed his father. The only thing he'd ever had in common with the asshole priest was their taste for warm blood. The silver flask, the single gift his father had ever given him, bore the inscription 'sanguis sues terrestres.' He had no idea what it meant. When he reached for the silver flask, he found it was empty.

The day was glorious, the scent of roses and irises emanating from gardens hidden behind old masonry. It didn't matter. Darth could see them in his mind. Though he'd never enjoyed the powers his sister had possessed, he could feel, and sense things others couldn't.

Now, he could smell the river and hear the music of the boats plying it. He loved the river, had an almost religious bond with it. He even wished his seven days were up and he was back on the Emma Lou on his way to St. Louis.

The headquarters of the Lower Mississippi Towboat Company was located in a large warehouse situated in an industrial area on the New Orleans side of the river. Sissy Boudreau, the cute receptionist from Chalmette, smiled, got up out of her desk and gave him a hug. Darth liked Sissy a lot though his backbone tightened when she hugged him.

Sissy was slightly taller than Darth, her dark hair straight, her complexion olive. Single, thirty years old and still looking for a man, she spoke the Chalmette-inflected accent that had strangers to the city mistaking her for a native of Brooklyn, New York.

"You about a shy one, you," Sissy said. "When you gonna put a smile on that cute face of yours and ask me out to go boot scooting?"

"I came for my check," he said.

Sissy straightened her ruffled blouse and black skirt as she returned to her desk.

"I got your check for you," "You never gonna loosen up, are you?"

Darth glanced around the open hall. "Where is everybody?" he asked.

"It's Sunday, sweetie," Sissy said. "Most people in church. I went to early mass before opening the office. You ever been to church?"

"More often than you'd think," he said. "Seen Sammy Ray around?"

"Haven't seen him and I hope I don't," Sissy said. "I can't stand that foul-mouthed man."

Darth glanced at his check. He still couldn't believe how much the Lower Mississippi Towboat

Company paid him. Except for a thousand dollars in hundred-dollar bills he kept in his wallet, most everything he'd ever earned was in a checking account at a local branch bank.

"I get off at three," Sissy said. "There's a jazz band playing on the Riverwalk later today. Ever ate an alligator po'boy?"

Darth glanced at the open top two buttons of Sissy's frilly blouse, and the glimpse of her lush breasts peeking up over the top of her red bra. There was nothing he'd rather do than fondle her abundant tits and have a taste of her blood. He averted his eyes and glanced at the floor.

"Gotta go," he said. "See you next time."

Darth could feel Sissy's stare on the back of his neck as he walked out of the office. Though he'd seen his beautiful sister's naked body many times, he'd never been with a woman other than his mother. She'd cradled him at night against her naked bosom, defiant when the drunken priest returned to the cell to punish her and him for their transgressions, either real or perceived.

Since the branch bank was closed on Sunday, Darth filled out a deposit slip and placed his check into the night depository. Unable to remember the last time he'd eaten, he bought a Lucky Dog from a vendor on the Riverwalk.

Darth had no driver's license and had never driven a car. He'd also never taken a cab. Feeling better after eating the Lucky Dog, he began the trek toward City Park. He loved the park. Even though it was several miles away, he'd decided to spend the rest of the lovely day beside one of the many lagoons there.

A light breeze was blowing when he reached City Park. The sky had darkened, and the sinister clouds signaled rain. When drops began sprinkling Darth's shoulders, he huddled beneath the draping branches of a giant live oak. Mostly shielded from the rain, he closed his eyes and fell into a deep, intoxicating sleep. When he awoke, the rain had ceased, the sky beginning to darken as the evening approached. He realized he wasn't alone. A young woman was kneeling over him, touching his forehead.

"Didn't mean to scare you," she said. "You were sleeping so soundly, and your skin is so pale, I thought you were dead. I'm Maeve. You're a vampire, aren't you?"

The woman's question caught Darth off guard. Dressed in khaki shorts, sleeveless Army green tee-shirt, and walking boots, Maeve looked as if she'd just finished hiking. Ringlets of auburn hair draped her bare shoulders and framed her pretty face highlighted by startling gray eyes. Her athletic legs and arms were equally as pale as were his. Hers were freckled.

"What the hell are you talking about?" he asked.

"It's okay," Maeve said. "I'm a vampire, too."

"I never said I was a vampire."

"But you are, aren't you?"

She laughed when he said, "What difference does it make? I'm not breaking any laws."

"Neither am I," Maeve said. "Liking the taste of blood isn't a crime."

"You've tasted blood?" Darth asked.

"Of course I have," she said. "I told you I'm a vampire. What's your name?"

"Darth."

"Are you from New Orleans, Darth?"

"Yes."

"I'm from Rhode Island," she said. "Lots of vampires in town are from other places. That's the reason I came here."

"There are other vampires in New Orleans?"

Maeve laughed again. "You kidding me? This is where it all started. Vampires came to America through New Orleans. You're a vampire. Surely, you knew that."

Darth shook his head. "I'm just part vampire and so was my dad. The only real vampire I know is my grandfather."

"Three generations of vampires? You can't be serious," Maeve said. "What about your mother?"

Darth shook his head again and said, "Nope."

"But your mom knew your dad was a vampire, right?"

"She knew."

"You're not much of a talker, are you?" Maeve asked.

"Nope."

"What do you do, Darth?"

"Seaman on a towboat," he said.

"I'm an actress," Maeve said.

"Then what are you doing in New Orleans?"

"There are more movies and television shows filmed in New Orleans, except for Hollywood and Bollywood than any place on earth," she said.

She smiled when he asked, "Are you famous?"

"I've gotten enough parts to make a living. I'm far from famous, though I've been in several movies you've probably seen. The biggest thing I'm proud of is that I haven't had to do any porn."

Maeve's jaw dropped when Darth said, "I've never seen a movie."

"You're lying. Everyone has seen a movie."

"I haven't," he said.

"Your parents never took you to one?"

"They didn't raise me."

"Why not?"

"My dad was a priest."

"Catholic priest?"

"Yes."

"Catholic priests are supposed to be celibate."

"This isn't a perfect world," Darth said.

With a gentle hand, Maeve brushed a strand of hair off Darth's forehead. He liked her touch and didn't move away.

"Who raised you?" she asked.

"An orphanage."

"St. Elizabeth's?"

"St. Elizabeth's was closed before I was born," Darth said. "They put me in a Catholic orphanage in the Lower 9th Ward."

"Were you abused?" Maeve asked.

The question made Darth laugh. "You kidding?"

"I don't know. Were you?"

"Me and everyone else in the orphanage. I was lucky because I kept running away and staying with my mother. They finally gave up on me. Guess the other kids weren't so lucky."

"I'm so sorry," Maeve said.

"Not your fault. I survived. I'm okay," Darth said.

"Would you like to exchange blood?" Maeve asked.

Darth couldn't believe what he was hearing. "Are you serious?" he asked.

"Of course I am," she said. "I wouldn't have said it if I wasn't."

"How do you want to do it?"

Maeve handed him a small knife with a carved handle.

"Use my ceremonial knife. It's sharp. You know how," she said.

Darth had never felt sexual desire like he was now feeling. Turning Maeve's hand, he made a small incision on the back of her wrist. Blood began oozing to the surface. He put his lips to the cut and began to moan.

"Suck it," she said. "Suck my blood."

Darth was snorting with desire, his face red with Maeve's blood when she pushed him away. It took him a moment to catch his breath. Grabbing the ceremonial knife off the grass, he cut a slit directly in the vein of his upturned wrist.

"Your turn," he said.

Maeve put her lips on the incision and began lapping Darth's blood. As she did, Darth began fondling her breasts with his other hand. Soon, they were tearing at each other's clothes as they rolled in the grass beneath the giant live oak.

A golden moon shined down on Maeve and Darth as they lay half-naked in the grass, panting beneath the ancient tree. Though Darth had been raped many times by his father, he'd never until that instant made love to a woman. For him, it was a transcendental moment.

"You're a wild man," Maeve said. "Have you ever been to Eden?"

"Eden?"

"A nightclub in the Quarter you won't believe. Will you go there with me?"

Chapter 11

Even after the long hike from City Park to the French Quarter, neither Darth nor Maeve was out of breath. Maeve was as young and athletic as Darth. When they reached the oldest area of the Big Easy, they were holding hands and smiling.

"Eden is off the beaten path," she said. "Few tourists even know it exists, though an occasional clueless visitor will wander in off the street. All the regulars are vampires."

"Real vampires?" Darth asked.

"Well, at least like you and me," Maeve said. "There are real vampires in New Orleans. It's always well after midnight when they come out. The regulars avoid them because they are dangerous."

"Why are they dangerous?"

"Have you ever known a real vampire?" Maeve asked.

"Just one," Darth said.

"I don't know about the vampire you knew, but real vampires will kill you."

"For sure?"

"That's what all the Eden regulars believe," Maeve said. "You knew a real vampire?"

Darth nodded. "Like I said before, my

grandfather."

"Your grandfather was a vampire? How did he die?"

"True vampires don't die," he said.

Maeve studied him, trying to decide if he were pulling her leg. He hadn't even the hint of a smile on his face. His comment created questions too numerous to ask. Saving them for later, she clutched his hand and pulled him forward.

Darth followed Maeve up a dark alleyway where they found a door marked by an unlighted sign that said, Eden. The tiny window on the heavy door sported uninviting bars. A sign said 'No cameras inside.' Darth didn't care because he owned neither a camera nor a cell phone.

Darth opened the door for Maeve and trailed her down a dark hallway. The walls were black. As soon as the door opened, they heard head-banging, heavy metal music emanating from speakers in the ceiling. The main room featured a bar painted with black enamel and was highlighted by kitschy black velvet paintings and old bones. Maeve waved when the bartender flashed a smile. She called to him above the dissonance of the music."

"Hi, Rocky. I'll catch up with you later."

"Too loud and too many tourists down here," Maeve said. "We're going upstairs. It's where all the regulars congregate. Hope you're not claustrophobic. A little stairway is the only way up to the second floor."

Maeve was correct. The stairs were so steep and narrow Darth wondered how fat people climbed it. Maeve laughed when he mentioned it.

"They don't," she said. "Vampires aren't fat."

The entryway at the top of the stairs opened into a room painted like the floor below. Even the bar was painted with black enamel. When the pretty bartender saw Maeve, she ran to hug her.

"Where the hell you been?" she said. "I was worried about you."

"Darth," Maeve said, "this is my bestie, Hope. She's the finest bartender in New Orleans."

Except for their hair, Maeve and Hope could have passed as sisters. Hope wore her blond hair in alpine braids. Like Maeve, Hope was dressed in shorts and tee-shirt, hers white and emblazoned in bright red with the word Eden. When Hope released Maeve, she gave Darth a hug.

"You about a stout one," she said. "You got some muscles under that shirt."

"Keep your hands off of him," Maeve said with a grin. "He's my property."

"Can't you share with your best friend?" Hope said.

Maeve was still smiling when she said, "I'll think about it. Can you make us a couple of Sazeracs?"

"You got it, babe," Hope said, returning to the bar.

"What's a Sazerac?" Darth asked.

"Absinthe, sugar, rye whiskey or cognac, and a couple of dashes of bitters. You're going to love it," Maeve said."

Maeve and Darth found a table. After bringing them their Sazeracs, Hope put her arms around Darth and pinched his nipple.

"I think I'm in love with this one," she said as she left the table.

Maeve was grinning and shaking her head. "You may have to do us both before the night is over. That girl's hot for you."

"You're joking, aren't you?" Darth asked.

"No way! She's my bestie."

Though the music was muffled, the room was dark as the one below. Maeve began exchanging smiles and waves with the other regulars. A young man whose long hair was as dark as

Darth's pulled up a chair at their table.

"Where you been, Maeve?"

"I took a hiking tour of Mississippi," she said. "Have you ever been to Oxford?"

"Can't say I have. What's it like?"

"Almost as mysterious as New Orleans," Maeve said. "I even found a few vampires there."

Focused on Darth, the young man wasn't listening to Maeve.

"I'm Ernesto," he said.

"Darth," he said, shaking Ernesto's hand.

Maeve put her arms around Darth's shoulders and kissed him on the neck.

"Darth's one of us," she said. "We've already exchanged blood."

"Have you now?" Ernesto said. "I haven't tasted any blood yet tonight. Would you share some of yours with me, Darth?"

Maeve nodded when Darth glanced at her. "How do you want to do it?" he asked.

"Take off your shirt. I'll make a small incision on your back with my knife," Ernesto said. "I promise the only pain you feel will be exquisite."

When Darth pulled off his shirt, the patron's at the other tables stopped what they were doing and gathered around to witness the bloodletting. One of the young women, a curly-haired blond named Janie, dressed like a Goth in all black gasped when Darth removed his shirt.

"My God!" she said. "Look at the body on that man."

Darth bent forward in his chair and allowed Ernesto to cut a small slit in his back. Ernesto squeezed the cut until blood began to ooze. When it did, he put his lips to the cut and lapped up the blood.

"Can I suck it?" Janie asked.

Ernesto wiped his lips and moved aside. Janie took his place and began tasting Darth's blood.

"Don't drain him," Maeve said.

Before Darth pulled his shirt back on, six people had tasted his blood. Soon, everyone in the room had pulled up their chairs to Maeve and Darth's table. Darth handed Hope a hundred.

"Drinks on me," he said. "If that's not enough, I have more."

The brown hair of a young man named Jim was long and straight, his skin pale. Even though the room was dark, he hadn't removed his sunglasses.

"All of us are working vampires," Jim said. "We have daytime jobs and earn livings like everyone else. That all changes after midnight."

"How so?" Darth asked.

A petite young woman named Peg, dressed in a floor-length skirt as if she were on her way to a medieval festival, said, "That's when the real vampires come out."

"Real vampires?" Darth said.

"A man named Malik comes here almost every night. He looks as if he's straight from Transylvania. He has fangs, and I don't mean prosthetic fangs," Peg's friend Joseph said. "He's almost seven feet tall, and he's a real vampire."

"He's definitely strange," Ernesto said. "He never talks to any of us. We've heard he has killed people."

Maeve had her arm linked through Darth's, not letting him stray from her. She could see the lust in Peg's eyes and the envy in those of all the men in the bar. Darth was truly a hunk. He was so short it had taken her a while to realize it.

Hope realized it. Every time she brought more drinks, she would drape her arms around his shoulders and rub his chest. Hope was hot for Darth, and so was everyone else in the room. After the bloodletting, Darth was definitely the center of attention. No one noticed when a large man walked through the door.

The man's thinning hair was long, draping to his shoulders. Even though the weather outside was mild, he was dressed in a black overcoat that draped almost to the ankles of his dark boots. He stopped at the bar, motioning to get Hope's attention, his eyes scanning the room.

"What'll it be, Mr. Malik?" Hope asked.

"Grim reaper with extra blood," he said.

Skulls, voodoo dolls and other macabre objects decorated the walls. Stuffed bats hung from the ceiling. Hope wasn't smiling when she brought Malik his grim reaper, drizzled with extra grenadine that looked like blood.

"Six bucks," she said.

The man named Malik counted out six ones for Hope, not bothering to give her a tip.

"Who's the little man at the table in the corner, and why is everyone standing around him?" he asked.

"His name is Darth," Hope said.

"Stupid name. Where did he come from?"

"Maeve brought him. He shared his blood with everyone up here. I even had a taste," she said.

"He looks like a fag," Malik said.

"Trust me," Hope said. "He's all man."

Malik drained his drink and ordered another as the crowd at Darth and Maeve's table continued to grow.

"Where you from?" a young woman asked Darth.

"New Orleans," he said.

"Most of us are from New Orleans. Where did you go to high school?" a dark-haired young man asked him.

"My mother home-schooled me," he said.

"From your accent, I thought you might have

gone to Jesuit," the man said. "Are you Catholic?"

"You could say that," Darth said.

"When did you first realize you were a vampire?" Peg asked.

"Don't know," he said. "I've never thought about it."

"What part of town are you from?" Ernesto asked.

"Whoa," Maeve said. "Darth is mine. Back off and let me spend some time alone with him. He'll be back. You can quiz him then."

Duly chastised, the group left Maeve and Darth's table. Maeve clutched Darth's hand and laughed out loud when Hope arrived with a new round of drinks. This time, Hope hugged Maeve.

"I love you, girlfriend," she said. "So sorry I have the hots for Darth."

"No problem. Love you too," Maeve said. "What are you doing later on?"

"I've been here since this morning and get off around one," Hope said.

"I'm taking Darth home with me. Want to come by the house?"

"Nothing I'd love more," Hope said. "Right now, I gotta get back to the bar. That scary dude Malik is drinking Grim Reapers, and he never stops trying to get me to share blood with him."

"Who's Malik?" Darth asked.

"The creepy guy almost everyone here, including me, thinks is a real vampire. Trust me when I tell you we give him a wide berth."

The laughter, ambiance of the bar, and the Sazeracs he'd drunk had combined to put Darth into a relaxed and happy mood. He didn't notice Malik until the large man clutched his shoulder in a vise-like grip. The crowd had gone quiet as Darth winced.

"Do I know you?" Malik said.

Darth grabbed Malik's hand, squeezing a

pressure point between the giant man's thumb and forefinger. Malik yanked his hand away.

"Don't ever touch me again unless I ask you to," Darth said.

"Then open your shirt and show me your mark," Malik said.

"I don't take your orders," Darth said.

"It isn't an order," Malik said. "I think I know you. I want to be sure."

"You're mistaken," Darth said. "We've never met."

"You were a baby when I saw you. You are the grandson of Louis, Le Petit Dauphin."

"My grandfather's name is Louis," Darth said.

"Then open your shirt. Show me your mark," Malik said.

Darth pulled up his tee-shirt, revealing a tattoo above his heart. It was a single drop of blood against a backdrop of elaborate scrollwork.

"Is this what you're looking for?" Darth asked.

Malik unbuttoned his shirt. The tattoo on his chest was identical to Darth's.

Malik's smile looked more like a grimace. "Now, you know I am for real."

"How do you know my grandfather?" Darth asked.

"We arrived in New Orleans together."

"My grandfather is from New Orleans," Darth said.

"Maybe now," Malik said. "He was born in France. So was I."

"When was that?" Darth asked.

"Centuries ago."

Before Darth could ask another question, Malik set his half-finished drink on the table and disappeared out the door. Maeve's eyes were opened wide until she finally blinked.

"What was he ranting about?" she said.

"Something I barely know myself," Darth said.

"Does he know your grandfather?"

"Maybe so," Darth said.

"That grotesque man doesn't look old enough to be anyone's grandfather," Maeve said.

"Real vampires don't age," Darth said.

Maeve smiled. "You're not a real vampire?"

It was Darth's turn to smile. "Vampires are the undead. As you already know, I'm very much alive."

"Then why do you have the same creepy tattoo as Malik does?" Maeve asked.

"I don't know. I don't even know where I got it," Darth said. "Or when."

"Are you serious?"

"Yes."

Maeve leaned back in her chair and sipped her drink.

"I hope Malik doesn't wait for us when we leave and drag us into a dark alley," she said.

Darth made a fist and rested it on the table. "If anyone ever lays a hand on you, they'll have to deal with me."

Chapter 12

Sister Lydia gave Bertram a solemn nod as she left the bar.

"I'm hungry," Rafael said. "I'm going to get something to eat, and then grab my laptop and head over to the research library at the convent. Anyone want to join me for lunch?"

"Count me in for both lunch and the research library," Avory said. "My laptop is upstairs. Should I take it now, or can we come back for it?"

"We'll put it in my car. The bistro I'm thinking about is on Magazine Street."

"See you guys later," Avory said as she and Rafael left Tony and me alone at the bar.

"You haven't said much. What's your take on all this?" I asked.

Tony sipped his scotch. "I'm kind of hungry myself," he said. "It wouldn't hurt us to finish our conversation over lunch. Been to Toukee's lately?"

"Not in a while," I said.

"It's not much more than a hole-in-the-wall, but their muffulettas are the best in town. We can talk about the case while we're chowing down."

"Why not?" I said.

Toukee's was on St. Charles Avenue, on the other side of Canal Street. Though it was far more than a hole-in-the-wall, it wasn't Brennan's. Still, every local knew about the little café. When we got there, we found people standing outside on the sidewalk waiting to get in. The line was moving fast, and our turn arrived quickly.

I glanced up at the ceiling where a half-dozen antique fans were spinning slowly, directing a cool breeze to the large room. Only one fan had a motor, and it was connected by belts to all the others. I lost my thought when a waiter recognized Tony and led us to an empty table. Tony ordered a Dixie, and I settled for iced tea. A friendly waiter who Tony apparently knew took our order.

"Two muffulettas, Joey."

"With extra olive salad," the waiter named Joey said.

"You know me too well," Tony said.

"Coming right up, Lieutenant," Joey said.

"Will people ever stop calling you Lieutenant?" I asked.

"Probably not," he said. "Old habits die hard."

The open door fronted St. Charles Avenue, people passing on the sidewalk slowing to catch a glimpse inside. A trolley turning off Canal rumbled past on its way to the Garden District and other parts of New Orleans. When our muffulettas arrived, Tony attacked his with enthusiasm.

"You're right," I said. "This muffuletta has the best olive salad I've ever tasted."

"Told you," he said. "You want my take?"

"On the muffuletta?"

"Our case," he said.

"Sure," I said. "I need the opinion of the best detective in town."

My solicitous remark brought a cynical grin to Tony's mug. Before responding to it, he lifted a finger to get the attention of a passing waiter.

"No need to kiss my ass, Cowboy," he said. "I'm going to tell you everything I know, anyway."

"Never a doubt in my mind," I said. "When we finish our muffulettas, I could go for some dessert. How about you?"

"You're reading my mind again."

When the white-smocked waiter returned, Tony gave him an enthusiastic thumb up.

"You did it again, Joey. Best muffuletta in town. You know, though, that ain't all we came for."

"Gotcha covered, Lieutenant. Coffee and lemon pie for two coming up."

The lunch crowd, rushing in and out of the little café, had been heavy. Most of the customers had hurried back to their day jobs as we enjoyed our lemon pie. The waiters ignored the remaining diners, clearing empty tables and clattering dishes.

"I'll tell you what I think," he said, sipping his strong coffee. "Sister Lydia isn't telling us everything she knows."

"My take exactly," I said. "Where do we go from here?"

"My Aunt Dot still lives in the Channel. She grew up with Sister Lydia. Let's go see her when we finish our lemon pie," he said. "Maybe she can tell us something we haven't thought of."

I was soon licking the last morsel from my fork. "Tasty," I said.

"Can't beat it," Tony said.

"Are you going to call your aunt before we head over there?"

"No need," Tony said. "She'll be happy to see us. She'll tell us everything she knows about Sister Lydia. At least if we can get her to stop talking long enough to give us a chance to tell her what we're there for. There might be a minor problem."

"Such as?"

"She'll have pie, and I promise you it will be the best you've ever tasted. We'll probably regret stuffing ourselves here."

"I'll try to hold up," I said with a smile.

"I bet you will," Tony said.

After leaving Toukee's, we waited at a streetcar stop on St. Charles. When an ancient streetcar rumbled to a halt, we climbed aboard. Lunch hour finished, we found the old rattletrap almost empty. Both Tony and I had ridden the route many times. No matter how many, it always took me back to my childhood. Tony pulled the cord, signaling the driver we wanted to get off at the next stop.

"We'll have to walk a few blocks," he said. "That'll be no problem for you. Me, I'm still not totally used to my artificial knee."

"Exercise is the best thing you can do for your bones," I said.

"That's what Lil says. Don't matter none cause neither of you has had a knee replacement."

"And I hope I never do," I said.

A sub-district of the Central City/Garden District area, the Irish Channel was largely a working-class neighborhood originally populated by Irish immigrants. Now, much of the population was either black or Mexican. Tony's Aunt Dot had never married and lived in the same shotgun house in which she'd grown up. After seeing Tony when she opened the front door, she grabbed him and gave him a hug.

"Tony, what in holy hell are you doing here? Did someone die?"

"No ma'am, they didn't. This is Wyatt Thomas. We're working on a case together and thought you might be able to answer some questions for us."

"I'm not a suspect in a murder, am I?"

Tony laughed. "I'm not with the N.O.P.D. anymore. We're helping Sister Lydia of the Greater New Orleans Archdiocese with a little problem they have. Since you grew up with Sister Lydia, we thought you might be able to tell us a few things about her."

"I can do that," she said. "Come in this house. I'll get you some coffee."

Tony's Aunt Dot was taller than him, her eyes as dark as his, her long hair gone to gray. The long print dress she wore was faded with age and too many cycles in the washer. She plodded to the chipped enamel stove in her small kitchen, hefting the little metal coffee pot to see if it was empty.

"Take a load off," she said.

After Tony and I had seated ourselves at her kitchen table, she brought the coffee and poured each of us a cup. Without asking if we were hungry, she served us slices of cherry pie.

"Sit with us, Aunt Dot," Tony finally said. "We didn't come to see you just to have you wait on us."

Aunt Dot brought her drink, the coffee pot, and pulled up a chair. When she tried to top up Tony's coffee, he stopped her.

"I'd rather have a glass of whatever it is you're drinking," he said.

"Just like your daddy," she said.

Aunt Dot got two tumblers out of a cabinet and grabbed her bottle of Irish whiskey."

"None for me," I said. "I'm a teetotaler."

"Don't know what you're missing," she said.

She laughed when I said, "Unfortunately, I do. I will have more of your wonderful coffee."

"You got to make it the right way: a metal percolator directly on the stovetop, and with a touch of salt and eggshell in the grounds."

"Take your word for it," I said as she poured me another cup.

"Two fingers, no ice," Tony said. "No use spoiling good whiskey."

"You are just like your old man," she said as she poured his whiskey. "Now tell me what it is you want to know about Lydia Stewart."

When Tony gave me a glance, I nodded for him to ask the questions. He was happy to oblige.

"The sister hired Wyatt to help the Archdiocese with a problem. Someone performed a satanic ceremony at a little altar at the Old Ursuline Convent," he said.

"Go on."

"Wyatt saw a young woman in the courtyard of the convent. When he told Sister Lydia about her, she got emotional, as if there was something she knew about the girl she wasn't telling us. Any ideas?"

Tony's aunt sipped her whiskey before answering. "Lydia and I were best friends growing up. She had some trouble during our senior year, and we lost touch."

"Trouble?" Tony said.

"She got pregnant and had to drop out of school."

"You know who it was that got her pregnant?" Tony asked.

Aunt Dot shook her head. "Lydia had a fascination with vampires. She used to drag me to every horror movie that came to town. When we were seniors, she got a part-time job at the Old Ursuline Convent."

"Because?" Tony prompted.

"I know you've heard about the Casket Girls and the rumors that there are vampires in the attic," Aunt Dot said.

"You think someone at the convent got Sister Lydia pregnant?" Tony asked.

"She never really told anyone who it was. Rumor has it, he was a priest."

When Aunt Dot hesitated, Tony said, "And?"

"Lydia never had a boyfriend her whole life. I didn't even think she liked boys. When I found out she was expecting, it hit me like a ton of bricks."

"I can imagine," I said. "Did she have the baby?"

"A boy," Aunt Dot said. "Lydia was always a devout Catholic. Her parents arranged to have the child taken."

"Taken? He wasn't adopted?"

Aunt Dot shook her head. "This was back in the seventies before they closed St. Elizabeth's. I heard the boy went there until he was old enough to leave."

"Any idea what happened to him after that?" I asked.

"I know exactly what happened to him," Aunt Dot said. "He went to seminary school and became a priest."

Tony gave me a glance and then quickly returned his attention to his aunt.

"You know his name?"

Aunt Dot nodded. "Luc Heaney. He used his mother's name until a family adopted him."

"He knew who his mother was?" Tony asked.

"Lydia was heartbroken when her parents made her give up the child. She became a nun, never finished high school, and never spoke to her parents again. She knew where Luc had gone and kept tabs on him."

"Sister Lydia's son was named Luc, and he became a priest?" I said.

"That's right," Aunt Dot said.

Tony gave me a glance. "You know Father Luc?" he asked.

"Avory, Rafael and I were at a music festival last night at Louis Armstrong Park. Rafael saw a priest he thought he recognized. The priest disappeared in the crowd when he chased after him. Father Luc was the name of the priest he thought he saw."

"Aunt Dot, do you have any idea what Sister Lydia's son looked like?"

"Short, stocky, dark hair, and eyes."

"Know where we can find him?" Tony asked.

"He went missing several years back," Aunt Dot said.

"Missing?" Tony said.

"Disappeared off the face of the earth," she said.

"How do you know so much?" Tony asked. "Are you still in contact with Sister Lydia?"

"I've already told you more than I should have. You're not going to rat me out, are you?"

"Our lips are sealed," Tony said. "You got my word on it."

Aunt Dot's arms were crossed tightly across her chest as she stared at me.

"Wyatt?"

"Unless you tell her yourself, Sister Lydia will never know we talked to you," I said. "One more thing. Do you know if Luc ever fathered any children?"

She hesitated before answering my question. "It's rumored he had two children out of wedlock; twins, a boy, and a girl."

"What happened to them?" I asked.

Aunt Dot refilled her whiskey glass and then topped up Tony's. Not forgetting me, she grabbed the coffee pot from the top of the stove.

"I've told you all I know," she said. "Another slice of cherry pie?"

Tony was already standing from the table, his arms up and his palms signaling no mas.

"No, ma'am," he said. "Your cherry pie is the best. Don't matter cause we got work to do and have to run."

"You just got here," Aunt Dot said. "I've so enjoyed your visit."

"We'll drop by again," Tony said. "I promise."

"But you haven't even talked about the family, or asked how your cousin Vincent is."

I sat back down, and so did Tony.

"How is Vincent?"

"Fat and sassy," she said. "Lost his job at the trucking company and had a little heart trouble last spring. Other than that, he and Millie are doing fine."

Aunt Dot continued talking as I had more coffee and Tony another drink. We had both eaten another slice of cherry pie before Tony looked at his watch and stood from the table.

"Gotta go," he said. "Got an appointment coming up I can't miss."

Aunt Dot was still talking when we waved from the sidewalk and started back toward the streetcar stop on St. Charles Avenue.

"You never cease to amaze me, Cowboy," Tony said. "You caught me by surprise when you asked Aunt Dot if Father Luc had children. Where'd you come up with that idea?"

"Sister Lydia," I said. "You saw how emotional she became when she talked about the possibility of the bird girl being a ghost. Considering her stoic demeanor, it seemed out of character for her."

"So what do you read into it?" Tony asked.

"This mystery started at the Old Ursuline Convent. My money's betting the convent is where it's going to end."

Chapter 13

Rafael and Avory were sitting at the bar when I returned alone to Bertram's. They'd changed clothes, Avory's royal blue dress emphasizing her bare shoulders while revealing a hint of her nice legs. Dressed in expensive dark slacks, white linen shirt open to the waist, black velvet blazer, and Gucci's with no socks, Rafael looked like a male model. I felt out of place in my khakis and a short-sleeved shirt.

"Going someplace?" I asked.

"Raf's taking me to a concert at City Park," Avory said.

"Under the stars at the Peristyle," Rafael said.

"Raf says I'll love it," Avory said.

"So it's Raf, now?" I said. "What happened to you and me?"

"Don't be a baby. Tell me about the Peristyle," Avory said.

"No place like it," I said. "An ionic-columned pavilion abutting a tranquil lagoon. Perfect for concerts. What time are we going?"

"You aren't invited," Avory said.

"I thought we were playing house," I said.

"Not tonight. Don't wait up for me," she said.

"I think I'm jealous," I said.

Avory grinned and patted Rafael's cheek.

"Don't be. You'll get your chance."

"No problem," I said. "Rafael and I had the same wife. I guess it's okay to have a communal girlfriend."

"That's the spirit," she said.

"Besides, there are things I need to do tonight."

"Such as?" she said.

"See if I can locate Father Luc."

Rafael focused on my words. "Wait a minute. How do you know Father Luc and why do you need to locate him?"

"You mean Sister Lydia's son?" I said.

When Rafael waved at Bertram, our Cajun bartender quickly arrived with fresh drinks and an icy glass of lemonade for me.

"Where you been?" he asked.

"The Irish Channel to talk with Tony's Aunt Dot."

"Maybe you should stop teasing and tell us what you know," Rafael said.

"Tony's Aunt Dot was Sister Lydia's best friend growing up," I said. "We quizzed her about Sister Lydia's life before she became a nun."

"We're all ears," Avory said.

Outside on the street, a carriage clattered past. One of the bar's regulars was already drunk when Bertram saw the man sneaking in the door. He called a cab and the hapless man's wife and then sent his would-be customer packing. Happily sensing Avory and Rafael's growing irritation, I sipped my lemonade, hesitating further before telling them about Aunt Dot.

"Seems Sister Lydia had a baby out of wedlock during her senior year in high school," I said. "His name was Luc Heaney. He became a Catholic priest."

"Are you making this up?" Rafael asked.

"Nope."

"I knew him," Rafael said. "Strange fellow. I could have sworn it was him I saw at Louis Armstrong Park last night."

"Aunt Dot said he disappeared several years ago."

"That's what I heard," Rafael said.

"What else do you know about him?"

"He was quiet, introspective, unassuming. He also had a well-disguised mean streak," Rafael said.

"How do you know that?" I asked.

"I once saw him kick a dog when he thought no one was looking."

"Maybe the dog was trying to bite him," Avory said.

"The old hound belonged to the seminary groundskeeper and was asleep in a flowerbed. Father Luc kicked him in the head. It looked to me like an act of pure cruelty."

"You think the man you saw last night was Father Luc?" I asked.

"Except for a single thing, he was identical in every way," Rafael said. "As I was chasing him through the crowd, I could see he was much younger than Father Luc would be. In his twenties, I'm guessing. Where do you think you might find him?"

"Maybe the convent," I said. "Could be he was the one who performed the ceremony."

"And your reasoning is?" Avory said.

"Louis Armstrong Park isn't far from the convent," I said. "Perhaps seeing him last night was a coincidence. We have little else to go on."

"He's too young to be Father Luc," Rafael said.

"About the same age as the bird girl who Sister Lydia insists doesn't exist," I said.

Rafael and I turned to Avory when she said, "Maybe they are brother and sister; Sister Lydia's grandchildren."

"Where do you come up with this idea?" Rafael asked.

"Women's intuition. It just seems to fit," Avory said.

"Funny you should say that because Tony's Aunt Dot seems to think Father Luc had sired twins. Fraternal twins, a boy, and a girl."

"Told you so," she said.

"Then use your powers and tell me what happened to the man who impregnated Sister Lydia," I said.

"Why don't we just ask her," Avory said.

"Why not?" I said.

It was past five, the bar already beginning to fill with tourists and locals who needed a drink before driving home. Two men in slacks and sports coats came through the front door, smiling when they saw me sitting at the bar. I slid off my barstool to shake hands with the two N.O.P.D. homicide cops Tommy O'Rear and Marlon Bando.

"You boys slumming, or dragging me downtown?" I asked.

Tommy grinned as he pumped my hand. "Neither," he said. "Tony asked us to help him with a case. We got some info for him."

"Avory Dorean, this is Tommy O'Rear and Marlon Bando, two of the N.O.P.D.'s finest homicide detectives."

Both bachelors, Tommy and Marlon, were instantly taken with attractive Avory, resplendent in her royal blue dress. Tommy was six-two, two hundred pounds, and could have passed as a linebacker for the Saints. He had to work at keeping his mop of unruly brown hair out of his eyes.

Marlon was slight of build, soft-spoken, quite ordinary looking, and his dark hair thinning. When it came to women, both men were painfully shy. Avory and her intuition picked up on their condition immediately.

Grabbing their hands, she said, "I love police officers. Can I buy you boys a drink?"

"Sure," Tommy said. "Bertram has Abita on tap. I'll take a tall one."

"Glass of juice for me," Marlon said.

Avory was still gripping their hands when she nodded, catching Lilly's attention.

"Bring my two new boyfriends a tall Abita and a glass of juice, pineapple if you have it," Avory said.

Neither Tommy nor Marlon was trying to free their hands from Avory's grasp.

"How did you know pineapple is my favorite juice?" Marlon asked.

"Though I've only known you a few minutes, I feel a certain common bond," Avory said, smiling as she gave me a wink.

"There isn't enough room at the bar," I said to Lilly. "We're moving to my booth."

"You got it," she said.

We were soon sitting in my 'office,' Avory in the middle with her arms linked through Tommy and Marlon's.

"What a lucky girl I am to sit with the four sexiest men in New Orleans," she said.

Tommy and Marlon were eating up the attention, both relaxing when Avory released their arms to nurse her martini.

"You have something for us, Tommy?" I said.

"A match on the blood sample you gave Tony," Tommy said.

"Already?" I asked.

Tommy downed half his glass of Abita before answering. "A former prisoner named Sammy Ray Nations. We found him in our DNA prison database. A perfect match."

"Is he still in prison?" I asked.

"Been out for a while," Tommy said. "Works on a towboat sailing out of New Orleans."

"At least he did," Marlon said. "Seems he has disappeared. He has no family. His employer's reported him missing when he didn't show up to collect his paycheck."

"Any ideas?" I asked.

"He has a little apartment in the Quarter," Tommy said. "Marlon and I aren't officially on the case. We checked it out anyway. Didn't look like he'd been there for a while."

"You found something else, though, didn't you?" Avory asked.

Tommy gave Marlon a glance and then returned his gaze to Avory.

"How did you know?" he asked.

"Lucky guess," she said.

"There was an incident at the music festival at Louis Armstrong Park last night," Marlon said. "A young woman was apparently molested."

"Apparently?" I said.

"There was an cut on her wrist," Tommy said. "She was anemic when she got to the emergency room."

"Loss of blood?" Avory asked.

"Exactly," Tommy said.

"What else?" I asked.

"She didn't remember much," Tommy said. "She had something in her hand."

"What?" I said.

"A priest's collar," Tommy said. "It was bloody. We ran DNA on it, and it came out positive for Sammy Ray Nation's blood."

"Dayum!" Avory said. "The girl was attacked by a priest who had the blood of a missing man on his collar?"

"That's about the size of it," Tommy said.

"Did the girl see who attacked her?" Avory asked.

"She was passed out in a pool of her own vomit and didn't remember much," Tommy said. "Where did you get the hundred-dollar bill?"

"Is this a police matter now?" I asked.

"If it wasn't for Tony, it would be," Tommy said. "Marlon and me are keeping it to ourselves for the time being because of him. We could be dealing with murder. We can't suppress this forever."

"Give us time," I said.

"You know something you want to share with us?" Tommy asked.

"We're working on some things. Right now, we don't know anything you don't know," I said.

"You didn't tell us where you got the bill," Tommy said.

"I can't tell you," I said.

"Why not?" Tommy asked.

"Tony and I are working for the Greater Archdiocese of New Orleans. We are sworn to secrecy. Though I don't know about Marlon, I do know you're Catholic, and that you understand. We need time to finish the job. When we do, we'll share everything with you."

"How long?" Tommy asked.

"No more than a couple of days," I said.

Tommy stuck his big index finger into my breastbone. "You got exactly two days," he said.

Tommy and Marlon left the booth without saying bye to Rafael or me. They both smiled and nodded at Avory before disappearing out the front door. Lilly was surprised they were gone when she appeared with more drinks.

"What happened? Did someone piss on their Post Toasties?" she asked.

"Not me," I said. "I'll drink Marlon's pineapple juice. Someone else will have to take Tommy's Abita."

"I'll drink the beer, though right about now

that seems the least of our problems," Avory said. "Where do you intend to go from here?"

"There's a link between Sammy Ray Nations and the person impersonating Father Luc," I said. "Fortunately, we're working with Tony, a man who's solved more gnarly murders than anyone I know. I doubt he's ever dealt with a vampire."

"Last night's assailant wasn't a real vampire," Rafael said. "He cut a slit in the woman's wrist."

"What's your point?" I asked.

"It probably means he doesn't have fangs," Rafael said.

"Vampirism is a cultural phenomenon," Avory said. "People who are otherwise normal commonly exchange blood these days. Have you ever been to Eden?"

Rafael and I shook our heads. "The biblical Eden?" Rafael asked.

"The vampire club in the Quarter," Avory said. "I'm not from here, and even I've heard of it."

"You mean there's a club in the Quarter where patrons pretend to be vampires?" Rafael asked.

"If drinking someone's blood is pretending to be a vampire, then yes," Avory said.

"We need to go there," I said.

"When Raf and I return from the concert," Avory said, "We'll meet you here. Eden doesn't get started good until after midnight."

"How do you know so much about it?" Rafael asked.

Avory finished Tommy's Abita and then returned to sipping her martini.

"I'm a screenwriter," she said. "Producers pay me big bucks to write realistic paranormal movies. It's my job to keep up with America's underbelly."

"Not to change the subject," I said. "Did you find anything promising at the convent's research library?"

"Several things," Rafael said. "I found the plans for the Old Ursuline Convent and a reference to Sister Lydia's comment."

"Refresh my memory," I said.

"When you showed Sister Lydia the old map you found in the coffin, she said the X marks the exact location of the entrance to hell. It's also the location of the Old Ursuline Convent."

"Is this a joke?" I asked.

"No joke," Rafael said. "The convent was built atop what Catholics at the time believed was the entrance to hell. The roof of the convent is significant because the Roof of Lucifer is the name given to the structure designed to keep the devil in hell."

"Wouldn't surprise me if certain Catholics still believe it's the cork in Satan's ass," Avory said.

"I found something else," Rafael said.

"Tell me," I said.

"A document that strongly suggests many of the priests back then were more than believers of the devil; they were followers. Their greatest desire was to destroy the obstruction blocking hell."

"They were closely aligned with the beliefs of the Freemasons though they had a name of their own," Avory said. "Rafael found the reference in a document, and I researched it on the Net."

"Ordre du Sang," Rafael said. "Order of the Blood."

"But that's French," I said.

"The Ursulines are French," Avory said.

The foot traffic was picking up on the sidewalk outside of Bertram's bar. When the door opened, music poured in off the street.

"How do you intend to occupy your time until we return?" Rafael asked.

"Don't know," I said. "Any suggestions?"

Rafael removed a folded sheet of paper from his sports coat. It was a hand-drawn map of the New Orleans city block between Chartres, Decatur, Iberville, and Bienville Streets. A hedge maze that looked a lot like the one at the Old Ursuline Convent occupied the northeast quarter of the city block

"Avory found this map, circa the 1720s, on the Internet," he said. "It's just down the street from here. We have plenty of time before the concert begins. Let's have a look."

Chapter 14

Chartres Street was hopping, tourists and locals enjoying the beautiful weather outside Bertram's bar. I felt like a slob as I followed Avory and Rafael. People on the sidewalk must have thought they were movie stars because everyone was turning to give them a look.

"I feel underdressed," I said.

"Quit whining," Avory said. "You look fine. How far do we have to walk?"

"Not far," Rafael said.

"Good," Avory said. "These shoes aren't the most comfortable pair I own."

She made a fist when I said, "Quit whining."

As Rafael had said, it wasn't far. When we reached the corner of Bienville and Chartres, we stopped and looked around. Having walked past the intersection many times, I already knew there was no hedge maze there. Commercial buildings occupied the entire block where the maze had once been. A man in a shop apparently noticed us gawking. Thinking we were tourists and needing directions, he opened the door of his shop and stepped outside.

The man was wearing dark slacks and a short-sleeved white shirt. He was probably in his seventies, though his full-head of hair and spry countenance made him seem much younger.

"Help you folks find something?"

"We really don't know what we're looking for," Rafael said. "Someone told us there was something to see at this corner."

"I'm Duane," the man said. "I've owned this gift shop for twenty years."

Rafael shook his hand. "This beautiful lady is Avory, and my friend is Wyatt. Maybe the person who told us was mistaken."

"Nope," Duane said. "There's a plaque right around the corner." He pointed. "This building was the Kolly House. Ursuline Nuns came to New Orleans in 1727 and used it as their convent until they moved up the street to the Old Ursuline Convent."

Duane pointed to the metal plaque we'd have probably never seen. The plaque's heading said: Kolly Townhouse, First Ursuline Convent, and Charity Hospital. It went on to explain that Jean-Daniel Kolly was a banking councilor to the Elector of Bavaria and a large investor in the West Indies Company.

A townhouse built by Kolly in 1718 was leased to the Ursulines in 1727 when they arrived in New Orleans, their last leg traversed by pirogue. They remained at that location until 1734. The maze across the street was built in 1731."

"I didn't know the Ursuline Convent wasn't at its original location," I said.

"Not many people do," Duane said. "Kolly was one of the first settlers of New Orleans and one of the owners of the West Indies Company.

"Did he also own the property across the street?" Rafael asked.

"Wouldn't doubt it. He owned lots of property around here."

"What happened to him?" Avory asked.

"Killed in the Natchez Indian Massacre."

"Interesting," Rafael said.

"Know anything else about him?" I asked.

Duane smiled. "Not much. Business is slow. When I saw you looking around like you were lost, I decided to help out in case the missus here might want to check out some of the souvenirs in my shop."

Avory snapped a few pictures of the plaque and the surroundings and then said, "Why not?"

Duane's shop was cheesy, though not like the tourist's traps on Bourbon Street. Avory bought a few tee shirts, postcards, and a self-published book written by a local author. She was smiling when we exited Duane's shop.

Back on the sidewalk, she said, "Check this out,"

The book was seventy pages of cheap copy paper stapled by hand. The cover page was a hexagram in a circle. The title said *Vampires and Numerology in New Orleans* by Count Sandor Vlad.

"A local authority," Avory said.

"I doubt it," Rafael said. "My guess is you just wasted fifteen bucks."

"You paid fifteen bucks for this?" I asked.

"Knock it off. It may be nothing other than articles you can easily find on the Internet. I won't know until I've read it," she said.

"That won't take you long," Rafael said.

"Yeah, well here's a picture of your hedge maze with an explanation."

"Let me see," he said.

Rafael began thumbing through the book. "Interesting," he said. "I better take this."

"Oh, no, you don't," Avory said, snatching it out of his hand.

"What's it say about the maze?" I said.

"Don't know yet," she said. "There's a reference to Philippe II, Duke of Orléans. He ruled

France after the death of Louis XIV for eight years, until Louis XV reached the age of twenty-three. New Orleans is named after him. He was also known from birth as the Duc of Chartres."

"The person whom this street was named after," Rafael said.

"I wonder if he was a Freemason," I said.

"We'll check it out later," Rafael said. "Avory and I need to head over to City Park. We'll catch you back at Bertram's around eleven. What are your plans until then?"

"I'll think of something," I said. "See you at eleven."

The foot traffic on the sidewalk had only increased as Avory and Rafael disappeared into the throng of tourists and locals getting off work. Thinking I may never see it again, I returned to Duane's souvenir shop and purchased my own copy of Count Sandor's tome about vampires and numerology. Duane was happy to see me and sold me his last copy of the book.

"Sell many of these?" I asked.

"You kidding? Sandor gives me twenty copies every Monday. They're always gone when he brings me more. I could sell a hundred if he could produce them faster."

"You know where he lives?" I asked.

"Sandor's a private man," Duane said.

"Does this help?" I asked, handing him a twenty.

Duane took the money. "I'm sure he won't mind if I give you his address," he said. "He lives in a Creole cottage on Burgundy, over in Faubourg Marigny."

The bells on the door tinkled as I exited Duane's shop, Count Sandor Vlad's homemade book under my arm, and directions to his cottage on Burgundy on a slip of paper. When I reached Jackson Square, I found a vacant park bench and began reading the book. It didn't take me long to realize that not only did Count Sandor Vlad know a lot about New Orleans, he also knew even more about the city's history, especially when it came to vampires and secret societies. I headed east after deciding to pop in on the count and pick his brain. I could have taken a cab, though Vlad's cottage wasn't far away, the weather perfect, and I was in no particular hurry.

Faubourg Marigny is the neighborhood due east of the French Quarter. Though not quite like Bourbon Street, the area has a vibrant nightlife along a stretch of Frenchmen Street. There were many good restaurants and even more music venues. Mama Mulate, my sometimes business partner, was a professor of English at Tulane University and a full-time voodoo mambo. Mama's favorite music club was in Faubourg Marigny.

When I got to Frenchmen Street, I followed it, catching the sights until I reached Burgundy and took a left. Daylight was waning when I found the address Duane had given me. The count's house was a Creole cottage, a colorful one-storied structure complete with a front porch and baby-blue shutters.

The house was neat, the colors inviting. It looked more like the home of a retired school teacher than the author of a book about vampires and Satanists. After knocking on the door and getting no results, I was beginning to think my trip was going to be for nothing. When someone opened the door a crack and peeked out, I realized I'd struck pay dirt.

"Count Vlad," I said, "I bought a copy of your book at Duane's Gift Shop on Chartres. He gave me your address and said he didn't think you'd mind if I dropped by."

"Out of the question," he said. "It's after dark."

"Sorry about my timing. I'm a writer and doing a story for a major publication back east. I'll pay you a hundred bucks for an interview, and it'll probably make a big difference in your book sales."

Count Sandor Vlad started to close the door, thought better of it and then opened it all the way. He was a tiny man, no taller than five feet. His gray hair was slicked back on his head, a black cape around his neck, draping the porch. I handed him the hundred-dollar-bill.

"Come in," he said.

The count's accent sounded more like an impersonation of Bela Lugosi in the movie Dracula than a local resident of Faubourg Marigny. The little man led me through the house to his messy office. He motioned for me to take a seat in a deteriorating office chair.

Furniture in the room included an ancient desk, a copy machine atop a folding table, and several boxes of copy paper. I could easily see making copies of his book was Count Sandor's primary enterprise. The lighting in the little office was dim, a candle in a holder flickering on the desk. When Count Sandor situated himself in the office chair behind the desk, I realized I'd seen him before and that I knew who he was. My first reaction was to suppress my desire to ask him for his autograph.

Noticing my grin of recognition, he said, "What are you smiling about?"

"I know who you are," I said. "When I was a boy, I never missed your show."

Count Sandor was an actor who had hosted a Saturday night show on a local station that highlighted old horror movies. The Count always appeared in character as a vampire from Transylvania named Sandor Vlad. He and other resident ghouls would perform skits during intermissions. On Saturday nights growing up, I rarely got to bed before two in the morning.

"I thought you said you were a writer from the east coast."

"I moved to New York after graduating from college. I grew up in New Orleans."

The room was dim, Count Sandor's facial expressions masked by dancing shadows. I didn't know if he knew I was lying or not, though he was apparently hungry for any accolades I might bestow. I didn't disappoint him.

"You're the primary reason that horror is my favorite genre. I never missed your show."

The hint of a smile flashed across the count's face. "I loved that gig," he said. "Unfortunately, it typecast me and ended up costing me dozens of acting roles I was otherwise qualified for."

"So you turned your talents to writing?"

"That's right," he said.

"Why haven't you self-published on the Net? A book like this would sell like hotcakes; far more than the twenty copies you sell to Duane's Gift Shop every week."

"I have my reasons," he said.

In a pile on the floor near my foot was a bound copy of a dissertation from Tulane University. When I read the title and the dissertation's author, I realized Count Sandor's primary reason for not publishing on the Internet. He wasn't the author of the book. He'd apparently stolen the dissertation from the Tulane library and had proceeded to plagiarize it for his own benefit. The room was dark, and I used my foot to scoot the dissertation toward me.

"You said you had questions," Sandor said.

"Sorry. Realizing I was meeting my childhood hero in person distracted me," I said. "How long did you do the show?"

"Eight years," he said. "New Orleans was just

becoming a movie-making Mecca when my gig ended."

"But it got you thinking about the possibilities of real vampires in New Orleans."

"Exactly," he said.

"Now I remember," I said. "Your real name is Bob James. You grew up in New Orleans and majored in drama at Tulane."

"Bravo," he said. "You're truly a fan."

It was apparent Bob James/Sandor Vlad knew little or nothing about the history of vampires and Freemasons in New Orleans. After asking a series of perfunctory questions, I handed him another hundred.

"Thanks, Count Sandor."

"Happy to help," he said.

I stopped at the front door. "One more thing. Can I get your autograph?"

Count Sandor smiled for the first time. Finding an old newspaper advertisement for his show, he signed it in a flourish with a gel pen. He didn't notice I had the Tulane dissertation cradled under my arm when I exited his Creole cottage.

Chapter 15

renchmen Street was rocking when I reached it, music pouring from open doors. Like no other place on earth, New Orleans was like a party that never ended. Since I had to walk past the Old Ursuline Convent on my way back to Bertram's, I decided to stop and retrieve the vampire's skull Avory and I had hidden in the second-floor library.

Long past dark, I was the only person on the sidewalk when I reached the convent. A bluesy saxophone holding court somewhere on Bourbon Street echoed in the darkness as I entered the compound through the back gate. It caused me to wonder what Avory, Rafael and I would find at the Eden Club. I left the dissertation in the bushes, the screech of the gate returning my attention to what I was doing.

Even in broad daylight, the old convent was creepy. Deserted of visitors and illuminated by auxiliary lighting, it took on the façade of a circus haunted house. Except for the creaky stairs on the way to the second floor, only the sound of mice gnawing on something in the walls disturbed the silence. After glancing around to assure myself I was alone, I used the passkey to open the door.

The library was dark, forcing me to fumble around until I found a lamp. Not powerful enough to light the entire room, the little lamp managed only to cast shadows on the bookshelves.

It took a moment to locate the row of boxes where Avory had stuffed the skull. When I found the box it lay behind, I pulled it out a bit. When I did, the light went out. I jumped when a hand in the dark touched my neck. Wheeling around, I reached for the hand. It was already gone

"Who is it?" I asked.

No one answered me. I couldn't hear a sound though I sensed someone was within arm's reach of where I stood. Without the candle, there wasn't even a flicker of light. A bead of sweat trickled down my forehead. My probing hands touched nothing but air.

"Are you there?" I said.

The room remained deadly quiet. I couldn't even hear sounds from the street outside, much less the saxophones on Bourbon Street. The darkness had turned me around. When I started for the door, I bumped into a bookshelf. I followed it until I found a wall. Though I had no idea which wall it was, I began feeling for a doorknob. When the lamp came back on, I was on the opposite wall from the library door. Someone was standing directly in front of me. It was the girl.

"I frightened you," she said.

"You did more than that," I said. "You scared the living hell out of me."

"I'm sorry," she said.

"I'll survive," I said. "Is Sister Lydia, your grandmother?" The young woman nodded. "I'm Wyatt. What's your name?"

"Leia."

"You mean like the Star Wars princess?"

"Yes," she said.

Until that moment, I'd only seen the young

woman from a distance. Standing close enough to me now that I could touch her, I saw she was incredibly beautiful, her pale skin glowing with an inner light. Her eyes were dark as her braids and the black feather in her hair. She was naked under the almost transparent chemise she wore. She must have realized the effect she had on me because the hint of a smile crept over her dimpled cheeks.

"Do you know who your grandfather was?" I asked.

"Of course I do."

"What was his name?"

"His name is Louis. Grandfather is still very much alive."

"What was his last name?" I asked.

"Dieudonné," she said.

Leia smiled when I asked, "He's not a priest?"

"Not of any god you worship," she said.

"Does Sister Lydia realize he's still alive?"

"Of course she does. They are married."

"You're kidding," I said. "Sister Lydia is a nun."

Leia's demeanor changed for a moment. "I don't want to talk about my grandparents any longer."

Her smile returned when I said, "I'm sorry."

"It's okay," she said. "We've only just met, and there are many things about me you don't know."

"Like how it is you manage to move around in the dark?" I asked.

"It isn't dark to me," she said.

She smiled when I asked, "Why do you wear a black feather in your hair?"

"There was no one for me to play with when I was little. My mom stuck this feather in my hair and told me to pretend I'm an Indian. I've worn it ever since."

"Are you. . . real?"

"Why would you ask such a thing?" she said. "You can see me, can't you?"

"You live alone in the convent. Your skin's so pale, it's all but aglow. You look supernatural, almost like a ghost."

"Do you believe in ghosts?"

"Does it matter what I believe?"

"I'm as real as the birds that fly outside in the courtyard," she said.

"Then it was you I saw lying in the grass."

"It was me," she said. "I love birds."

"I'm not sure I believe my eyes," I said.

Leia was standing so close to me, I could hear her gentle breathing. She raised her chemise, took my hand, and cupped it to her breast.

"Can you feel my warmth and the beating of my heart?"

My own heart was in my throat when I said, "Yes."

"You're touching me," she said. "Do I feel real to you?"

"Like the most wonderful thing I've ever felt," I said.

I bit my lip, thinking I might be dreaming. If I were asleep, the pain didn't wake me. Though Leia released my hand, I continued clasping her soft breast, not wanting to let go. Moving closer, she put her arms around my shoulders, drew me to her, and kissed me. Closing my eyes, I relished the moment, hoping if I were asleep that I'd never wake up.

Leia finally pulled away and said, "I have something to show you."

"You have my undivided attention."

Leia led me out of the library toward the nun's cells on the second floor. Stopping before we reached the first door, she pushed a spot on the wall. As if by magic, a panel opened and she pulled me into the darkness.

"Most people don't know this building is laced with secret passageways," she said.

My brain had entered some stasis between reality and a dream world. I didn't know where I was as Leia led me down a long passageway. Totally dark inside the passage, I didn't see the door she opened. After pulling me inside behind her, she found a candle and lit it. When she'd lighted several candles, the little room glowed with a flickering radiance and dancing shadows.

The air in the room was stale. Someone had recently thrown up on the floor beside the bed, the reek of vomit tickling my nose. Strewn bones lay on the bed. Human bones. The fear I'd felt when the lights had gone out in the library returned, my dream morphing into a potential nightmare. Had Leia turned into a demon at that moment, it wouldn't have surprised me. She didn't.

"Is this where you live?" I asked.

"It's my mother's room," Leia said.

"Where's your mother?"

"On the bed," she said.

"Those bones. . . ?"

"My mother, Mona Marie."

"How long has she. . . ?"

"Been dead?" Leia said.

"I don't mean to sound insensitive."

"Mother worked at the convent as the cleaning lady. We lived here. Nuns brought us food. Mother died years ago," Leia said. "Almost as long ago as I can remember. Darth never accepted her death."

"Darth?"

"My brother."

"You and your brother are named Darth and Leia?"

"One of my father's cruel jokes," she said.

"What was your mother's full name?" I asked.

"Mona Marie Alphonsi."

She nodded when I said, "She was Italian?"

We were standing in front of a water basin with a broken mirror behind it. What looked like dried blood caked the sides of the basin. Leia stood behind me, her arms laced around my chest, exerting gentle and sensuous pressure against the small of my back. When I glanced into the mirror, I could see my own image but not Leia's. Like a waking dream, the thought flew from my brain as I turned to see if she were still there. She was.

"Did your mother die after she'd raised you?"

"My brother and I raised each other."

"Darth?" Leia nodded. "Is he alive?" I asked.

"Very much so. He was here earlier."

"Who is your father?"

"Father Luc," she said.

"The priest?"

"Yes."

"Where is he?"

"Dead," she said.

"What happened?"

"Darth killed him."

"Your brother killed your father?"

"My twin brother," she said.

"Where is Darth?"

"Near. He's the reason I brought you here."

"Tell me," I said.

"My father was abusive."

"Abusive?"

"He took physical advantage of Darth and me from the time we were very young. Mother protected us as long as she was able. I barely remember when he beat her to death."

"You can't be serious! Father Luc beat your mother to death? Didn't the nuns take action."

"They never knew what had happened to her. They thought she'd left the convent to go someplace else," Leia said.

"And Father Luc?" I said.

"Darth hated him from that moment, though he was too young to do anything about it. The state took him when he got older. He kept escaping and returning here. When he became strong enough, he killed our father."

"What about you? Were you placed in a home?"

Leia didn't answer my question. "You're from Louisiana. You know what possession is."

"Of course I do," I said. "Is this about voodoo?"

Leia smiled again. "You don't know much about religion, do you?"

"I thought I did."

"Voodoo isn't the religion that came from West Africa. It's a mixture of Vodoun, West Indies Indian beliefs, and Catholicism. Catholics believe in possession. That's why they perform exorcisms."

"I never thought about it," I said.

"Evil sometimes possesses Darth. When it does, he becomes Father Luc. Though Darth's not a perfect person, he's a good man when he's not possessed. He doesn't deserve to die. At least not before his time."

"You think he's destined to die soon?" I said.

"This old convent has a dark secret," she said. "It was placed at this exact location because it overlies a gateway to hell."

"You believe that?"

"It's true," she said. "The convent is the door to the Roof of Lucifer. Some wish to destroy it and release the hounds of hell on the earth. Grandfather is one of those people. Father Luc was another. I'm afraid that when Darth is possessed, he will carry out the destruction of the roof. That must never happen."

"Can't you do something to stop him?" I asked.

"I can't, but you can, though you'll need my help. There is something we must do first, and we have little time to do it. Once the act is consummated, you and I will be as one."

"You intend to possess me?"

"Exactly what I intend to do."

"And then what do you want me to do?" I asked.

"Whatever it takes, even if it means your own death," she said.

Leia was still holding my hand as she pulled me toward the bed, her chemise dropping to the floor before we reached it. Some voice deep in my brain told me to protest. I couldn't. We began rolling on Leia's mother's bed, not worrying about the loose bones.

"You're entrancing me," I said, the sound of my voice gurgling in my throat.

She didn't answer, and I was too possessed to protest.

❦

When I came to my senses, I was alone in the little room. All the candles had gone out except one. Its flame was flickering as if it had little time left. I was naked, my clothes scattered across the floor, a human bone poking me in the back. There was also a white rose in my hand. I got out of bed, careful not to step in the vomit, and got dressed. Before leaving the room, I had a closer look around.

Taking the flickering candle, I followed the secret passage to the spot where I vaguely remembered entering through a secret door. Sweat dripped down my forehead and the back of my neck as I searched for the button to open it. I was about to panic when I found it, cooler air chilling my face as I leaped into the hallway of the

132

convent's second floor.

Dim lighting illuminated the building's interior as I bounded down the stairs. I exited the backdoor of the convent and was soon back on Chartres Street. I'd walked no further than a hundred feet when I realized I'd forgotten both the dissertation and the vampire skull.

I returned for the dissertation I'd left in the bushes but decided to forget about the skull. Some unknown dread was squeezing my gut, and I wasn't going back for it.

Chapter 16

When I reached Bertram's, I found Avory and Rafael waiting at the bar for me. Rafael didn't look happy as he glanced at his Rolex.

"We've been waiting almost an hour," he said.

"What time is it?" I asked.

"Midnight. You were supposed to be here at eleven."

"Perfect," I said. "No need arriving at Eden before the witching hour."

Avory was shaking her head. "Whatever! Where have you been, and what are you doing with that rose?"

I'd forgotten I had the white rose. The sight of it sent a wave of nostalgia cresting across my bow. I didn't bother telling Avory where I'd gotten it, showing her the Tulane dissertation instead.

"Seems the booklet you bought at Duane's Gift Shop was plagiarized from this."

"Where did you get it?" she asked.

"Duane gave me the address of Count Sandor Vlad. He lives in Faubourg Marigny. I paid him a visit."

"Find out anything?" Rafael said.

"That Count Sandor is a charlatan. You're from New Orleans and about the same age as I am. Did you ever watch Spook Fest on Saturday nights?"

"You kidding? I never missed it. I was in love with the station's Elvira knockoff, Katrina and her monstrous tatas."

"You and every other teenage boy in town," I said. "Surely, you remember Count Sandor."

"Oh, my God! You're right! Is that who wrote the book Avory bought?"

"That's who stole the book from its rightful author. He's made a living plagiarizing it for years. The real author got his Ph.D. at Tulane. I intend to check him out and see if he still lives around here."

"Where else have you been?" Avory asked.

"You wouldn't believe it if I told you," I said.

"Try me," she said.

"I stopped at the Old Ursuline Convent on my way here. I was going to retrieve the skull and bring it with me."

"But you didn't?" she said.

"Something happened while I was there," I said.

"Such as?" Rafael said.

"I was probably at the convent for a couple of hours, and I don't remember a damn thing except. . ."

"Except what?" Avory asked.

"When I left the convent, I had a feeling of dread I haven't experienced since I was a child, and used to think there was a monster under my bed."

"And you didn't get the skull?" Avory said.

"Afraid not," I said.

"Sounds like you had a stroke," Rafael said. "Perhaps we should take you to the emergency room."

"I'm fine," I said. "I didn't have a stroke. Something else happened, though I'm unsure what it was."

Both Avory and Rafael finished their drinks and ordered fresh ones. Rafael gave me a glance.

"If you're confident about your senses, we need to visit the Eden Club. Are you well enough to accompany us?" he asked.

"Stop it," I said. "I'm fine. Let's do it."

Lilly brought our tab and winked as Rafael cleared it. "Seen Quin lately?"

"No, and I hope I don't," Avory said.

"I was wondering if he'd come up with any ideas about where we should start our script," Lilly said.

"Don't worry, girlfriend. The project is half-finished. After tonight, we may be looking at it in the rearview mirror," Avory said.

"Anything you want to share with me?" Lilly asked.

"Not yet. Have fun with Bertram. I've got this one covered."

Avory and I waited in the bar while Rafael went for his car. She turned away for a moment to extract something from a sack on the floor. When she glanced up at me, she was wearing an ornate gold Mardi Gras mask.

"What do you think?" she asked.

"Love it. Looks expensive. Where did you get it?"

"Quin bought it for me when he was filming his last movie here in New Orleans," she said.

"And you have it on now, because. . . ?"

"I'm wearing it tonight. It just seems right."

I thought about it a moment. "Probably not a bad idea," I said. "It sets the mood. Maybe it's what we need to get us in the door with the regulars at Eden." I motioned Bertram. "Got a question for you."

The bar was packed with tourists and regulars, a zydeco band setting up on Bertram's little stage preparing to perform. Stopping what he was doing, he propped his elbows on the bar across from us and stared at Avory.

"Well, ain't you pretty?" he said. "Going to a costume party?"

"Something like that," she said.

"Rafael and I will be with her, and I was wondering if you had any Mardi Gras masks we could wear?" I asked.

"At least a hundred," he said. Bertram pulled a box of decorative Mardi Gras masks, collected over the years, from under the bar. "Take your pick."

After digging through the box, I chose the two flashiest masks in the pile.

"Thanks, Bertram. I knew I could count on you."

"Yeah, yeah," he said with a backward wave. "Don't call me if you get thrown in the pokey. I ain't bailing your ass out."

Before we got off our stools, Lilly arrived with fresh drinks in roadie glasses for Avory, Rafael and me. We waved goodbye to Lilly and Bertram when we heard Rafael honking outside the door.

Eden was in walking distance, but Avory was still wearing her uncomfortable shoes. Rafael's expression was all the comment we needed when he saw our masks.

"Thanks, I guess," he said when I handed him his exotic mask decorated with purple rhinestones and peacock plumes.

"No questions," Avory said. "Just put it on."

In the French Quarter, it's often easier to walk to where you are going than to find a parking spot. Rafael was grumbling about having to leave his Escalade on a dark side street. We looked as if we were on our way to a Mardi Gras ball when we exited his big vehicle.

The entrance to Eden was down a darkened

alleyway off Toulouse Street. A young man with female friends attached to both arms was leaving as we reached the front door. They either didn't notice our masks or else didn't care. Rafael turned and watched them go.

"People you know?" Avory asked.

"That young man reminded me of someone," Rafael said. "Maybe the priest I saw last night."

"I think you're seeing things," I said.

"Are we going inside, or stand out here in the alley and shoot the shit?" Avory asked.

"After you, milady," Rafael said.

He held open the door for Avory and me, and then followed us down the narrow hallway. The head-banging music was overpowering. The bartender pointed to the stairs.

"You folks look as if you're ready to party. It's quieter and lots more fun upstairs," he said.

We thanked him and quickly headed for the steep and narrow stairway. The bartender was right. It was quieter upstairs, the loud music ebbing as we reached the bar.

We entered a dark little room painted in black enamel. "I'm Bradley," the man behind the bar said. "What can I get you?"

"Martini for me," Avory said.

"Scotch, neat with a single cube of ice," Rafael said. "And make it a double."

"Water for me," I said.

Bradley fixed our drinks. "Have a seat anywhere you like. We don't have waiters or waitresses up here so I'll be taking care of you. Just wave when you need another."

We found an empty table in a dark corner. It was messy and looked as though it had just been vacated. When we glanced around, we noticed the people in the room were checking us out. Bradley cleaned our table with a bar rag and removed the empty drink glasses. A young man with long hair that matched his dark eyes scooted his chair beside us.

"I'm Ernesto," he said. "Are you from New Orleans, or out of town?"

"From here," Rafael said.

"Love your masks," Ernesto said. "Don't know if you heard. Most everyone here is a working vampire."

"What does that mean?" Avory asked.

"We all have day jobs. None of us have real fangs. Don't matter cause we all like the taste of blood. What about you?"

"We'd like to know more about vampires," Avory said.

"Sorry," Ernesto said. "If you're not vampires, then you're probably not going to fit in up here."

"Who said we aren't vampires?" Avory asked.

"Do you share?" Ernesto asked.

The young man's question must have caught Avory by surprise because she took a moment to answer him.

"Maybe," she said.

"Then can I taste your blood?"

When Avory glanced at Rafael and me, our Mardi Gras masks covered our expressions.

"What do I need to do?"

"I have a ceremonial knife," he said. "It's sharp and sterile. I'll make a tiny cut on your back. Just enough to taste your blood."

"Will it leave a scar?"

Ernesto laughed. "Just a superficial cut. "No scar, I promise."

"Okay," Avory said.

Everyone in the little upstairs bar, including Bradley, the bartender, had apparently been listening to the conversation. When Ernesto raised his thumb, they crowded around our table. Though I couldn't see Avory's face because of her mask, I knew she must be frightened. Her royal blue dress was secured by a bow tied around her neck. The top dropped to her waist, exposing her breasts when Ernesto untied the bow. Suddenly, everyone's attention was focused on bare-breasted Avory.

Along with a ball of cotton and a vial of rubbing alcohol, Ernesto produced his little knife. After swabbing a spot between Avory's shoulder blades with the cotton ball, he used it to clean the knife blade. Everyone around the table gawked as Ernesto made a cut, squeezing it until a drop of blood appeared, and then touching it with his tongue.

Avory had flinched when Ernesto made the cut. Her head was lowered, and her eyes hidden by the Mardi Gras mask. When she grabbed my hand and squeezed, I knew for sure she was frightened. There was little I could do except give her hand a reassuring pat.

After tasting Avory's blood, Ernesto stood from his chair, relinquishing it to a young woman in glasses who was dressed in black. Before the spectacle ended, Avory had shared her blood, except for Rafael and me, with everyone in the room.

"No thanks, we've already had the pleasure," I lied after everyone had finished tasting Avory's blood.

Avory retied her blouse, and just as quickly regained her senses.

"Did everyone get a taste?" she asked.

"Thank you," Ernesto said.

Ernesto began introducing us to everyone who had crowded around our table. Avory's performance had earned us acceptance. We introduced ourselves and took off our masks so everyone could see what we looked like.

"Maeve, one of our regulars, brought in a vampire earlier tonight who we hadn't met before," a woman named Peg said.

"Darth also shared his blood with us," Jim, a man with long hair and dark sunglasses, said.

"Darth?" I said. "That's a strange name."

"He was strange," Peg said, "but what a body."

"When did he leave?" I asked.

"Just before you got here," Ernesto said. "He left with his girlfriend, Maeve and Maeve's girlfriend, Hope."

"How tall is Darth?" I asked.

"Short," a woman named Jane said. "Probably five-six, or so."

Rafael was apparently thinking the same thing I was. When I glanced at him, he gave me a nod.

"Who is Hope?" he asked.

"One of our bartenders," Bradley said. "The owner's doing inventory this week, and Hope was here all day helping him. I took over for her before you got here."

"There was an incident," Peg said.

"Oh?" I said. "What happened?"

"There's a man who comes in here who everyone thinks is a real vampire," Jim said.

"A real vampire?" I said.

"Not like us. A vampire who sleeps in a coffin and only comes out at night."

"You mean like Dracula?" Rafael asked.

"Exactly," Ernesto said. "His name is Malik. He's big and strong and always arrives at the club well after midnight."

"He was here tonight as we tasted Darth's blood. He apparently didn't like the attention Darth was getting. He grabbed Darth's shoulder with the intent of hurting him," Peg said.

"Darth latched on to Malik's hand and squeezed it so hard he all but went to his knees," Jim said.

"Darth and Malik, strangely enough, had identical tattoos," Ernesto said.

"Interesting," Rafael said. "What did their tattoos look like?"

"A drop of blood against a background of scrollwork," Ernesto said.

"What sort of scrollwork?" I asked.

"Like on the back of a dollar bill."

Seeing Avory was acting disjointed, Rafael called for our tab.

"Bradley, bring us go cups. I have to work in a few hours. Oh, and put a drink for everyone in here on my tab."

Avory was clutching Rafael's hand tightly as we descended the narrow stairway.

"Are you okay?" I asked when the heavy door of the Eden Club shut behind us.

"It's beginning to hit me what I just did," she said. "I think I may get sick."

"You're a trooper, and I applaud your bravery," Rafael said. "I couldn't have done what you did."

"Me either," I said. "We got what we came for and if not for you we wouldn't have."

It was late when we made it back to Bertram's, and I climbed out of Rafael's big Escalade. Avory was huddled in a fetal position, her arms around her knees, her head lowered between them. She looked as if she were about to throw up.

"Are you going to make it?" I asked.

"Let her come home with me," Rafael said. "What Avory needs is the services of a priest who can perform an exorcism and rid her of her demons."

Something about what Rafael had said jogged a dim memory in my brain, and I was almost able to retrieve it. It wafted away like a waking dream as their taillights disappeared in the darkness.

Chapter 17

Darth awoke in a strange bed, his clothes strewn across the floor. Two naked women were in bed with him, and it took him a moment to remember he'd gone home with them after his visit to the Eden Club. Hope awoke to the persistent ringing of a cell phone on the table beside the bed.

"Oh shit!" she said. "I'm supposed to be at the club helping with inventory. They're going to fire me."

Maeve rubbed her eyes. "No one's going to fire you. Jump in the shower. You'll have a clear head when you get to work."

Hope was rummaging through the clothes on the floor, dressing quickly when she found hers.

"No time," she said. "Hope I got my own underwear and not yours."

Maeve giggled, her hand over her mouth, as she watched Hope hurry out the door. After hopping out of bed, she didn't bother getting dressed. Darth watched the athletic young woman set a pot of coffee on the stove in her little kitchenette. When it started percolating, she sat on the bed and put her arms around him.

"I hope you had a wonderful time last night and don't think Hope and I are weird."

"It was the best night of my life," he said.

"My little water heater runs cold before you can say scat," Maeve said. "Want to shower with me?"

"Nothing I'd like better," he said.

Maeve shrieked when the hot water turned colder. They were both still covered with soap and had to try hard to keep from shivering as they finished their showers beneath a stream of mostly tepid water.

"That's enough to destroy a warm and fuzzy mood," Maeve said as she toweled off.

"Not for me," Darth said.

Maeve glanced at him with a grin. "You're insatiable. Doesn't matter because I have an audition in an hour. You'll have to cool it until tonight."

"Please don't go," he said.

"I'll be back. Will you wait for me?"

"I'll be here when you return," he said.

"You sure?" she asked.

"Wild horses couldn't drag me away."

"I've heard that line before."

"Not from me, you haven't," Darth said.

Darth watched as Maeve got dressed, and then finished her coffee before kissing him and hurrying out the door.

Before closing it, she said, "I'll miss you."

"Miss you too," he said.

Darth listened to her footsteps as she ran down the stairs. When the room was silent, he grabbed his head and sank to his knees. It was the last thing he remembered for a while.

❧

Father Luc was kneeling on the floor of a strange room when he opened his eyes. He was naked, his hair damp, and his clothes lying in a pile on the floor beside a strange bed. He had no idea where he was or what he was doing there.

After getting dressed, he found a pot of coffee on the stove in the little kitchen. It was hot, and he looked around to see if he was alone before pouring himself a cup. The tiny apartment had a single window overlooking a French Quarter courtyard. It had rained sometime during the night and birds were bathing and preening their feathers in a concrete birdbath. He finished his coffee and put the cup in the sink, not bothering to lock the door on his way out.

The little priest had no idea why he wasn't dressed in his clergy vestments. His clothes felt familiar though he had no idea why they did. Except for being somewhere in the French Quarter, he didn't know where he was when he exited onto the street outside the apartment.

When he reached the intersection of Burgundy and Dauphine, he realized where he was and knew he wasn't far from the Old Ursuline Convent. There was a warehouse near the river, and he needed to go there. When he reached the warehouse and knocked on a side door, someone peered at him through a peephole.

"Who is it and what do you want," a voice behind the door asked.

"Luc Heaney," he said. "You know me."

The person did know him. It didn't matter. The questions were always the same whenever he came there.

"And what do you expect to find here?" the voice asked.

"People of a like mind," Father Luc said.

"What people?"

"Ordre du Sang."

The man on the other side of the door hesitated a moment before asking, "Are you a brother?"

"Not only a brother. I'm the son of a Disciple."

"Are you now?" the man behind the peephole

said. "Which Disciple?"

"Le Petit Dauphin."

"Louis is dead," the man said.

"He is immortal," Father Luc said. "He cannot die."

"If what you say is true, then display your mark."

Father Luc opened his shirt, showing the man behind the door the drop of crimson blood against a backdrop of scrollwork tattooed on his chest. When the door opened, the priest was motioned to enter. The magnificent interior of the warehouse was unlike what its simple exterior suggested. Father Luc had been there many times and had never ceased to be awed.

The man who'd opened the door was stocky and not much taller than Father Luc. He had dark hair and eyes and a Gallic nose and complexion. He was also slightly bow-legged. He was dressed in a dark suit with a blue tie decorated with a gold fleur de lis.

"How are you, Orson?"

"Passable," the man said. "We've been expecting you, and we have some good news. Please come with me."

Father Luc followed Orson down a hallway lined in gray marble. Elaborate oil paintings of French rulers and colorful tapestries lined the walls. The interior of the warehouse emulated a grand palace. Orson knocked twice when they reached a massive double door with carved moldings, and antique door handles. Not waiting for an invitation, he pushed open the doors.

The room was elegant, an elaborate office decorated in the manner of French royalty. A man in a dark suit and red tie, and looking enough like Orson to be his brother, sat behind an antique desk. Smiling when he saw Father Luc, he left the desk, taking a seat on a red velvet divan.

"So good to see you again," he said. "Join me."

Orson and Father Luc joined him on the divan. Sitting beside each other, it was easy to see Orson and the man were brothers.

"Veston has good news," Orson said.

The man named Veston said, "We've managed to obtain explosives. Our dream of destroying the Roof of Lucifer is near at hand. And Darth, you will have the honor of carrying out the mission."

"I'm Luc, not Darth."

"It doesn't matter who you think you are," Veston said. "What matters is you are available."

Father Luc suppressed a frown as he nodded. He didn't know why Veston persisted in calling him Darth though decided to let the remark pass. As Veston had said, what mattered was his availability to carry out the mission. Orson handed him a glass of water.

"Where did you get the explosives?" Father Luc asked.

"That's a detail to which you have no need to know the answer. What you should know is that one of our brothers is a demolition expert. He has studied the architectural plans of the convent and has drawn a schematic detailing how and where to place the explosives to bring it to the ground," Orson said.

"He will instruct you on how to carry out the mission," Veston added.

"When?"

"Now," Veston said.

The double doors opened, and a short man with a shaved head entered. From his looks, he was probably in his fifties. A Manila folder was tucked under his arm, and he extended his free hand to shake Father Luc's.

"Darth, this is Paul. You will go with him. He

will instruct you how to place the explosives to destroy the Roof of Lucifer."

"We have much to discuss and little time to do it," Paul said. "Please come with me."

Paul led Father Luc down the long hallway to a tiny room with a single table. Once there, he spread out maps and diagrams from the Manila folder under his arm.

"Orson told me you are extremely intelligent," Paul said. "Please have a seat, and I'll get you up to speed."

"I'm ready."

Father Luc shook his head when Paul asked, "Were you ever in the military?"

"I'm a priest, not a soldier."

"Too bad," Paul said. "It would have made our task much easier if you already knew the basics of demolition."

"I'm sorry."

"Not your fault," Paul said. "Bringing down a building, even though we are using explosives to do it, is a precise and daunting task. Every factor must be planned in great detail. A miscue could result in damage of the offset property, or worse."

"Such as?"

"We don't want to kill any of the neighbors." Paul pointed to a document on the table. "Do you know what a blueprint is?"

"Yes."

"This is a blueprint of the Old Ursuline Convent. We obtained it from records kept in France. The building has been modified more than once, and I've added the modifications to the schematic."

As Paul began pointing out various parts of the blueprint, Father Luc noticed the tattoo on his forearm. It was the insignia of the 101st Airborne Division. Paul, it seemed, had learned his demolition skills while in the U.S. Army. From the blueprint and the present-day photos of the convent, Father Luc began to see where the explosives needed to go.

"That's about it," Paul said. "Think you can handle it?"

"What happens once the explosives are in place?" Father Luc asked.

"You'll set the timer to explode sometime late at night when there's no one in the building," Paul said. "I'll be available for consultation every step of the way."

"I look forward to completing the task," Father Luc said.

"You must do more than you think you can. If you have any doubts, then tell me now."

"I have no doubts," Father Luc said.

"Good. You now know as much as I do about the demolition of the Old Ursuline Convent," Paul said. "The weight of the Order of the Blood is on your back."

"I won't let anyone down, I promise," Father Luc said.

"Just remember if you run into problems, I'm available to help you solve them. The explosives are in a backpack which you must carry to the convent."

Paul dragged a heavy backpack out of a closet.

"That can't be all I need," Father Luc said.

"It's not," Paul said. "A single pack is all a man, even a strong man, can carry in one trip. You'll have to return here several times to get it all."

"Is that it?" Father Luc asked.

"None of the authorities must stop you and ask to look in the backpack," Paul said. "If you are stopped, you must not allow that to happen. Am I making myself clear?"

Father Luc could only nod as Paul helped him

lift the pack to his shoulders. It was heavy, likely more than a hundred pounds, though no problem for him as he returned to the Old Ursuline Convent. When he reached the convent, he stood on a trashcan and peered over the wall. Seeing it was clear of tourists, he opened the gate and entered the compound. It was late, and no one saw the little man bearing a heavy pack on his back.

Father Luc wasn't used to seeing the old convent during daylight hours. Though still well-lighted, the rooms were vacant of tourists. He pushed a button hidden on the wall behind a painting and entered the maze of secret passages.

Though he couldn't see in the dark, he didn't have to. He'd been in the hidden hallways so many times he could traverse them with his eyes closed. After climbing the stairs to the second floor, he opened the hidden door to Mona Marie's room and lighted a candle. After glancing around the room, he knew someone had been there. It didn't matter. He was exhausted.

Father Luc slid the heavy pack off of his shoulders and let it drop with a thud to the floor. Without bothering to remove his clothes, he rolled over on the bed, closed his eyes, and fell fast asleep.

Chapter 18

Tony Nicosia was waiting for me at the bar the morning after my visit to the Eden Club. Instead of my usual cup of coffee, I asked Bertram if he could make me a bloody mary.

"Fall off the wagon, Cowboy?" he asked.

"Still on it," I said. "Sometimes you just need a bloody mary because they taste so good, even without the alcohol."

"You want me to make you a Shirley Temple bloody Mary?"

"Please," I said.

Bertram was shaking his head as he began mixing my drink.

"Hard night?" Tony asked.

"Only if watching someone lap up human blood bothers you," I said.

"Maybe you'd better tell me about it," he said.

Bertram brought my bloody mary and stayed to hear about the Eden Club.

"I don't know how Avory did it," I said. "She was overwhelmed by the experience. So were Rafael and I, though at least we didn't have to give blood."

"Your story don't surprise me none," Bertram said. "I heard lots of strange things go on there after midnight."

He laughed when I said, "Hell, Bertram, strange things go on here after midnight."

"The price of that bloody mary is the same, even without the vodka," he said.

"Put it on my tab," I said.

Bertram smiled and winked. "Call me when you need another."

Tony was laughing as Bertram hurried away to wait on a couple who had wandered into the bar.

"Did you leave something out of the story?" he asked.

"You're good, Tony."

"I've had lots of practice," he said.

"When we arrived at Eden, we saw a young man leaving with two women. Rafael said the man looked familiar, almost like the person he'd chased through the crowd at the festival."

"And?"

"I think the young man was Darth, the two women with him his girlfriend Maeve, and Hope, the bartender.

"What makes you think so?" Tony asked.

"They fit the descriptions of Darth and the two young women the patrons of the Eden Club described to us. It seems likely to me that Darth and Father Luc are related."

"Is Darth Sister Lydia's grandson?" Tony asked.

"Maybe we should ask her, and it wouldn't hurt to question the young woman, Hope," I said.

"Good idea," Tony said. "Maybe she caught his last name."

"Among other things," I said. "I'm thinking we should find out."

A mule-drawn carriage, laden with happy sightseers passed outside on the street. It prompted a bevy of picture taking as tourists on the sidewalk used their cameras and camera phones to record the event. Having seen it all before, Tony sipped his scotch without bothering to glance out the window.

"You must have had a good time last night if you already want to go back there," he said.

"Someone at the club told me they're doing inventory this week, and that Hope is helping. We could pop over on our way to visit Professor Fredrickson."

"Professor Fredrickson?" Tony asked.

"Rafael and Avory spent much of yesterday at the Old Ursuline Convent library. They found a map that showed a hedge maze like the one in the courtyard of the convent. In 1737, it was located at the intersection of Chartres and Bienville."

"You mean just down the street from here?"

"Yes. The owner of a souvenir shop saw us looking around, came out on the sidewalk and asked if he could help. He showed us a plaque on the wall that said it was the site of the Kolly Townhouse. The townhouse was leased to the Ursuline nuns when they first arrived in New Orleans."

"Interesting," Tony said.

"The man who leased it to them was Jean-Daniel Kolly, one of the owners of the West Indies Company. The townhouse was built in 1718, the same year New Orleans was founded."

"Was this Kolly fellow a Freemason?" Tony said.

"Funny you should ask. Avory and Rafael also found a reference to a secret society called Order of the Blood. Though akin to Freemasonry, its main goal was to destroy the physical barrier barring Satan from the earth."

Tony smiled and waved to get Bertram's attention. When he did, he raised two fingers to indicate we needed new drinks.

"My parish priest would say that door has

already been breached," he said. "What else you got?"

"Duane, the owner of the souvenir shop, was having a slow day and pulled us into his place. Avory bought some postcards and tee shirts and found a book titled *Vampires and Numerology in New Orleans*. It was handmade, cobbled together using standard copy paper by a local author named Count Sandor Vlad."

"Why does that name sound familiar?" Tony asked.

"Ever watch Spook Fest when you were growing up?"

"Me and every other kid in New Orleans," Tony said. "Damn! That Count Sandor Vlad?"

"One and the same," I said.

"He's still alive?"

I quipped, "Vampires live forever."

"Funny."

"I paid the count a visit yesterday. He didn't write the book. It's from a dissertation written by a Tulane doctoral candidate. I figured it out when I saw the dissertation on the floor. Vlad probably came across it at the Tulane library. He kiped it and has been plagiarizing and living off the profits ever since."

"Too bad we don't have the name of the real person who wrote it," Tony said.

"One step ahead of you. I took the dissertation with me when I left the count's house."

"Professor Fredrickson's dissertation?"

"You got it," I said. "He teaches history at Tulane. Strangely enough, he has a house in Bywater not far from where Count Sandor lives."

"Small world," Tony said.

"I'd planned to return the dissertation to the library and look up Fredrickson while I was there. I found out it is semester break, so I called him instead. Nice man. He invited me to drop by his house and offered to share his knowledge with me."

"When do you want to go?" Tony asked.

"After we finish our drinks."

The almost perfect weather was holding as Tony and I left Bertram's. There wasn't a cloud in the sky, tourists out in droves. Like every other New Orleans insider, Tony had a favorite spot to park when he visited the Quarter. We had to walk down a dark alleyway to get to it.

"One of these days I'm going to buy a bicycle," he said as he maneuvered his red Mustang convertible out of the narrow and probably illegal parking spot.

"It's not that far," I said. "We should just walk."

"Not an option," he said. "I got an artificial knee. Remember?"

Even if it took us longer to find a parking spot than it did to walk to Eden's, I protested no further. Instead, I showed him where Rafael had parked his Escalade. The spot was still open, and Tony gave me the high sign.

"Thanks, Cowboy. Now, how far do we have to hike from here?"

"Not far," I said. "I only hope they let us in the door."

The alley leading to the Eden Club seemed dingier and not as mysterious in the light of day. Even the skull painted on the door looked less menacing. I rapped on the entryway with no answer and was about to leave when Tony pushed by me and began banging on the door.

"N.O.P.D.," he said. "Open up!"

Someone immediately peeked through the peephole.

"Who is it?" a man's voice asked.

"Detectives Tony Nicosia and Wyatt Thomas.

We're here on business."

The door opened a crack. "Show me your badges."

"Screw you," Tony said as he yanked open the door and stepped inside. "We want to talk to Hope."

The black enamel walls were still dark though there was no head-banging music. The man frowning at Tony was shorter than he was, probably in his mid-fifties, and had closely-cropped hair and a cookie duster mustache.

"Not until you show me your badge," he said.

"You know me, Harold," Tony said. "I had to shut this place down and run you in a few years back. You want another dose of lockup?"

"I haven't done anything wrong," Harold said.

"Didn't say you have. Neither has Hope. Wyatt and me just need some information. Won't take more than a few minutes, unless you want to take it downtown."

"Hope's upstairs," Harold said. He called up to the other floor. "Baby, there are some men who have a couple of questions for you. Got a sec?"

"Send them up," a female voice answered.

Harold watched as we climbed the narrow stairway to the second floor of the Eden club. A young woman dressed in a white Eden Club tee shirt and khaki shorts was waiting for us behind the bar. Her blond braided pigtails made her look more like someone's pretty daughter than a bartender in a French Quarter vampire club.

"I'm Hope," she said. "How can I help you?"

"A scotch for me and lemonade, if you have it, for my partner here," Tony said.

"Drinking on the job, officer?" Hope asked with a grin.

"Enjoy life when you can," he said. "In our line of work, you may never get another chance."

"Amen to that." After making our drinks, she

rested her elbows on the bar. "Now, what else can I help you with?"

"You left the club last night with a man and a young woman," Tony said. "We have some questions about the man."

"You're the police, right?" she said.

Tony evaded Hope's question. "This isn't serious. No one's in any trouble. We just need a few answers, and then we're out of here."

"Such as?" she asked.

"The name of the couple you left with," Tony said.

"My best friend Maeve Wickes and her boyfriend Darth Heaney."

"You spent the night with them?"

"What difference does it make if I did?" Hope asked.

"No difference," Tony said. "What can you tell me about him?"

"He's short."

"And?"

"I couldn't believe how strong he was," she said. "Maeve and I work out every day, but I've never met anyone with muscles like Darth's. He felt almost. . ."

"Almost what?" Tony asked.

"Superhuman," she said. "He's a vampire, you know?"

"You mean like the vampires that frequent this bar?" Tony asked.

"I mean he's a real vampire," she said.

"With fangs?" I said.

"Not exactly," Hope said. "His canines are longer than normal, though not as sharp as the movies portray them."

"Does he have any tattoos or other distinguishing marks?" Tony asked.

"A gorgeous set of dimples and a tattoo just over his heart," Hope said. "A drop of red blood surrounded by scrollwork. I asked him what it meant, and he said he didn't know."

"Can you draw it for us?" Tony said.

Hope grabbed a pen and a scrap of paper from under the bar and quickly drew us a picture of Darth's tattoo. At least how she remembered it looked. Tony gave it a glance and then handed it to me.

"Any ideas?" he asked.

"Don't know about the drop of blood. The scrollwork looks like the pattern on the little altar at the Old Ursuline Convent," I said.

Tony pulled his wallet out of his pocket and removed a dollar bill. After comparing the scrollwork on the back of the bill to the drawing Hope had made, he handed them to me.

"Let me see," Hope said. After staring at the dollar bill for a moment, she said, "That's it. Darth's tattoo looks exactly like the scrollwork on this bill. What's it supposed to mean?"

I shook my head. "I'd like to know myself. Did Darth say anything you might consider odd?"

"Such as?"

"Like bragging about killing somebody," Tony said.

"Or ranting about conspiracy theories," I said.

Hope glanced at the black enamel paint on the walls as if trying to recall something she might have forgotten.

"He's an intelligent young man," she said. "We were too busy with other things to talk about politics or religion."

"Did he say where he works?" I asked.

Tony and I exchanged glances when she said, "He's a seaman on a towboat sailing out of New Orleans."

"You know the name of the towboat?" Tony asked.

"He didn't say," she said. "Is Darth in trouble

for something?"

"No trouble," Tony said. "What's does your friend Maeve do for a living?"

"She's an actress."

"I haven't heard of her," Tony said.

"Maeve's a great actress and drop-dead gorgeous. So far, she's only had a few bit parts. Someone will spot her and give her a lead role."

"There are lots of beautiful actresses in New Orleans," Tony said. "They don't all become stars."

"Maeve will," Hope said.

"Does Darth have a house?" Tony said.

Hope shook her head. "We didn't ask."

"Where does Maeve live?"

"In a flat near Burgundy and Dauphine."

I could tell Hope was a native of New Orleans because she pronounced the street name Burgundy with the accent on the second syllable instead of the first. She jotted down Maeve's address for us on the back of her drawing of Darth's tattoo.

"Is Darth a local?" I asked.

"An orphan," Hope said. "He had a traumatic childhood."

"How so?" Tony said.

"His father was abusive to him and his sister."

"What else did he tell you about his family?" Tony asked.

"He said his mother's name was Mona Marie and that he had a sister named Leia."

Chapter 19

Tony had a fresh go cup when we left the Eden Club and was less grumpy during our half-block walk to his car. Not even out of breath, he took a drink before buckling the seatbelt.

"Good job, Cowboy," he said after cranking the engine. "That girl was an information goldmine."

"If we learn half as much from Fredrickson, it'll be a good day."

Tony turned onto N. Rampart. The day was gorgeous as he lowered the top of his convertible.

"Hope the wind and noise don't bother you," he said.

"I love it. If I owned a car, it would be a convertible. I'd never put the top up."

"A New Orleans rainstorm would change your mind on that one," he said.

"Maybe. One of us needs to call the towboat company where the missing man works. See if he and Darth work on the same boat."

"What's it going to prove?" Tony asked.

"It'll suggest Darth was the person who performed the satanic ceremony at the Old Ursuline Convent," I said. "Makes sense because part of the tattoo Hope drew for us looked like the scrollwork of the cabinet holding the altar."

"And the scrollwork on the back of a dollar bill," Tony said. "What do you make of that?"

"Don't know. Add it to our list of questions for Professor Fredrickson."

Tony turned south into the New Orleans neighborhood known as Bywater. The area had been largely renovated after Hurricane Katrina, colorful shotgun houses and Creole cottages selling for astronomical prices and causing Bywater to become the hottest real estate market in the metroplex. An influx of upscale music venues and internationally known musicians had only accelerated the growth and rising home prices.

Professor Fredrickson's house was a beauty, a light blue Creole cottage complete with yellow storm shutters. The fresh paint wasn't the only attractive thing about the house. It was on a corner lot, had off-street parking and a covered patio in back.

Tony parked the Mustang on the street, and Fredrickson answered on the first knock. After opening the massive oak door, a slender man fully four inches taller than me extended his hand.

"David Fredrickson," he said. "You must be Mr. Thomas."

"Just Wyatt," I said. "David, this is my partner Tony Nicosia."

"Are you the police?"

"Why, have you done something wrong?" Tony asked with a snicker.

"Don't mind Tony," I said. "He used to be a lieutenant with the N.O.P.D. Neither of us is a cop anymore."

"We have some questions about New Orleans, and we heard you're an authority," Tony said. "Sorry about my bad joke."

"No problem," Fredrickson said. "Good to know you're not dragging me downtown."

"Not happening," I said. "We only want you to share your knowledge with us.

Dressed in faded jeans with holes in his knees, and an old Tulane teeshirt, David Fredrickson didn't look very professorial. His curly hair was uncombed, his beard and mustache scruffy. Since he had no gray in his brownish hair and beard, and no discernible facial wrinkles, I guessed his age as forty-something. He opened the door and beckoned us in.

"This house is one-hundred-eighty years old," he said. "Contractors took it down to the studs after Katrina. Brenda and I adore the restoration."

"I see why," I said. "Your wood floors are beautiful, and the antique furniture looks authentic."

"It's my wife Brenda who has an eye for authenticity. The sofas, side chairs, rugs, and paintings are all Antebellum originals or precise reproductions."

A yellow tabby came around the corner, padding across the wood floors to see who David was talking to. I let him smell my hand and then gave him a few full-body strokes.

"You like cats, Wyatt?" David asked.

"Very much so. I have a kitty named Kisses."

"That's Lucky," David said. "He has the run of the place."

David led us into the kitchen where an attractive woman was stirring a savory pot of beans on the stove. Though her hair was snowy white, she was no older than David. I realized as much when she turned around."

"Honey, this is Wyatt Thomas and Tony Nicosia. They aren't the police, and they're not here to run me in."

"I'm Brenda," she said, shaking our hands with a firm grip. "I see you've met Lucky."

When she glanced at my foot, I saw why. Lucky had followed us into the kitchen and was rubbing against my leg. I reached down and petted his head.

"Beautiful cat," I said.

"Rescue cat," she said. "Adopt, don't shop."

"My sentiments exactly," I said. "My Kisses is a rescue cat. My partner, Mama Mulate, has three rescue cats."

"Professor Mulate?" David said.

"Yes," I said.

"How is it she's your partner?" he asked.

"Long story," I said. "Maybe you'd better ask her."

"Mama's a close friend of ours," Brenda said. "She's been to our house, and we've had dinner together on several occasions. We see her at every Tulane function. We're aware she's a practicing voodoo mambo."

"Small world," I said.

"David's dissertation dealt briefly with voodoo," Brenda said. "He's somewhat of a local authority."

"David's dissertation is why we're here, though today we're not interested in voodoo."

"I have red beans and rice with andouille sausage cooking on the stove," Brenda said. "Can I get you a cup of coffee or a drink?"

"I see a bottle of scotch on your cabinet," Tony said. "I'd love scotch and water."

"Wyatt?" Brenda said.

"Better stick with coffee. I'm a working alcoholic. In New Orleans, it's never easy staying on the wagon."

"You got it," Brenda said. "Though David loves his gin and tonic, I'm a teetotaler."

David was grinning when he said, "Malaria can be rampant in these subtropical climes. Everyone knows tonic is a natural preventative."

"There hasn't been a case of malaria in New Orleans in well over a century," Brenda said. "You just like your gin and tonic."

"No use taking any chances," David said.

"Take them to the patio," Brenda said. "I'll bring the drinks."

We followed the slender man through the house to the cypress deck of the patio in back. A ten-foot fence surrounded the small backyard complete with palm trees, a working fountain, and the ambiance of a French Quarter courtyard. Ceiling fans rotated slowly above us, the air chilled by a misting system on the eave of the roof. We were barely situated in overstuffed deck chairs when Brenda brought our drinks.

"I'll leave you men alone to talk business," she said.

"Please don't go," I said. "Nothing we have to discuss is in any way secret. We just want to pick David's brain a bit."

"Well, if you don't mind," she said.

David sat his gin and tonic on a little table beside the two-seater he and Brenda were sharing. Lucky had jumped into my lap, and they were both smiling.

"You're not from New Orleans?" Tony asked.

"Not even from Louisiana. I grew up in Ohio. Being interested in French History, the Civil War, and the culture of New Orleans, I applied for my doctorate at Tulane. When they offered me a scholarship, I came as fast as I could. I've been here ever since."

"What about you, Brenda?" Tony said.

"I'm from New York. Since my pet topic is southern history, Tulane seemed like the perfect place to get my master's degree. David and I met in grad school. When I learned he loves many of the same things I do, we grew attached."

Tony glanced my way. "Looks to me like you may lose Lucky to Wyatt."

"I'm not worried," Brenda said. "He knows who fills his food bowl every morning."

"Since you haven't returned north, you two must like New Orleans," Tony said.

"More than like it," David said. "We love it here."

"And your relatives?" I said.

"We have two spare bedrooms, and they're usually filled with visitors," Brenda said. "We go back to Ohio and New York several times a year, usually in July or August. New Orleans is our home now."

"I hear you," I said. "Wish I could get out of town during July and August."

"It's not hard. Just do it," David said. How did you learn about my dissertation? Did Professor Mulate mention it to you?"

"Mama's out of town. I actually lifted it from the person who stole it from the Tulane library," I said.

"Really! The library originally had four copies. I was aware one had gone missing."

I removed David's dissertation from the bookbag I'd brought with us and handed it to him.

"Here's your dissertation," I said.

"Where did you find it?" David asked.

I showed him the drawing of the hedgerow maze located down the street from Bertram's bar.

"We found this drawing on the Internet and walked to Chartres and Bienville to see if we might find something interesting," I said.

"Of course," David said. "The location of the Kolly House and the site of the first Ursuline Convent."

"There's a souvenir shop near there. The shop was selling a book with the same title as your dissertation and supposedly written by a man named Count Sandor Vlad."

"You're kidding," David said.

"I'm not. The shop owner provided me with Vlad's address. When I called, he agreed to talk to me. When I saw your dissertation on his floor, I realized he was pirating it."

"Thank you, Wyatt. I'm grateful."

"You may want to have a lawyer send him a cease and desist letter," I said.

"Better yet, I may turn the dissertation into an e-book and paperback and have Vlad market it for me. Seems he has the knack."

I laughed and said, "Might be something to consider."

"Now, please tell me how my dissertation, *Vampires and Numerology in New Orleans*, is of interest to you."

"Tony and I are private investigators. We were recently hired by the Archdiocese of New Orleans to delve into an incident that occurred at the Old Ursuline Convent."

David's smile disappeared, and he scooted forward in his seat.

"Go on," he said.

"It appears a satanic ceremony was performed there," I said.

"Oh, my!" Brenda said.

"Tell us about it," David said.

"In the museum, there's a little room not much larger than a closet. The altar in the room is similar though much smaller to the other altars. Someone had left a white rose in a vase and a hundred dollar bill marked in human blood with the number 66. That only begins the mystery," I said.

"What else?" David asked.

"Sister Lydia, our liaison with the Greater Archdiocese of New Orleans, let me explore the attic of the convent."

"And?"

"I found a coffin."

"You didn't!" Brenda said.

"Yes, I did. I didn't tell Sister Lydia what I'd found, at least not then. I returned after dark with a crowbar and opened the coffin."

"You're a brave man," Brenda said.

"Or stupid," Tony said.

"Thanks, partner," I said.

"What was in the coffin?" Brenda asked.

"A nun's habit, plans for the convent, several skeletons, and a priceless religious relic."

"Vampire skeletons?" Brenda asked.

"I didn't bother checking. When I returned later with a colleague, the coffin was gone. We found a skull that had fangs."

"You can't be serious," Brenda said.

"Yes, I am. For some unknown reason, a window in the attic was open. Police on the street outside saw our light, gained entrance to the convent, and arrested us. They let us go when Sister Lydia provided us with an alibi."

"You said you found a religious relic in the coffin. What can you tell me about it?" David asked.

"Hold that thought," Brenda said. "I'm getting hungry. We can resume this conversation after lunch."

Chapter 20

I'd missed breakfast and hadn't realized how hungry I was until Brenda returned from the kitchen with fresh drinks and steaming bowls of red beans and rice.

"Hope you're not vegetarians," she said.

"One of my daughters is," Tony said. "Every time we eat together, she gives me hell."

"Don't let Brenda fool you," David said. "She's a vegetarian. I'm a lucky man because it hasn't stopped her from cooking scrumptious meals fit for a meat-eater like me."

"My cat Lucky is also a carnivore," Brenda said. "I understand the way of the world though I don't like the abuse heaped on animals. Someone has to stand up for them."

David clasped Brenda's hand. "Baby, no one does more to help animals than you do. Brenda's tireless," he said. "She puts up pictures on social media every night of New York death row cats needing to be rescued. A piece of Brenda's heart dies every time a cat is killed."

"Which is why I need to leave this conversation and get to work," Brenda said. "It was nice meeting you. You're both welcome back anytime. I'd love to meet your wives."

"I'm not married," I said.

"Then bring your cat."

"Thanks, Brenda," Tony said. My wife Lil would love your house. She, by the way, has a cat."

"I'd love to meet her," Brenda said. "There's more red beans and rice on the stove. Help yourself. David will refresh your drinks."

Tony waited until Brenda was gone. "That one's a prize. Never let her out of your sight."

"Don't I know it," David said. "Before eating, we were talking about a relic you'd found in the attic of the Old Ursuline Convent."

"A very old wooden cross," I said. "Sister Lydia told us it was made from the wood of the actual cross on which Christ was crucified."

"The Cross of Gilead?"

"Yes," I said.

"You have to be kidding. It disappeared from the Vatican in . . ."

"1738," I said. "The same year the Old Ursuline Convent was constructed, and the same year as the Papal Ban of Freemasonry."

"You've apparently done your homework. Where is the cross now?" David asked.

"Can't tell you. Upon penalty of eternal damnation, Tony and I are sworn to secrecy."

"Sister Lydia told us the cross has the power to change lives forever," Tony said. "She warned us against even touching it. Her warning was too late for Wyatt."

I had to smile. "My soul isn't worth much. I'm not losing any sleep over it."

"You know a lot about what you're dealing with. What else can I add?" David asked.

"Two other people are helping us with the investigation: Rafael Romanov, a priest knowledgeable about Catholicism, and Avory Dorean, a screenwriter."

"Is this going to become a movie?" David asked.

"Maybe," I said, "Though it's not a goal of my own. Rafael assured me while there may have been Satanists who occupied the Old Ursuline Convent, they are long gone. Whoever performed the ceremony may or may not be associated with them in any way."

"And then again, maybe they are," David said.

Tony was working on his second bowl of red beans and rice. He stopped eating and set the bowl on the table.

"Maybe you'd better explain," he said.

"You mentioned the Kolly House. Jean-Daniel Kolly was an investor in the West Indies Company. He arrived in what is now New Orleans in 1716. Before he died in 1715, Louis XIV had arranged for Kolly's investment."

"The French ruler known as the Sun King?" I said.

"One and the same," David said. "Louis XIV was Catholic though he didn't always agree with the views of the Vatican."

"Was he a Freemason?" I asked.

"Let's just say Louis XIV shared many common beliefs with the Freemasons," David said.

"What about the maze at the Kolly House?" Tony asked. "Who put it there? Kolly or the Ursulines?"

David hesitated a moment before answering. "I've done extensive research of the era toward the end of the Sun King's reign, and the years following his death. Much of what I know, or think I know, isn't publishable because there's too much conjecture involved. Doesn't matter because I have strong views about what may, or may not have happened during that era."

"Can you share them with us?" I asked.

"Of course. Just don't attribute them to me. They are controversial, and I could lose my job."

"You can't be serious," I said.

"The academic community is firmly set in its ways. Suggestions for changes in history can become career-torpedoing moves. So sorry for being such a poor host. Our drinks need refreshing. Brenda will kick my butt."

David slugged his gin and tonic as he got out of his chair. Tony handed him his empty scotch tumbler. The professor was still visibly shaken when he returned from the kitchen with fresh drinks. It made me wonder what we were about to hear.

"Are you okay?" I asked.

Sensing his human's need, Lucky left my lap. After jumping into David's, he began rubbing against his chest. David's grimace mellowed into a smile.

"I'm fine," he said. "I mentioned my theory about alternate French history to a colleague once and received a severe dressing down. Because of that rebuke, I stopped researching that particular era and changed my focus to the Civil War. Thinking about it reminded me how I felt following the scolding I received from the senior professor who was, and still is, my superior."

"You have nothing to worry about from us," I said. "Mama Mulate is the only other Tulane professor I know. I doubt you could tell her anything that would shock her."

David laughed. "I suspect you're right about that. Doesn't matter. The rest of this conversation is off the record."

"You got it, doc," Tony said. "Tell us what you know."

David took a long drink of his gin and tonic before beginning.

"The Sun King ruled longer than any other European ruler, either before or since," he said. "One of the reasons for his longevity was his attention to detail."

"Such as," Tony said.

"During his reign, Louis XIV was a war hawk, instigating numerous conflicts and all but bankrupting France in doing so. It didn't stop him from building the Palace of Versailles, commonly referred to as the most expensive residence ever built."

"You seem interested in Louis XIV," I said.

"There's a reason. One of Louis' insiders was André Le Nôtre, the landscape architect responsible for the geometrical designs of the palace gardens. Pierre Charles L'Enfant, who designed the master plan for Washington, D.C. was influenced by Le Nôtre's sunburst style. Many believe the designs of both the Palace of Versailles and Washington have Freemasonry influences."

"So the Sun King was a Freemason," Tony said.

"A good possibility," David said. "He was also into absolute security. Ever hear of the French Ciphers?"

Tony and I both shook our head. "Some form of code?" I asked.

"Every letter Louis XIV sent or received was written in code. Many of the ciphers have long since been broken, although in the Sun King's time they were quite formidable. That brings me to the point of my story."

"Which is?" Tony said.

"Immortality," David said. "The Sun King was looking for the Fountain of Youth, a way to live forever. He never achieved immortality, though perhaps his heirs did."

"No man is immortal," Tony said.

"Vampires are," David said.

"Vampires aren't real," Tony said.

"Do you know that for a fact?"

"I've never seen a vampire."

"Have you seen everything there is to see?" David asked.

Tony sipped his scotch. "No one has."

I interjected a thought. "Tony and I were at the Eden Club before coming here. If you're talking about otherwise normal people who exchange blood, then there are lots of vampires in New Orleans."

"The people who frequent the Eden Club are normal," David said. "Normal people exist in the light of day. Normal people live and breathe. Vampires are the undead. You never see them because they don't exist in day-to-day life."

"Are you serious?" Tony said.

"Vampires walk at night. They rely on warm blood to continue to exist," David said. "Louis XIV had unholy desires to live forever and brought vampires from Bavaria. His favorite heir was his grandson Louis, Duc de Burgundy who was briefly known as Le Petit Dauphin. Louis supposedly died of measles at the age of thirty."

"Supposedly?" I said.

"There's a possibility Le Petit Dauphin is still alive or at least undead, and living right here in New Orleans," David said.

Tony was counting on his fingers. "He would have to be. . ."

"More than three-hundred years old," David said.

"What proof do you have?" I asked.

"Let me tell you a story," David said.

"Maybe you'd better give me a refill on my scotch before you begin," Tony said.

David smiled. "Of course. What about you, Wyatt?"

"I'm fine," I said.

"You following this?" Tony asked when David disappeared into the kitchen.

"I'm trying," I said. "Let him tell his story. If we need to, we can ask for clarification."

Tony had no time to reply as David returned. He not only had Tony's refreshed drink, he'd also brought the bottle with him.

"Don't worry," he said. "I promise there will be no pop quiz about what I've told you."

"Good," Tony said. "History was never my strongest subject."

"Then you had the wrong teachers," David said.

"None of them ever told me a French monarch was a vampire," Tony said.

"How's your drink?" David asked.

"Good," Tony said. "Hopefully, it'll help me bend my head around your story."

"That's why I brought the bottle," David said. "If my tale grows too outlandish, feel free to help yourself to more scotch."

"Thanks," Tony said. "I'll take you up on that offer. Now, please, finish your story."

"Around 1800, there was a heinous murder in New Orleans. The daughter of a prominent politician was found in her bed, drained of blood and quite dead. At least they thought."

"She wasn't dead?" Tony asked.

"Quite the contrary," David said. "She popped out of her coffin the night before her burial. All but scared the life out of an undertaker. The young woman disappeared and was never seen again."

"What about her would-be murderer?" Tony asked.

"Detectives followed a trail of blood. The sun was coming up when they found a large man in a state of near stupor. There was dried blood on his shirt."

"Did the cops arrest him?" Tony said.

"They tried. The man came around physically as they cuffed him. He broke the cuffs and tossed one of the policemen against a wall. If not for a priest who happened by on the sidewalk, he would have escaped."

Tony laughed. "Did the priest tell him to get on his knees and repent his sins?"

"He wore a cross around his neck and pressed it against the crazed man's forehead. It dropped him to the ground. More police arrived while the man writhed in pain."

"Then what?" Tony said.

"Louisiana housed state prisoners here in New Orleans until 1835. It was little more than a dungeon. The man the police had captured was never identified. For some reason, they called him the Duke. Because of his size and violent nature, the Duke was placed in solitary confinement."

"What became of him?" I asked.

"He spent thirty-five years in solitary confinement," David said.

"You're shitting me!" Tony said.

"In a room with no windows. They fed him through a slot in the cell's metal door. The jailers were afraid to go into the cell."

"Why didn't they just use a cross, like the priest on the street had?" Tony asked.

"They tried it. Even other priests had no success. The cross trick apparently only works for those possessing extraordinary faith. The prison was shut down in 1835, and the prisoners moved to Baton Rouge. All the prisoners except for the Duke."

"What happened?" I asked.

"The jailers thought he was too weak to resist when they took him from the cell. They were wrong. He escaped and was never seen again."

"What does your story have to do with the Old Ursuline Convent and the King of France?" Tony asked.

"The Duke left behind his personal diary he'd kept while in prison. It was written in French ciphers."

"And?" I said.

"Give me a moment," David said. He slugged his gin and tonic before going into the house, returning shortly with a bound volume, and then dropping it on the table in front of Tony and me. "This is the Duke's diary."

Chapter 21

Maeve felt unbelievably happy as she strolled down Burgundy Street on the way to her apartment. Her audition had gone well. Now, her fingers were crossed a major part in an upcoming historical thriller would be the lift her acting career needed. Even if it didn't, Darth, the man of her dreams, would be waiting for her. She took a backward step when she reached the doorway to her apartment and found it ajar.

Maeve didn't live in a bad neighborhood. Seeing the open door was no reason to suspect foul play. Still, her good mood had disappeared as she stepped through the doorway. Perhaps Malik, incensed at being humiliated by Darth at Eden, had followed them to her apartment. Maybe Darth was lying wounded, or worse, dead on the floor. Other distressful thoughts crossed her mind as she began looking around.

She found nothing amiss, at least that she could see. When she didn't find Darth's lifeless body in the corner of the room, elation returned, though only for a brief moment. Her euphoria began draining away, replaced by dark thoughts and pallid cheeks.

Darth had lied to her. He'd taken her love and

crushed it beneath his foot. He was probably sitting in a bar right now, telling his buddies how he'd had the fuck of his life from some woman too stupid to know he was only taking advantage of her.

"Damn it, Maeve, get a grip!" she said aloud. "He was nothing to me but a swinging dick!"

With the back of her hand, she wiped away the single tear rolling down her cheek. She used a half-empty gallon jug of spring water in the pantry to fill her grandmother's old teapot on the stove. As she sat on a kitchen stool, tears began to flow. When the teapot whistled, it took a moment before she heard it. She was on her second pot of tea and still crying when Darth came through the door.

"Maeve, are you okay?"

Darth dodged the teacup Maeve threw at him. "You betrayed me," she said.

"What are you talking about?" he asked.

"You said you would be here when I returned. You lied to me. You left the door open for anyone off the street to come in. My apartment could have been burglarized. A rapist could have been waiting for me. You don't care about me, and it's obvious."

"That isn't true," Darth said.

"The hell it's not! Don't try to explain. Just get the hell out!"

Maeve slapped at him when he tried to touch her hand. Her face was red, and he could see she'd been crying.

"I brought you something," he said.

Darth held a single crimson rose in his hand. The aromatic blossom filled the room with its sweet fragrance. Instead of reaching for it, Maeve clasped her arms tightly around her chest, her red curls bouncing as her head sagged.

"I'm so sad," she said. "This morning was the

best day of my life. I thought I'd met the man of my dreams. Now. . ."

"Please," Darth said. "Hear me out. I have spells I can't explain. I sometimes blackout for a day or so. When I awoke in my bed, I knew hours had passed. There are hours I don't remember. What I couldn't forget is you. I think I love you. Please don't turn me away."

Maeve's arms relaxed and her hands went to her face. When Darth put his arms around her and squeezed, she didn't pull away.

"Oh my God, I hate you!" she said. "Today could have been the best day of my life."

"It still is," he said. "How did your audition go?"

Her voice cracked when she said, "I think I got the part."

"I was praying you would," Darth said.

"You prayed for me?" Maeve asked.

"With every breath I have."

David Fredrickson dropped the heavy book on the table in front of Tony and me. I opened it and began thumbing through the fragile old pages. As David had said, it was written in code.

"Has someone interpreted this text?" I asked.

"I have," David said.

I'd already sensed there was something important in the diary. David's smirk confirmed it to me.

"You've been waiting a long time to show this to someone, haven't you?" I asked.

"Longer than you know. Brenda won't even talk to me about it. She says if I don't have the balls to bring it up to the faculty, then she doesn't want to hear me carp about it."

"Tony and I want to know," I said. "We can't help the relationship with your faculty. Please, tell us what the diary says."

"I interpreted the entire diary left in the cell," David said.

"Where did you get it," Tony said.

"I stole it," David said.

Tony glanced up from his scotch glass. "Pardon me?"

"It was in storage at the Tulane museum. I'd looked for the diary ever since I heard the story about the Duke. When I finally found it, I took it because I knew no one else had a clue what it was," David said, "I have no regrets."

I gave Tony a dirty look. "Neither Tony nor I care how you came by the document. What we want to know is what it says."

"It tells the story of how vampires came to America and how French royalty was involved," David said. "As I've already told you, the Sun King was searching for immortality and had brought a vampire from Bavaria. It was the primary reason Kolly got a concession."

"The king of France believed in the supernatural?" Tony asked.

"Every unexplained thing isn't necessarily supernatural. There can be other reasons."

"Such as?" Tony said.

"The Sun King was quite progressive. Not only was he surrounded by great artists and musicians, but by physicians, mathematicians, architects, and every manner of progressive scientists. Though knowledge of bacteria and viruses hadn't yet been discovered, even the country-folk knew the bite of a diseased animal sometimes resulted in the contraction of something deadly."

"If they knew about vampires, then why don't our scientists know about them now?" Tony asked.

"Unless it's recorded for posterity, knowledge is ephemeral. Who knows what priceless information was lost or destroyed through the ages? Vampirism, for all we know, could be caused by a virus. Who's to say it isn't?"

"If there is such a thing as a vampire," Tony said.

David ignored Tony's skepticism. "Louis XIV's scientists apparently realized vampirism was contracted through blood exchange. The king died before he could become one himself. Others in his court actually saw his plan through to fruition. The Duke was one of those persons."

"Then you know who the Duke was, or perhaps still is," I said.

David placed his palm on the handwritten document. "By his own words, Duke proclaimed himself to be Louis XIV's grandson, Louis, Duc de Burgundy, also known as Le Petit Dauphin."

Tony thumbed through his notepad. "You told us he died of measles at the age of thirty."

"That's what the history books say. What really happened is something quite different," David said.

"Like what?" Tony asked.

"Le Petit Dauphin was married when he was fifteen. He was devoted to his wife. When they were stricken by measles, Louis was open to anything to save himself, his wife and sons. History states he died of measles in 1712."

"But he didn't?" I said.

"Louis XIV's experiments on immortality using vampires were close to fruition. Hoping to save the lives of himself, his wife and two sons, Le Petit Dauphin agreed that they would participate in the vampire experiment."

"What's the timeline here?" Tony asked.

"Garbled, at best," David said. "The historical records and the actual facts differ more than you might imagine. One thing is certain: when Louis decided to participate in the vampire experiments, he agreed they would leave France forever and start a new life in the colonies."

"Then give us a rough estimate," Tony said.

"First, let me give you some background. The colonies were short of women suitable for marriage. France had cleared out their prisons sending criminals and prostitutes to the New World. You can imagine how that turned out."

"How does this relate to the Casket Girls?" I asked.

"The Casket Girls were an attempt to send a higher class of women to the colonies. Though they didn't know it when they were recruited, they ended up playing a large part in bringing vampires to America. They served as hosts and provided sustenance to the vampires. That's why they looked so pale and wan when they arrived."

"You mean . . . ?"

"They actually had little knowledge of their participation in the experiment. The vampires drank their blood, but the keepers were the ones who drew the blood from the Casket Girls. There was never any direct contact with the vampires, and this is what prevented the hosts from becoming infected."

"Are you sure about that?" I asked.

"How can you be completely sure of something that happened centuries ago?" David said.

"History says the Casket Girls first arrived in New Orleans in 1728."

"Yes, but the first vampire to arrive in New Orleans was Le Petit Dauphin. The Duke's wife and sons died of measles and never made the trip to the new world."

"So when do you think Louis arrived in New Orleans?" Tony asked.

"My best guess is around 1716, four years or so after the Duke's reported death. The convent wasn't even built yet."

Absorbed in telling us his story, David hadn't noticed my coffee had grown cold. Brenda did and appeared from the kitchen with an iced glass and a pitcher of tea.

"Try this," she said. "It's my proprietary blend of strawberry-mango tea."

I took a sip, and then another. "This is the best tea I've ever tasted," I said.

"You don't have to say that," she said.

"I'm not kidding. It's good."

"David was so engrossed in his tale of vampires, he totally neglected his guests."

"No way," I said. "I can't remember when I've enjoyed myself so much."

Brenda was smiling and enjoying my praise when she said, "Poof!"

"I'm sorry, baby," David said. "Forgive me?"

"Hey, I married you for better or worse. If that's the worst I have to deal with, then I don't have much to complain about."

David was beaming. "I've been waiting to tell that story for ten years. Thanks for hearing me out."

"You're the one to thank," I said. "One more thing. What does any of this have to do with Satanists performing secret ceremonies at the Old Ursuline Convent?"

"The Edict of Nantes guaranteed freedom of religion to everyone in France," David said. "Louis XIV revoked it. He was a devout Catholic, and the revocation of the Edict of Nantes resulted in a ban of all religions in France and the colonies except for Roman Catholicism."

"Then where does the Satanism come in?" I asked.

"Although Louis XIV was a Roman Catholic, he didn't believe in all the views of the Vatican. As we've discussed, he likely adhered to many

Freemason principles. Many Catholics and Freemasons at the time believed in Satan. There was a belief that there was a duality between the heavens and the netherworld. To many, Satan was a god."

"I'm guessing modern Satanists still believe that way," I said.

"Louis, Duke of Burgundy, had a much different view of the world than did his grandfather," David said. "After studying his diary which spanned decades in prison, I feel the Duke began to change, perhaps sink into madness."

"What do you think became of him?" I asked.

"It's my opinion he's still in New Orleans."

Tony finished his scotch. "Is he the person responsible for the ceremony at the Old Ursuline Convent?"

"I'd say yes," David said.

"What's his intention?" I asked.

"Ever hear of the Roof of Lucifer?"

I glanced at Tony. "Maybe," I said. "Please tell us what you know."

"It's a spiritual barrier over the entrance to hell that keeps Satan from returning from the netherworld and reaping havoc. Some believe the Old Ursuline Convent is situated over the entrance to hell and is, in fact, the structure known as the Roof of Lucifer."

"And the Duke wants to destroy it?" Tony asked.

"In any way possible, at least that's my opinion," David said.

Chapter 22

Since Tony's wife Lil was cooking gumbo for dinner, he went straight home after dropping me off in front of Bertram's. I found Avory and Rafael waiting at the bar. Both of them had an attitude.

"Where have you been?" Avory asked.

"Tony and I interviewed David Fredrickson, the real author of *Vampires and Numerology in New Orleans*."

"I thought we were all in this together," Avory said.

"You and Rafael were elsewhere so Tony and I carried on without you. It doesn't mean you're no longer a part of the investigation," I said.

"Then what does it mean?" Avory asked.

"This case is far from over. Let me catch you up on what Tony and I learned and then we can decide where to go from here."

Rafael rested his hand on top of Avory's wrist. "Let's hear him out," he said.

"Not to change the subject," I said. "But you two seem awfully cozy. Am I no longer participating in our game of house?"

"Rafael saved my life last night," Avory said. "I don't recall having ever been so low."

"What exactly did Rafael do?" I asked.

"You sound jealous," Avory said.

"Do I have reason to be?"

"Maybe," she said. "Rafael is the most understanding male I've ever known. He helped me regain my self-esteem."

"Oh? Exactly how did he do that?" I asked.

"None of your business," she said.

Avory's words made me smile. "Just asking."

"You should be explaining where you were and what you were doing and not worrying about Rafael and me."

"Tony and I checked out a couple of leads. I was going to tell you about it," I said.

"Sure, you were!" Avory said.

Bertram saved me, bringing me lemonade and fresh drinks for Avory and Rafael.

"You three looking mighty intense," he said. "Maybe it's time for me to start mixing some of my specialty cocktails."

"Your martinis are the best," Avory said. "I'll stick with them."

"And I'll have another scotch," Rafael said.

"Yes ma'am, and yes sir," he said as he stepped away to mix Avory's martini.

Rafael finished his drink, rattled the remaining ice, and sat the tumbler on the bar.

"Now, tell us what you and Tony learned today," he said.

"We went back to Eden and talked to Hope, the upstairs bartender.

"What's she look like?" Avory asked.

"A young beauty with blond pigtails, long tanned legs, a gorgeous smile, and she doesn't need makeup. Her friend Maeve Wickes is a would-be actress, and Darth's last name is Heaney. Darth has a sister named Leia."

"What else?" Avory asked.

"Hope said Darth was short though strong as a bull. He has dimples and a tattoo over his heart. Here's a picture of it she drew for us."

"A single drop of blood," Rafael said.

"With a scrollwork background," Avory said.

"Scrollwork that looks like the carved altar where the ceremony was performed." I pulled a dollar bill from my wallet and showed them. "And like the scrollwork on a dollar bill."

"Freemasonry," Rafael said. "Or some form of it."

"Fredrickson thinks so," I said. "According to the professor, Louis XIV believed in many of the same things as Freemasons."

"Interesting," Rafael said. "Where did he come up with that idea?"

"He says Louis XIV was interested in immortality and imported vampires from Bavaria because they were supposedly immortal."

"Get out of here!" Rafael said.

"According to Fredrickson, the first vampire to come to America was Louis XIV's grandson, Louis, Duke of Burgundy."

"I'm calling bullshit on that one," Rafael said. "Le Petit Dauphin died of measles before turning thirty."

"Maybe not," I said. "Fredrickson has a diary he stole from the Tulane archives. It was handwritten by a man kept in solitary confinement here in New Orleans for decades. It was written in code."

"Seriously?" Rafael said.

"Professor Fredrickson thinks the inmate dubbed the Duke was actually Le Petit Dauphin. He'd acquiesced to the vampire experiments to save his life and the lives of his wife and son. David thinks his family died of measles and that the Duke was the first vampire to come to America. There are problems."

"The timeline doesn't fit," Rafael said.

I gave him a thumb up. "Exactly. If he came with the Casket Girls, he wouldn't have arrived here until 1728, and the Old Ursuline Convent wasn't even built yet."

"I'm missing the implication here," Avory said.

Bertram appeared with fresh drinks before I could answer. Avory was drumming her polished nails on the bar.

"According to the history books, the Casket Girls didn't land in New Orleans until 1728. If they were the vampire's hosts, then vampires couldn't have arrived until then," I said. "Where were their coffins stored? The convent wasn't even built yet."

"I love you both though neither of you has any imagination," she said.

"What are you talking about?" Rafael asked.

"I haven't had anything to eat all day. I'm starving," she said. "Let's get something, and I'll share my ideas on the subject."

"Does anyone other than I crave charbroiled oysters?" Rafael said.

"Eew!" Avory said. "I was thinking about steak, or maybe tacos."

"Have you ever had charbroiled oysters?" Rafael asked.

"I've never had oysters of any kind," Avory said. "They're slimy."

"You have no clue what you're talking about," Rafael said.

Avory gave me a glance. "Wyatt?"

"Rafael is right. Charbroiled oysters are yummy."

"You two are being macho. Oysters can't be good," Avory said.

"Tourist," I said.

"There's an oyster house on Bourbon Street. Try one of their charbroiled oysters. If you don't like it, I'll take you to the most exclusive steak joint in the metro," Rafael said.

"What if I gag and lose my appetite?" Avory said.

Rafael grinned. "I promise you won't. Let's finish our drinks and head that way."

Avory had changed out of her flowing dress and was wearing shorts and a tee-shirt. Replaced by comfy walking shoes, her uncomfortable pumps were history.

"Let's walk," she said.

"Driving is easier," Rafael said.

"This is the French Quarter," Avory said. "It's unlike any place on earth and the whole Quarter is no more than a square mile. I say, let's walk."

"I second that emotion," I said.

"Okay, Smokey Robinson," Rafael said.

After Rafael had cleared the tab with Bertram, we left the bar and headed toward Bourbon Street. Neither Rafael nor I realized Avory had never experienced the iconic venue and was like a kid in a candy store.

Mardi Gras, Lent, and Easter were long since past. Still, we were on Bourbon Street, and people on the balconies were calling for Avory to show her tits.

"They can't be serious," she said.

"They're serious," Rafael said. "You can earn yourself some nice beads if you acquiesce."

"If I was sloshed out of my mind and had hundreds, maybe thousands of people egging me on, then I might. Right now, there are only you two, so forget it."

"I'm crushed," I said.

"Shut your mouth, Wyatt Thomas," Avory said. "You've seen plenty of tits in your life. You don't need to see mine."

"You can never see too many bare breasts," I said with a grin.

Avory ignored my wry comment with a frown. "Where is this oyster house?"

"Not far," Rafael said.

The sun was sinking below the horizon, crimson colors of dusk melding with the Quarter's flashing neon. The sprinkle of rain that began falling caused us no problems. It wouldn't have mattered anyway as we reached the Bourbon Oyster House Rafael had raved about. The aroma of fried goodness greeted us when we entered the restaurant.

With its black and white tile floor, slow-moving ceiling fans and a full-time oyster shucker plying his trade behind the bar, the oyster house was eclectic. A happy couple sitting at the bar was consuming the tasty mollusks as fast as the man could shuck another dozen for them.

"Now that's the life," Rafael said.

"Disgusting," Avory said.

We were seated at a table covered with a red and white plastic table cloth. Rafael ordered cold mugs of Abita for himself and Avory. I opted for unsweetened iced tea.

"Got to drink cold beer if you're going to eat oysters," Rafael said.

"I'm not sure about this," Avory said. "Do they have an alternate menu?"

When the waiter returned with our drinks, Rafael requested a dozen raw and an order of charbroiled oysters.

"Just keep an open mind and try one," Rafael said. "If you don't like them, I'm sure there are other things on the menu."

When our food arrived, Rafael sopped up some butter sauce on a piece of French bread and plopped a charbroiled oyster on top. He held it to Avory's mouth.

"I don't know about this," she said.

"Close your eyes and open up," he said.

"Last time a man said that to me, I got up and ran," Avory said.

"You won't run if you take a bite of this," Rafael said. "It's a little taste of heaven."

Avory bit into the charbroiled oyster atop the savory French bread. Rafael and I waited for her reaction.

"Oh, my God! This is so good!" she said.

I doctored the raw oysters with fresh lemon and then mixed the red sauce with horseradish. I forked an oyster and put it on a cracker.

"Try it?" I said.

When Avory opened her mouth, I fed her the oyster on a cracker.

"Well?" Rafael asked.

"It's good. I think I'm hooked."

We'd soon consumed the oysters. When Rafael ordered more, I asked the waiter to bring us three cups of gumbo.

"You need to taste the gumbo before you slather on the hot sauce," I said.

"You didn't," Avory said.

"Because it's never too hot for me," I said. "You may have a lower tolerance to pepper sauce than I do."

Despite my warning, Avory added too much hot sauce to her gumbo and quickly finished her beer to lessen the burn. The waiter was smiling when he showed up with two more icy mugs of beer and more iced tea for me.

"Is this the best place in New Orleans for seafood?" Avory asked.

"Heavens, no!" Rafael said. "There are hundreds of restaurants in the metro that are this good or better."

"I love this cuisine," Avory said. "What'll I do when I return to Hollywood?"

"Suffer until you return to the Big Easy," Rafael said. "My ship is sailing soon, and I have an early morning meeting tomorrow with the crew. Are you coming with me, Avory?"

"You're on your own, big boy," she said. "I'm hot on this story and have places to visit tonight. If Wyatt doesn't join me, then I'm going alone."

"You sure?" Rafael said.

"Don't get that gorgeous nose of yours bent out of shape. Last night was a transcendental experience for me. This is tonight, and things are different."

Rafael kissed her on the cheek. "Then, will I see you tomorrow?"

"Of course you will," Avory said. "We're working on this story together. We'll probably have lots to discuss."

"Then adieu," he said. "I paid for dinner and left the tab open, so enjoy."

Avory and I could see the rain pelting the street outside as Rafael borrowed an umbrella and hurried through the restaurant door.

"I think you just broke the poor man's heart," I said.

"Then take it as a lesson and don't get too attached. If you remember, we've already talked about this scenario."

"I've sworn off women," I said.

"What about Leia?"

"I don't know if she's real, or if I was just dreaming."

"Though my shorts already need loosening, I'm craving something sweet," Avory said.

"They have coconut cream pie on the menu. Southern goodness and a hot cup of Creole coffee sound like heaven to me."

Avory smiled. "I'd like a martini, though no one can mix them like Bertram. Any suggestions?"

"When I was a drinking man, I liked mango daiquiris with my desserts."

"You think they make them here?" she asked.

"You kidding? We're on Bourbon Street. It's illegal to tend bar here unless you can mix anything and everything."

Avory was smiling when she said, "You're so full of shit!"

I summoned the waiter and put in our order. Avory relaxed, unfolding her arms from around her chest.

"I want to go back to the upstairs bar at the Eden Club. Maybe Mauve and Darth will be there. I'd like to talk to them, and to the bartender, Hope."

"Sounds like you've thought this out."

"What about you?" she said. "What's hanging you up about this case?"

"The timeline. What seems to have happened doesn't match the dates in the history books."

"You're worrying too much about it," Avory said. "Maybe they stayed on a ship docked in the Port of New Orleans. They might have transferred the coffins to a warehouse. Though I don't know as much as you do about this old city, I find it amazing the number of people who disappear without a trace. NOLA was so crazy back then, it's hard to imagine now what might have happened. Brothels, pirates, murderers, thieves. . . It was a dangerous place."

"Still is," I said. "Let's eat our pie and then head over to the Eden Club."

Chapter 23

Rain was no longer drumming the roof as we finished our coffee and desserts. The ephemeral storm had managed to chase away many of the usual French Quarter crazies. What was left was a steamy mist rising off the street.

Bent on reaching the Eden Club before the darkened sky unloaded on us, Avory hurried down the stoop at a race walker's clip. I was grinning to myself as I strived to keep pace.

"Slow down," I said. "You'll give me a heart attack after all the rich food we just ate."

"Suck it up. You look healthy to me," Avory said.

"Even so," I said. "It's still early. No one will be at the Eden Club yet."

"Hope will be," Avory said. "It'll give us a chance to talk to her alone."

She frowned when I said, "You the boss, Miss Avory."

It didn't take us long to reach the dark alleyway leading to the entrance of the Eden Club. Although well after dark, it was earlier than the witching hour. As I'd predicted, the regulars had yet to arrive. As we stood in the doorway of the mostly empty upstairs bar, I saw someone I recognized. Hope was sitting with a young woman, the two of them immersed in an intense conversation. The eyes of the woman talking to Hope were as red as her curly tresses.

"Is that Hope?" Avory said.

"Yes, and from the look of things, maybe we should try this another time."

"Screw that!" Avory said.

I followed her to the table. Resting her hand on the pretty bartender's shoulder, she said, "Hi, Hope, is this Maeve?"

"Do I know you?" Hope asked.

"Wyatt told me your name. We were here last night. You had already left before we arrived. I shared blood with almost everyone in the bar."

"Are you Avory?" Hope asked.

"Yes."

"Maeve and I are having a personal conversation," Hope said.

"I can see that," Avory said. "I promise I won't be intrusive. Wyatt informed me Maeve is an actress."

Even larger tears filled Maeve's eyes. "What started out so well has become the worst day of my life."

Avory knelt beside Maeve's chair, put her arms around her and cradled her head.

"I can see your sadness. What's the matter, baby?"

Hope answered for her. "Maeve's boyfriend Darth left thirty minutes ago and hasn't returned."

"That's only the half of it," Maeve said. "I've been trying to get a speaking part in a movie for almost a year now. Today, I thought I'd gotten lucky and had finally broken through."

Avory continued hugging Maeve, lightly patting her back. "Tell me what happened," she said.

More tears welled in Maeve's eyes. "No one bothered calling to let me know their decision. I found out I'd lost the part from a grip on the set."

"You have the looks and body of a movie star," Avory said. "But can you act?"

"My college degree is in drama," Maeve said. "I've acted in plays since I was ten. I'm a good actress."

"Baby, I'll take your word for it. I'm a Hollywood screenwriter. I'll get you a gig."

Maeve lifted her head and stared at Avory. "Are you serious?"

"It's not what you know, it's who you know." Avory had pulled her cell phone out of her purse. "Have you heard of Quinlan Moore?"

"You mean the hottest producer in Hollywood?" Maeve asked.

"He's my boyfriend. His next picture will be filmed right here in New Orleans. He's in town checking out locations on a movie I'm writing the script for. I'll call him and get you a part."

Hope glanced at me. "You're not her boyfriend?" she asked.

"We're just playing house," I said.

Avory was smiling when she got off the phone. "Baby, you have a guaranteed talking part in Quin's new movie. If you don't flub it, you're going to be a star."

Maeve clutched Avory's hands. "Are you kidding me?" she asked. "What part?"

"Don't know yet. I'll create a character with you in mind. I promise the role will be juicy."

"Is this a bad joke? Are you going to get my hopes up and then yank the rug out from under me?"

"Absolutely not," Avory said.

Though Maeve's eyes were still red, she was smiling as she put her arms around Avory and hugged her.

"Thank you so much," she said.

"Not so fast," Avory said. "I expect something in return."

"Just ask me," Maeve said. "I'll do anything you want me to do."

"No casting couch required, though we could start with a drink," Avory said. "It was a long walk over here, and I'm a bit dry right now."

Hope got out of her chair, giving me a look before she headed for the bar.

"Is she for real?" she asked.

"You can count on it," I said. "Maeve has the part if she wants it."

Hope had a mile-wide grin as she headed toward the bar.

"Grim Reapers coming up," she said. "On the house."

"Make mine a Shirley Temple," I said. "I get crazy when I've had a little alcohol."

Hope gave me a wink. "Might be fun to see that happen," she said.

"Please, iced tea, lemonade or coffee for me," I said. "I'm not a pretty sight when I'm drunk."

Hope winked again as she disappeared behind the bar. Maeve's face was still red though her tears had turned into laughter.

"Who do I have to kill?" she asked.

"No one," Avory said. "This is going to be a perfect part for you because I'm going to write it with you in mind. I just need you to answer a few questions."

"Ask me," Maeve said.

"Where's your boyfriend, Darth?"

Maeve's eyes reddened again. "You know Darth?"

"Never met him," Avory said. "Why are you crying?"

"Darth is the best man I've ever met," Maeve said. "He has a problem."

"What problem?" Avory asked.

"He's a real vampire, and he has spells."

"What kind of spells?"

"Though I'm not from New Orleans, I've lived here long enough to know it's unlike any place on earth," Maeve said.

"Please explain," Avory said.

"Vampires are real here. So is voodoo. Do you know about possession?"

I gave Avory a knowing nod when she glanced at me. "Someone is possessing Darth?" I said.

Maeve's curly red tresses bounced when she nodded her head. "One minute he's the nicest person on earth, the next he's a complete stranger."

"Have you seen him when he becomes possessed?" I asked.

Maeve nodded again. "He thinks he's a Catholic priest."

"A priest named Father Luc?" I said.

Maeve's red eyes opened wide. "How did you know?"

"Darth's dad, Father Luc, is dead. It's someone else who possesses him," I said.

"Who?"

"Don't know for sure," I said. "I suspect it's his grandfather, Louis. Has he ever talked about him to you?"

"Darth was with me most of the day today. We were having a wonderful time enjoying each other's company when he clutched his head and dropped to the floor. When his eyes cleared, he looked at me as if he'd never seen me before. When I called his name, he ignored me and ran out the door."

"Where do you think he went?"

Maeve rubbed her eyes. "I don't know. What I suspect is he's not coming back."

"It's okay," Avory said. "Everything will work out, and you'll see Darth tomorrow."

"I'm not so sure about that," Maeve said.

"Let's backtrack," I said. "What did you mean when you said you learned something last night about Darth's grandfather?"

"That monster Malik confronted us here at the club."

"Who is Malik?" Avory asked.

"A giant of a man who wears clothes and boots from another century and who everyone believes is an actual vampire," Hope said. "He has real fangs, and I'm not just making it up."

"Malik knows Darth's grandfather?" I asked.

Maeve nodded. "He told Darth he knew him, and that they had come to New Orleans together."

"Oh?" I said.

"He said it was centuries ago. I don't think he was exaggerating," Maeve said.

"So Darth's grandfather is a vampire?"

"Yes," Maeve said.

"What does that make Darth?" I asked.

"Part vampire, I guess," she said.

Hope returned to our table with a tray of drinks.

"Grim Reapers," she said. "Drizzled with extra blood."

Avory was smiling as she tasted the mixed drink.

"Love it," she said.

"The blood is actually grenadine," Hope said. "This is the best-selling drink at the Eden Club."

"What's in it?" Avory asked.

"Kahlua, 151 proof rum, grenadine, and ice," Hope said. "Not yours," she said, looking at me. "You have a Chocolate Soldier on ice."

"Thanks," I said.

"Do you share blood?" Hope asked.

"Maybe," I said. "I'm selective."

"Can I taste it?" she asked.

"Don't be a chicken shit," Avory said. "Share a little blood with Hope. I need to talk to Maeve."

"No way," Hope said. "If he shares his blood with me, he shares with everyone at the table."

Avory glanced at the ceiling and said, "Here we go!"

"Unbutton your shirt," Hope said.

Not expecting the sudden turn of events, I was starting to feel a bit queasy. Hope helped me when I fumbled with the top button of my shirt.

"What now?" I asked when my chest was bared.

"This won't hurt," she said. "I promise. Nice chest, by the way. Are you an athlete?"

"Jogger," I said.

"You have quite the body on you," she said. "You could make some big money as a Chippendale dancer."

With a queasy feeling in the pit of my gut, I didn't bother replying as Hope made a small cut on my right shoulder blade. Although I couldn't see, I felt her soft lips and tongue working on the incision. Despite my revulsion, I felt a strong sexual sensation pulse through my body. It was almost like a rolling orgasm.

"Girls?" Hope said when she'd had her fill of my blood.

Maeve's eyes were no longer red. My own eyes were closed as she licked the blood from the wound in my shoulder.

"Avory?" Maeve said.

"I . . . don't know," Avory said.

"Taste it," Hope said. "I need to know you're one of us.

"Please," Maeve said. "Then I'll truly know you're a sister."

My eyes were still closed when Avory touched my oozing wound with her tongue. She did her best not to show her revulsion and smiled as she reclined back into her seat. She finished half of her Grim Reaper before slamming it on the tabletop. The bar was still empty, Hope smiling as she hurried to the bar, returning with four chocolaty shots.

"Buttery nipples," she said. "Vodka, butterscotch schnapps, Irish crème, and coffee liqueur."

Hope, Maeve, and Avory were smiling as they drained their shots.

"I can't," I said.

"Yes, you can," Hope said. "You're about to taste the blood from my own buttery nipple. This is a rite of passage. Drink the shot."

I put the shot to my mouth, closed my eyes, and drained the glass.

"That was so good," Avory said.

"Then let's have another," Hope said. "We have some celebrating to do."

Hope returned from the bar with eight buttery nipples. Two for each of us. The vodka from the last shot had already smacked me in the face. When Hope, Maeve, and Avory hoisted their glasses in a toast, I was powerless not to raise my own. When I finished my third shot, I was feeling no pain. Hope must have sensed my weakness as she pulled her tee-shirt over her blond braids.

"Wow!" Avory said. "Maybe it's you who should be the new movie star."

Maeve was giggling. "Or an exotic dancer. My girlfriend Hope has the best bod in New Orleans."

Hope's stare focused on me. With my psyche infused by three quick shots of vodka, I couldn't quit staring at Hope's nipples. After making a tiny incision near the top of her left breast, she put her arms around my head and pulled me toward the red blood beginning to seep from the cut. I didn't pull away.

I had entered into an elevated sense of consciousness, my mind focused on one thing. Maeve and Avory were whispering to each other. Someone had entered the bar. When I glanced up, I saw a giant man with hair that draped his shoulders. He was smiling wickedly as he stared at Hope's bare breasts.

Chapter 24

ope hurriedly pulled her tee-shirt over her head. After flashing Maeve and Avory a confounded look, she rushed to the bar to greet the large man with an obvious leer on his face.

"What'll it be, Mr. Malik? Grim Reaper with extra blood?"

"I'll have the same thing he was having," he said.

"Fresh out," Hope said. "Sorry about that."

"Then I'll settle for my usual," he said.

Hope ducked under the bar and grabbed a bottle. "Coming right up."

Maeve was whispering something in Avory's ear. I was too busy buttoning my shirt and trying to cope with the effects of the three buttery nipples to worry about what they were discussing. My head was swimming when Hope returned from the bar with another round of shots.

"Someone will have to drink mine," I said.

"You're not getting away with that," Hope said. "Open your mouth."

"I can't," I said.

"Yes, you can," Hope said.

Alcoholics are who they are because they

don't know when to stop. I knew when; I just didn't have the willpower to follow through. The shots were working on Avory and Maeve as well, both giggling as Hope opened my mouth and poured one of the shots into it. We were all laughing when Avory's cell phone rang.

"That was Quin. He wants Maeve and me to join him at the bar in the Roosevelt Hotel."

"I don't get off work until midnight," Hope said.

"Good," Avory said. "If Quin saw that body of yours, he'd be offering you a part in his next picture instead of Maeve."

Maeve clutched Hope's hand. "Sorry, girlfriend," she said.

Hope was grinning. "No problem. Wyatt will take me home."

I'd already had too many buttery nipples to worry about the winks Maeve and Hope exchanged. Avory gave me a peck on the cheek.

"Don't wait up," she said.

We watched them walk out the door, leaving us with seven untouched buttery nipples. The man named Malik noticed. Hope's smile disappeared when he approached our table. She had little time to fret about it as customers began filing into the little area.

"I'll be back," she said.

Hope ducked under the bar, the big man standing behind me.

"I'm Wyatt Thomas," I said.

The man ignored my hand. "Malik," he said.

"Happy to meet you, Mr. Malik."

"Just Malik."

When he opened his mouth to speak, I could see the glint of his teeth. Hope wasn't kidding; he had fangs. I suddenly regretted my state of inebriation.

"Hope and Maeve were telling me about you,"

I said.

"Oh? What did they say?"

"That you know Darth's grandfather."

"How do you know Darth?" he asked.

"Casual acquaintance," I said. "Seems we have way too many buttery nipples. Would you like one?"

Malik grabbed a shot glass, opened his mouth, and downed it. He smiled, curling his upper lip when he saw me staring.

"Fangs," he said. "Real vampires have fangs."

"So you're a real vampire?" I asked.

It was my turn to smile when he said, "Want me to bite you on the neck?"

"No, thanks," I said. "If you and Darth's grandfather are real vampires, what does that make Darth?"

"He's part vampire, a hybrid," Malik said.

I let Malik's words sink in for a moment, and then said, "Have another shot. No use letting them go to waste."

Malik grabbed a shot glass and downed the velvety drink. After slamming it to the table, he wiped his mouth with the sleeve of his floor-length coat.

"What are you doing here, Mr. Thomas?"

"Just Wyatt," I said. "My girlfriend is a screenwriter. She's writing a movie about vampires to be filmed here in New Orleans."

"Someone beat her to it," he said.

"That was a while back. There's still lots of interest in vampires. If you have a minute, I'd like to talk to you about it."

"Talk?"

"An interview," I said.

"What exactly do you want to know?"

"Many things," I said. "I'll buy your drinks if you'll grant me an interview."

"I don't do my talking in bars," he said.

"Then, where?" I asked.

After searching the pocket of his coat, he handed me a card. They only thing on one side of the card was a picture of a drop of blood against scrollwork. His address was embossed in raised print on the back.

"I've seen that picture," I said. "Mind telling me what it means?"

"I'll explain during the interview," he said. "This is my home."

"Sometime tomorrow?" I asked.

"Vampires never give interviews in the light of day. I have some hunting to do. If I'm lucky, I'll be back home around two."

"Two in the morning?" I said.

"Is that past your bedtime?"

"I'll be there."

Malik killed another shot. "If I'm running late, wait outside on the stoop for me. I'll be there soon as I can."

Another couple was entering the bar as Malik left. He brushed past them as if they were insignificant. Hope knew all the customers by their first names. After taking care of their drinks, she joined me at the table and sat in my lap.

"I'm off work in thirty minutes. I don't live far from here. You can take me home."

From the way she was hugging me, I realized she had more in mind than just an escort.

"I'll see you home. I can't stay," I said.

"And why not?"

"There's something else I have to do."

"It's almost midnight. What do you have to do tonight that can't wait until morning."

I showed her the business card. "I'm interviewing Malik at two."

"You're going to his den?"

"To his home," I said.

Hope made a face, shook her head, and then

killed a shot.

"You apparently have a death wish," she said. "Malik's a vampire; a real vampire. He'll drain your blood and leave you for dead on the sidewalk."

"I think you're exaggerating," I said.

"You're drunk. I can't let you go to Malik's."

"You're the one who got me this way," I said.

"Doesn't matter. Malik will kill you."

"No, he won't. Lots of people, including you, saw me with him. If I turn up missing, he'll be the prime suspect. He's not that stupid."

"Fine, then I'm coming with you," Hope said.

"You're off work in another thirty minutes. I'm not meeting Malik until two."

"No problem," she said. "I'm a night owl. We can do some club hopping on Bourbon until then."

"Fine, then pass these shots out to the people at the next table and please bring me a cup of strong coffee. Maybe I'll be half sober when we make it to Malik's."

Hope drained another shot. "You may want to sober up. It's not a problem for me."

Tolerance to alcohol turned out to be one of Hope's strengths. I was grateful when she brought me an espresso so strong it could have peeled the black lacquer off the walls. It didn't really matter. As I'd learned during my drinking days, coffee does little more than make you a wide-awake drunk. When the midnight bartender arrived, Hope clocked out and joined me.

"You think Darth is a real vampire?" Hope asked.

"Malik called him a hybrid, a part vampire," I said.

"He has a taste for blood, and he's very much alive," she said. "His fangs are longer than most people's though I doubt anyone has ever noticed."

She gave me a funny look when I asked, "Can vampires father children?"

"I have no idea. What made you think of that?"

"I know, or at least think I know, Darth's grandmother. She's definitely not a vampire."

"I've been in this club since ten this morning. I'm sick of the place. Let's get the hell out of here," she said. We can talk about vampires someplace else."

The weather was mild when we exited the Eden Club to the outside alleyway. It didn't stop Hope from clutching my arm and snuggling close to me. Still unexpectedly bewitched by the taste of her blood, I didn't protest. It wasn't far to Bourbon Street, and we found the venue hopping.

Bourbon was blocked off to automobile traffic, the sidewalks and street crowded with people walking in both directions. Music poured from the open doors. When we passed a strip club, the barker at the door called to Hope.

"Hey, babe, need a job? You got tits bigger than any of my girls."

He smiled when Hope flashed them for him.

"Having fun?" I said.

"Tits are like rose blossoms," she said. "You need to enjoy them before they wilt and fade."

"Can't argue with that," I said. "Where are you taking me?"

"A patio club that opens up to the street. We can have a drink and watch the head cases walk by on the sidewalk."

Though I'd passed the club many times, I'd never been inside of it. Hope knew one of the waiters. He seated us at a table with a great view of the sidewalk.

The waiter who didn't look old enough to be serving alcohol, asked, "What are you drinking?"

"Club Special," Hope said.

"Just coffee for me," I said.

"Wimp," Hope said.

When the waiter returned, I gave Hope's drink a quizzical glance.

"I've never heard of a Club Special. What's in it?"

"You pour vodka, limeade and Sprite in a tall glass of ice, top it up with club soda and then garnish with a lime and lemon wedges. Want to taste it?"

Since my better judgment had already flown out the window, I took a sip.

"I could get addicted. I thought I'd heard of every cocktail there is."

"Invented in Oklahoma," she said. "I had a boyfriend from there once."

"You mean they have something in Oklahoma besides cattle and football?"

"You don't travel much, do you?" she asked.

"Guess not," I said.

When the waiter returned to check on our drinks, Hope ordered another Club Special for herself and one for me.

"You're already lit," she said. "Enjoy yourself. I'll make sure you don't do anything crazy."

"I want to be halfway coherent when we talk to Malik."

"We're visiting a vampire's digs at two in the morning, and you want to be sober? Myself, I need a few more drinks."

"You're a vampire," I said.

"While it's true I'm a working vampire, Malik is a suck-your-blood right out of your neck member of the undead. If you aren't scared shitless of him, you should be."

"I'm not so sure," I said.

"Malik is a real vampire. Real vampires can't survive without blood. Lots of blood. Ask him if you don't believe me."

"I believe you. That's why I want to talk to him. I have questions I haven't been able to find answers to. Who better to ask than a real vampire?"

"Just don't let him share blood with you."

"Even though I don't intend to, why do you say that?"

"Because you'd become a vampire," she said.

"I think you've seen too many vampire movies. Almost nothing you see on the big screen is real."

"And how would you know? You had never even heard of a Club Special until I gave you a sip. No one knows everything."

Duly chastised, I drank my Club Special. "You're right about that," I said. "I'll have to ask Bertram to start making these for me without the vodka. It could be my new favorite drink."

"Who is Bertram?"

"My landlord. He owns Bertram's Bar over on Chartres Street."

Hope grinned. "Love the place. Been there lots of times. Bertram is your landlord?"

"I live in an apartment at the top of the stairs."

"Do you have a wife or girlfriend waiting there for you?"

It was my turn to grin. "Just my cat Kisses."

"What does Kisses do when you stay out all night?"

"Nothing. She understands tomcatting better than I do. If I'm gone too long, Bertram checks on her food and water for me."

"You don't sound like a good parent," Hope said.

"Cats are as different as humans are. While some cats dote on affection, Kisses will tolerate just so much before she scratches me."

"That's so sad," Hope said.

"No, it isn't. She gives me my space, and I give her hers. We make the perfect couple."

"Good thing I'm only interested in your body and not your mind," Hope said.

Feeling no pain, I ignored her pointed remark.

Malik's house wasn't far away, Bourbon's flashing neon replaced by the darkness of the French Quarter as we walked toward it. The vampire lived in the northern corner of the Quarter, near the intersection of Governor Nicholls and Dauphine. Since there were no streetlamps, I had to guess the color of his Creole townhouse as red with black shutters. Though the paint scheme was different, even by French Quarter standards, I doubted it even raised an eyebrow in a neighborhood where every house had a different and distinctive paint scheme.

There were no lights on in the house, probably not unusual for a vampire. I sensed Malik wasn't home yet so we waited on the sidewalk, listening to a stray cat rattling the trashcans in a nearby alleyway. I jumped, and Hope squealed when someone put their large hands on our shoulders.

"Good thing my hunt was successful," Malik said. "You two would have made easy victims."

Chapter 25

Malik's house was warm, the air stale. It became even more evident when he lit a candle. Unlike the perfectly renovated cottage of David and Brenda Fredrickson, Malik's abode looked as if it had never received a coat of fresh paint. There was also no electricity. Malik smiled when Hope sneezed.

"Sorry about the dust and mold," he said. "The undead care little about such things."

After removing his long coat, he settled into an old chair and pulled off his boots. The only other furniture in the little room was two rickety cane-backed chairs. Hope and I seated ourselves without waiting for Malik to offer. I asked the first question.

"You said you had a successful hunt. What were you hunting?"

"Not what," he said. "Who. New Orleans has a problem with transients, derelicts, and homeless people. They come and go. The city doesn't know how many there are, nor do they care. They have no clue when one goes missing. It's a perfect scenario for me."

"You kill them and then drink their blood?" I asked.

"Actually, they die from loss of blood. There's

a sedative in vampire saliva that renders the victim helpless while they are being drained."

He laughed when I asked, "How do you dispose of the bodies?"

"There are storm drains all over town. Although the covers are too heavy for an average person to remove, it's no problem for me."

"You throw the bodies into a storm drain?" I said.

"Once a body disappears inside the storm system, it's never seen again. As far as the city is concerned, no body, no problem, good riddance."

"How many people have you killed like that?" I asked.

"Hundreds. I make a kill once or twice a month."

"And you have no remorse?"

"Do you have remorse when you eat a chicken leg?"

"It's not exactly the same thing," I said.

"I don't choose to drink blood to survive. It's a necessity, not a choice. If you're here to judge me, then please leave now."

"Okay," I said. "I get it."

"What exactly is it you want from me?" Malik asked.

"I'm a private investigator working on a case for the Greater Archdiocese of New Orleans."

"What sort of case?" Malik asked.

"Someone performed a satanic act at the Old Ursuline Convent. I've been retained to find out who and why."

"So why are you asking me?" Malik said.

"Because two things keep popping up."

"What two things?"

"Freemasonry and vampirism. I can't quite put my finger on the connection between the two. Can you help me?"

"My story is long, and there are only a few

hours until dawn," Malik said.

"What happens then?" I asked.

"I must return to my coffin before first light."

"Please tell us what you can until then," I said.

Malik rubbed his hand through his hair, stretched out his long legs and reclined back into the old chair.

"I was born in 1680 during the reign of the Sun King, Louis XIV."

"That would make you. . ."

"More than 300 years old," Malik said.

"How is that possible?" I asked.

"I'm a vampire. Vampires can't die because they are already dead. For practical purposes, I am immortal."

"Were you born a vampire?" I asked.

"I was born a normal human. In 1712, I was purposely infected with the virus that causes vampirism. I was thirty-two."

"Vampirism is caused by a virus?" I said.

"I know that now as a fact," Malik said. "In 1712, we didn't know what a virus was. Louis the Great, the Sun King, was the longest-reigning monarch in history. He was an intelligent man who sought to control everything, even his own mortality."

The dark little room was lit by the flickering light of a single candle. Malik paused his story when several noisy motorcycles raced past on the street outside his house. When I glanced around the room, I saw the black blinds covering the windows.

"Damn cycle gangs," Malik said. "They wake the dead with their loud mufflers."

When the rumble died away down the street, I said, "You were talking about the Sun King."

"Louis the Great assembled a group of scientists to work on the question of immortality.

He'd brought together the greatest minds in Europe to solve the problem. What they found, unfortunately, is there is no such thing as immortality. Every living thing ages and eventually dies, except. . ."

"Vampires?" I said.

"Therein lies the rub," Malik said. "To achieve immortality, you must first die. It wasn't a solution the Sun King wanted to hear."

"How did vampires come into the equation?" I asked.

"There were always rumors of vampires who existed in eastern Europe. When one was captured in Bavaria, Louis the Great paid dearly for it."

"How did they control the vampire?" I asked.

"By limiting its intake of blood. They drew blood from hosts and gave the vampire just enough to let it survive while preventing it from achieving its full strength. It was the same technique France employed when they sent us to the New World."

"So the Casket Girls did more than provide females for the colony," I said.

"Much more," Malik said. "They kept us alive, and I use that term loosely, on our journey from France."

"If the Sun King rejected vampirism as a means of achieving immortality, why did others go forward with the experiment?"

"The option was always available," Malik said. "Every member of the crown was aware of the experiments. Though the scientists had no clue they were dealing with a virus, they did know that vampirism could be transmitted by the exchange of blood."

"What prompted someone to try the experiment?" I asked.

"Measles," Malik said. "In 1711, a disease that

today has been virtually eradicated was spreading through France. Le Petit Dauphin, the Sun King's grandson, along with his wife and one of their sons, was infected. Desperate to save his wife and progeny, Louis, Duke of Burgundy decided to become a vampire. He succeeded, though not before his wife and child had succumbed to measles."

"And you?"

"I was Louis' cousin and his best friend. We were inseparable. I elected to join him in the experiment. Ten others were infected along with Louis and me. The twelve of us were known as the Disciples."

"What did Louis look like?" I asked.

"An imposing man. I'm six feet ten inches tall. Louis was taller. He had dark black hair he kept in a pigtail. When he was younger, there was nothing he wouldn't do for a friend."

"And now?" I said.

"He has changed. His hair turned snowy white during his stay in prison. The fencing scar on his cheek that was once a mark of honor has turned red and raw. He's become an angry man."

"Why did you come to America?" I asked.

"Because even though we were royalty, we were deemed too dangerous to remain in France."

"The Casket Girls were your hosts. Someone must have known about them and the Disciples."

"Though Louis XIV was a good Catholic, he didn't believe all the dogma coming out of the Vatican. He wasn't officially a Freemason, even though he'd studied it fervently in his search for immortality. At the behest of the Sun King, a group with ties to Freemasonry became powerful."

"The Order of the Blood?" I said.

"They were already ensconced in the colonies. Many of them, Jean-Daniel Kolly for one, had amassed great wealth, much of which he and other members of the West Indies Company attributed to the practice of Freemasonry. Heirs of the Sun King became members and eventually took control of the Order of the Blood."

"They took care of you on the trip from France?"

Members of the Order of the Blood were involved in the vampire experiments from their inception. They accompanied us from France and knew how to control us. Though we didn't realize what was happening, we ultimately became their pawns."

"How did Louis survive his years in solitary confinement without blood and a coffin?" I asked.

"Louis learned how to achieve dormancy. Most of his incarceration, he hibernated like a bear."

"He didn't spend his entire twenty-five years hibernating. He was coherent enough to write a nearly seven-hundred-page diary. How did he survive without blood, and where did he get the paper and ink?"

Malik chuckled. "Rats," he said. "They were rampant in prison."

"Louis survived on rat blood?" I said.

"He was in a weakened state; that is without question. He had coins on him when he was captured. He used the gold to buy paper, pen, and ink from his jailers."

"How did he escape?" I asked.

"Louisiana began transferring prisoners to a new prison in Baton Rouge. The first jailer to enter Louis' cell revived him when he became his first human victim in twenty-five years. Louis escaped because he was too powerful to stop."

"I was told a passing priest used a cross to capture Louis. How is that possible?"

"Like his grandfather, Louis is a practicing Catholic, though Satan is his savior and not

Jesus. It took a powerful priest and a religious icon to sedate Louis long enough to capture him. Not just any priest would have been successful."

"Then it was the Order of the Blood that stole the Cross of Gilead from the Vatican."

"Yes, and it was that theft that prompted the Papal ban of Freemasonry. The Cross of Gilead was what the Order needed to control the Disciples."

"Louis' kryptonite," I said.

"And, unfortunately, mine," Malik said.

Hope was listening intently to every word we spoke. Her eyes soon grew even larger.

"Is this Order of the Blood pro vampire or anti-vampire?" she asked.

"They are Satanists. They believe there's an opening to the netherworld capped by the Vatican centuries ago. Their goal is to destroy the Roof of Lucifer."

"What exactly is the Roof of Lucifer?" Hope asked.

"The Old Ursuline Convent. That's why Jean-Daniel Kolly plotted to house the Ursuline nuns at the Kolly house. He knew the intent of the Vatican and attempted to thwart it. He was almost successful."

"Then the Ursulines aren't Satanists?" I asked.

"No, though some of the priests associated with the convent through the years were. The altar where the ceremony you asked about was performed is a satanic altar. It's an original part of the convent."

"The convent wasn't built yet when you arrived in New Orleans," I said. "Where did you stay?"

"Aboard ship," Malik said. "It remained docked in New Orleans until our coffins could be transported to a warehouse on the river. Members of the Order owned the warehouse and attended to us."

"Does the Order of the Blood still exist?" I asked.

"Though the Order is a secret society, it's politically viable here in New Orleans. It might surprise you how many prominent local politicians are both Catholic and Satanists."

Hope gave me a look. "I'm Catholic, and I'm not a Satanist. I'm finding all this hard to believe."

"Centuries ago, there was a schism between Catholics who accepted Jesus and those who followed Satan," Malik said. "Jesus prevailed though there are many who still believe otherwise."

"My own research seems to bear that out," I said.

"The night is growing old," Malik said. "I only have time for another question or two."

"What happened to the Disciples?" I asked.

"Except for Louis and me, the rest are dead, really dead."

"How did that happen?" I asked.

"The brothers who run the Order had them disposed of because they grew too frightened of their power."

"How do you feel about that?" I asked.

"The Disciples were my brothers. If I could avenge their deaths, I would."

Seeing that Malik was becoming emotional, I changed the subject.

"Tell me what you know about Darth and Father Luc," I asked.

"Luc was the son of Louis and a woman who became a nun."

He nodded when I said, "Sister Lydia?"

"But Sister Lydia isn't a vampire. What does that make Father Luc?"

"As I told you at the Eden Club, he's a hybrid. In his case, he's half vampire."

"What about Darth?"

"Darth was born out of wedlock to Luc and a cleaning woman who worked at the Old Ursuline Convent."

Malik nodded when I asked, "Then Darth is a hybrid vampire? Does he have a sister named Leia?"

"A twin sister," Malik said.

"How has she managed to survive all these years alone at the convent?" I asked.

"She hasn't," Malik said. "Father Luc killed Leia in a rage, just as he had killed her mother."

"Leia can't be dead," I said. "I saw her. . ."

"Who you saw was a ghost," Malik said. "She is unique because she's the ghost of a hybrid vampire."

When I opened my mouth to speak, words refused to issue forth. Hope asked a question for me.

"Was Darth's father caught and punished?"

"Darth killed him," Malik said.

I'd managed to regain my composure enough to say, "Father Luc's body has never been found. He's officially missing though still not pronounced dead. Where is his body?"

"His bones, along with Leia's, a woman I knew, and several priceless objects reside in a coffin hidden in the attic of the Old Ursuline Convent."

"A woman you knew?"

"Her name was Eva. She was a Casket Girl who had taken personal care of me during my journey to New Orleans."

"What happened to Eva?" Hope asked.

"I was in love with her and she with me. Eva became a vampire when I purposely infected her. The Order of the Blood put her to death."

"But why?" I asked.

"Their need for complete control. They killed her by driving a stake through her heart and then cut off her head with a guillotine."

"The skull Avory and I found near the casket," I said.

"They use torture as a way of keeping their members under control. If someone strays from their dogma, such as I did by falling in love with a Casket Girl, they are punished by having to see a loved one tortured and killed in the vilest manner."

Hope and I could barely believe what we were hearing. "That is so barbaric," she said.

"And the reason I escaped their control," Malik said. "The Order of the Blood maintains a torture chamber. The iron maiden, the breast ripper, the rack. There's often a torture spectacle at the meetings."

"Horrible," Hope said.

"Those who control the Order of the Blood are more than Satanists, they are sadists. At least once a year they steal an infant, drink its blood, and eat it."

"You have to be kidding me?" I said.

Malik shook his head. "I'm a vampire by design. Members of the Order of the Blood are sadists by choice."

Malik pulled himself out of his chair. He took the candle with him, and we followed him into another room where the only object was an ancient coffin. After opening the top of the coffin, he climbed inside it, handed me the candle stub and lowered the top.

Before it was completely shut, he said, "Beware the Order of the Blood. They are more bloodthirsty than I will ever be."

"What now?" Hope asked when the lid closed on Malik's coffin.

"Get the hell out of here."

The French Quarter was still dark and cloyingly warm for such an early spring night. Though the dawn was near, we could hear music coming from the direction of Bourbon Street.

"I'm going with you," Hope said. "That experience scared the hell out of me. After what we just heard, I may not let go of your hand for days."

I'd had a similar reaction, and after hearing what had happened to Leia, Hope's presence was comforting. When I started in the direction of Bertram's, she shook her head and gave my hand a yank.

"I need a drink," Hope said. It isn't far to Bourbon Street and this day is already shot."

"Why not?" I said.

The night was all but history when Hope and I reached the sidewalk in front of Bertram's bar. Bertram had locked up, all his customers gone home. We were still sharing the Hurricane we'd bought from a street vendor as we climbed the stairs to my apartment. Hope released my hand and began unbuttoning my shirt.

"There's one thing that will take my mind off Satan and real vampires," she said.

Hope's warm body and all the strong alcohol I'd consumed were all the convincing I needed. It was still dark, and we hadn't bothered turning on the lights when amid squeals and love talk we climbed under the covers. We quickly learned we weren't alone, nor were we the only naked ones in the bed.

Chapter 26

Father Luc couldn't understand why his head wouldn't stop hurting as he climbed in the rafters of the Old Ursuline Convent. He'd been stringing detcord since early that morning, trying to complete his task before the meeting that night. As even stronger pain surged through his head, he fell to the floor. When he opened his eyes, he saw his father, Louis, standing over him.

Louis was a tall and powerful man. A breeze blowing through an open shutter rustled his snowy white hair. The angry scar on his left cheek said volumes about his demeanor. After more than three centuries in New Orleans, Louis spoke with a clipped, almost Cajun accent.

"You about a lazy one. People are counting on you. Get off the floor and finish the wiring."

"My head is killing me," Luc said.

"I can make the pain even worse. Don't fail me on this," Louis said.

As if struck by a bolt of lightning, Father Luc's body shook. Like a will-o'-the-wisp, Louis disappeared, the pain slowly ebbing from the little priest's head.

Having followed the engineer's plans to perfection, he was almost done and everything in place. All that remained for him to do was to attach the final strand of detcord to the detonating device. Once done, he would wait for his orders to set the timer. The Old Ursuline Convent would come crashing to earth, exposing the entrance to hell. Maybe then his father Louis would accept him unconditionally as the perfect son he thought he was.

There was another presence in the attic of the Old Ursuline Convent. Leia, his daughter, couldn't, for some reason, get his name straight.

"Darth, you can't do this," she said. "Grandfather has lost his mind. What he is trying to force you to do is wrong. Evil people are controlling him. He is controlling you. You must fight it."

"I'm not Darth; I'm Luc, your father."

"No, you aren't. Our father is dead. You are my brother Darth."

Father Luc's temples pounded harder, and he grabbed his head again.

"Release me from this pain. I can't take much more," he said.

"I'm not the cause of your suffering, nor can I free you from it," Leia said. "It's Grandfather. You can't go through with this spiritual travesty. You must fight the pain."

"I'm bound by oath. I have to carry this through to the end."

"What you're doing is wrong. I have no power over Grandfather. Only you can save the convent. You must find a way to resist him."

Luc writhed on the floor of the attic. "I can't."

Leia's image dissolved as the pain in Father Luc's head abated. When it did, he began tying the hanging strands of detcord to a common line. Soon, there would be nothing left for him to do except set the timer and await the detonation.

❧

Hope had lost her mind, and mine wasn't far behind. We hadn't bothered turning on the lights as we tumbled into bed like tangling wildcats. We quickly had a surprise. Someone was in bed with us. When the person turned on a lamp, we saw it was Avory.

Hope giggled when Avory sat up, her arms crossed tightly across her bare chest and an abashed look on her face. Stoked by the already tense events of the night plus my own overindulgence, I also began to laugh.

"What's so funny?" Avory demanded.

"The look on your face," Hope said. "It's priceless."

"I didn't expect this," Avory said.

"And we never thought we'd find you here. You told Maeve the Hollywood producer is your boyfriend. We expected you to be with him."

"Is that true, Wyatt?" Avory asked.

"It's a reasonable assumption, and you told me not to wait up," I said.

"You're both drunk. Where have you been?"

"You don't sound exactly sober," I said.

"Maybe not," she said. "You can still tell me what you were doing."

"Interviewing a vampire," Hope said.

Avory glanced at Hope, and then at me. "You're not serious, are you?"

"Malik offered to tell me how he arrived in New Orleans and invited me to his house to hear his story. Hope was off work and came with me."

"Why did you interview him alone?" Avory asked. "Don't you know what this story means to me?"

"It was either last night or never. Malik gave me no other choice. It's okay because I'll tell you everything," I said.

"Did you record it?" Avory asked.

"No, but I remember what he said."

"I can't believe you," Avory said. "I thought you were a professional."

"I'm a private dick, not a journalist," I said.

"You're a dick, all right," Avory said.

"Where's Maeve?" Hope asked.

"That asshole Quin came on to her," Avory said.

Hope grew agitated. "Does that mean she lost the part?"

"She has the part. I left her at the bar with Quin. They seemed pretty cozy."

"Are you crazy?" Why did you leave her alone with him?" Hope asked. "She's Darth's girl."

"I got angry when Quin hinted we should try a threesome," Avory said. "Quinn's my boyfriend; not Maeve's. I know he plays around. Doesn't matter because I refuse to participate in it."

"You left Maeve with a pervert?" Hope asked.

"Quinn's neither a pervert nor a rapist. He'll back off if Maeve tells him to," Avory said.

"She may feel she's obligated," Hope said.

"She doesn't," Avory said. "I talked to her about it on the way to the Roosevelt. Maeve's just fine. It's you two I'm worried about."

"Wyatt's not your boyfriend. You said so. Have you changed your mind?"

"No . . . I just. . ."

"I think you're making a mountain out of a molehill," Hope said. "How about having a threesome with Wyatt and me?" Avory's arms relaxed when she began to giggle. "Why are you laughing?"

"Because," Avory said. "I've never participated in a threesome, and I've been offered the chance twice tonight."

"Well?" Hope said.

Avory didn't answer. Her inebriation showed when she got out of bed and staggered to the open door of my balcony overlooking Chartres

Street. She met Kisses coming in the door. Avory picked her up, clutching the cat to her chest.

"Looks like everyone here has been doing a little tomcatting," she said.

"It's okay," I said. "It's a tomcat's paradise here in the French Quarter."

Dawn had arrived in the Quarter, the room growing lighter as Avory placed Kisses on the floor and stumbled out to the balcony.

"It's lovely this time of the morning," she said.

"You better put some clothes on if you're going to stand out there," I said.

"You weren't a prude a minute ago. Don't be one now. I love your balcony. If I lived here, I'd watch the sun come up every morning with my coffee."

Hope got out of bed and followed Avory to the balcony. "I want to see," she said.

When Kisses jumped on the bed, I gave her a few full-body strokes, got up, and filled her food bowl on the floor of my little kitchen. I started a pot of coffee and then went into the bathroom to take a shower. The pot had finished perking when I emerged dressed in my old blue robe. I took the tray of coffee to the balcony.

Avory and Hope had moved away from the railing and were sitting in my deck chairs, soaking up the ambiance. Their smiles lit up when I served them.

Your coffee is the best I ever tasted. What's it got in it that I don't recognize?" Avory asked.

"Chicory," I said. "Once you get used to it, it's hard to settle for plain coffee."

Avory savored another sip. "You aren't getting out of telling me about your visit with the vampire."

"Don't you want to get dressed first?" I asked.

"Am I disturbing you?" she asked.

"A little," I said. "Actually, quite a lot."

"I enjoy nudity. It's so relaxing, and we're away from the balcony. No one can see me except you," Avory said.

"Then I'll try to persevere," I said with a smile.

Nudity was no problem for Hope. She'd finished her coffee and had dozed off while soaking up the rays in a sunny corner of the balcony.

"I'm waiting," Avory said.

"Malik claimed to be more than 300 years old and former best friends with the grandson of Louis XIV."

"The Sun King? Get the hell out of here," Avory said. "I studied French history in college, and I never heard such an assertion as that."

"He claimed vampirism is caused by a virus and that even in the 1700s French scientists knew how to transmit it. And you were right about the Casket Girls. They were hosts to the twelve vampires who came to America from France."

"Where did they keep the coffins?"

"First in a ship docked in the Port of New Orleans. Later, they were moved to a warehouse near the river," I said.

"Told you so," Avory said. "Someone other than the Casket Girls must have helped them."

"You're a step ahead of me," I said. "How'd you know?"

"Quit patronizing and finish the story," she said.

"The Order of the Blood, the group you and Rafael found a reference to in your research."

"Freemasons?" she asked.

"Something like that. They were the ones who stole the Cross of Gilead from the Vatican. It resulted in the Papal Ban of Freemasonry."

Avory topped up her coffee from the carafe on the tray and laced it with extra cream.

"Why did they steal the cross?" she asked.

"The vampires were powerful and deadly. The Order needed a way to control them. The cross provided that control."

"How did they lose the cross?"

"Don't know," I said. "I do know after talking with Malik the Order of the Blood is a dangerous organization and not to be trifled with."

"What about Leia?" Avory asked.

"I won't lie to you. I was beyond shocked when Malik told me Leia is dead. He said Father Luc murdered her in a fit of rage and that's the reason Darth killed him."

"Then the young woman you thought you saw was a ghost?"

"The ghost of a hybrid vampire, according to Malik," I said. "Even if she is a ghost, I saw her, and she was real to me."

"Sister Lydia isn't a vampire," Avory said. "What does that make Luc and Darth?"

"Luc was half vampire. Malik called them both hybrids. They have great strength and a taste for blood but they are alive, can have children and exist in the light of day."

"Interesting," Avory said. "Where are the bodies of all these missing people?"

"In the casket in the attic of the Old Ursuline Convent. I'm guessing Darth put them there. The vampire skull we found was of a Casket Girl who fell in love with Malik. When the Order learned she'd become a vampire, they made an example of her."

"What did they do?"

"They beheaded her with a guillotine and then killed her by driving a stake through her heart. It was apparently done in a solemn ceremony witnessed by all the members. It's what prompted Malik to escape and live on his own."

"Oh, my God!" Avory said.

"The Order of the Blood is into torture and

more sick things than you can even imagine."

"How does Malik survive?" Avory asked.

"He attacks derelicts. After draining them of blood, he throws their bodies into storm drains," I said. "God only knows where their bodies wind up."

"Storm drains?"

"They're all over the city," I said. "They feed into the Bonnet Carre Spillway."

"What's that?" Avory asked.

"A way to deal with flooding when the river gets too high. The Spillway drains excess water out of the city and into the surrounding swamps."

"Interesting," Avory said. "I'm starving," Have anything to eat in that little kitchen of yours?"

"Some day-old croissants I bought at the French Market. Would you like a toasted croissant with cream cheese and strawberry jam?"

"Sounds like heaven," Avory said. "I could eat a dozen."

"I don't have that many," I said.

"One will do. Need help?"

"I'll get them. Won't take a minute."

I returned with three toasted croissants slathered with cream cheese and strawberry jelly. I gave one to Avory and placed another on the stand beside the sleeping Hope.

"This is wonderful," Avory said. "I may have to relocate to New Orleans and move in with you."

"You'd change your mind. Croissants and coffee are pretty much the extent of my culinary talents."

"You have other talents," she said.

She blushed when I said, "And I'd like to demonstrate them for you sometime."

"Is sex the only thing you ever have on your mind?"

"Only at times like this," I said.

"What I meant are your detective talents."

"Oh," I said.

The ringing of my cell phone interrupted our thoughts. It was Bertram calling.

"Where are you?" he asked. "Sister Lydia is here and wants to talk to you."

"Now?" I said. "It's barely seven."

"Don't matter," he said. "Get your butt down here."

"Who was that?" Avory asked.

"Bertram. Sister Lydia is downstairs and wants to talk to me. Got to go."

"Not without me you aren't," Avory said.

Avory hurried to my closet and began searching through her clothes.

"What about Hope," I said. "We can't just leave her here alone."

"She's a big girl," Avory said. "She can find her way out without our help."

Chapter 27

Sister Lydia was sitting at the bar, nursing one of Bertram's martinis, when Avory and I made it down the stairs from my apartment. She wasn't smiling when Avory took the stool on one side of her and me on the other side.

"You haven't reported to me in two days," she said.

"I've been busy on the case and have lots to report. Let me catch you up."

Bertram gave me a dirty look when he brought Sister Lydia a fresh drink, my lemonade, and a martini for Avory.

Sister Lydia ate the olive, sipped her drink, and said, "Then maybe you'd better fill me in."

"I interviewed a vampire last night. His name is Malik. He claimed to be more than 300 years old."

"I'm a Catholic nun. I don't believe in vampires," Sister Lydia said.

Since I had reason to disbelieve her, I ignored her assertion and kept talking.

"Malik came to America with eleven other vampires. They called themselves the Disciples. One of the Disciples was Louis, Duke of Burgundy, also known as Le Petit Dauphin."

"Where are you going with this?" Sister Lydia asked.

A Freemason-like group that calls itself the Order of the Blood, along with the Casket Girls, made sure the vampires stayed alive until they reached New Orleans."

"And?" Sister Lydia said.

"It was members of the Order of the Blood who stole the Cross of Gilead from the Vatican."

"For what purpose?" Sister Lydia asked.

"To control the vampires who they knew were powerful beyond imagination."

Sister Lydia was listening intently to my story, though she kept her gaze directed on the bar in front of her martini.

"So tell me, what does this order, or vampires, have to do with the ceremony performed at the convent?"

"Members of the Order of the Blood worship Satan and believe the Old Ursuline Convent is built directly over the entrance to hell. They call it the Roof of Lucifer."

"Please continue," Sister Lydia said.

"Many Catholics and even some members of the clergy belong to the Order of the Blood. It's my opinion one or more of its followers performed the ceremony."

Sister Lydia looked at me for the first time. "If that's the case, then you've completed the task for which I hired you. The Greater Archdiocese of New Orleans thanks you. I thank you. Your services are now terminated."

When she finished her martini and started to leave, I said, "Not that easy. There's more to the story."

"I've heard all I care to hear," she said.

"Your grandson may have conducted the ceremony."

Sister Lydia was scowling when she stared

into my eyes.

"I'm a nun, Mr. Thomas. I have never been married."

"You had a child out of wedlock before you became a nun."

Avory gave me a go-to-hell look and put her arms around Sister Lydia when she grew visibly deflated.

"Wyatt, how dare you," Avory said.

"Your son was a Catholic priest named Father Luc. He got a cleaning woman at the Old Ursuline Convent pregnant."

"Please," Sister Lydia said.

"Stop it," Avory said. "Can't you see you're upsetting her?"

"The woman, Mona Marie Alphonsi, had twins with your son. Luc and Mona Marie named them Darth and Leia," I said.

Sister Lydia's hands were over her ears. "I don't want to hear anymore," she said.

"Have you lost your mind?" Avory said.

"Father Luc killed Mona Marie. He also killed Leia while in the process of sexually abusing her. Because of Luc's abuse, your grandson Darth beat him to death. Your son's and your granddaughter's bones are in the coffin that disappeared from the attic of the Old Ursuline Convent."

By now, Sister Lydia was in a state of full-blown tears. She ran out of Bertram's and started up the street.

"You're a fucking asshole!" Avory said. "How could you?"

Avory hurried out the door, trying to catch up with Sister Lydia. Bertram stood about ten feet away, polishing a glass with a bar rag. He walked over and took my lemonade away from me.

"Miss Avory is right, Cowboy. You're an asshole. Most drunks aren't as mean as you."

"Sorry to involve you in this. Everything is going to work out."

"When it does, I'll bring you more lemonade," he said. "Till then, you're cut off."

"Thanks," I said.

Tony came in the door, joining me at the bar. "What's up, Cowboy? You look like you just wrecked your mama's new car."

"Something like that," I said. "I told Sister Lydia I knew about her illegitimate child."

"Damn!" Tony said. "You didn't tell her how you found out about it, did you?"

"You and Aunt Dot are safe. Sister Lydia didn't ask how I knew. I didn't volunteer."

"Where is she?"

"She started crying and ran out of the door. Avory went after her," I said.

"Damn!" Tony said.

Bertram walked over without bothering to bring Tony's usual.

"If you need a drink, you might think about sitting somewhere else," I said. "Bertram saw the whole thing, and I'm in the doghouse with him."

When Tony moved over a stool, Bertram nodded his approval.

"Smart, Lieutenant," Bertram said. "Cowboy's going to hell. Ain't no use letting him drag us down with him."

Rafael came through the front door and hurried over.

"I passed Avory and Sister Lydia on the sidewalk," he said. "What happened?"

Bertram answered for me. "Cowboy, here, done lost his mind."

"What'd he do?" Rafael asked.

"Made a nun cry. If you ask me, you can't go much lower than that," Bertram said.

"Just doing what she hired me to do," I said. "I've come as far as I can in this case. She has information she doesn't want to share. I played my hole card."

"Yeah, well it looks like your little plan backfired on you," Bertram said.

Before the words were barely out of his mouth, Sister Lydia and Avory walked through the front door. Sister Lydia's tears had dried though neither she nor Avory was smiling.

"Maybe not," I said.

Rafael went to meet them, clutching Sister Lydia's shoulder and squeezing her hand.

"Are you okay?" he asked.

"Father Rafael, there is something I need to confess. Will you hear my confession?" she said.

"At once," he said. "Let's go to Wyatt's booth."

Avory sat on the empty stool to my right, refusing to speak to me. I waited, occasionally glancing at the animated conversation between Sister Lydia and Rafael. After several uncomfortable minutes, Rafael got Bertram's attention and raised two fingers. When Bertram returned from taking them their drinks, he tapped my shoulder.

"They want all of you to join them," he said.

As we crowded into the booth, Avory made a point of not sitting close enough to touch me.

"I have a confession to make to all of you," Sister Lydia said. "It was I who killed Luc, my son."

Avory glared at me when I said, "You beat your son to death?"

"That's right. When I learned he had killed my granddaughter Leia, I couldn't contain my anger."

"No one's accusing Darth of having killed his father. Father Luc isn't even considered dead, only missing."

"Doesn't matter," Sister Lydia said.

I looked at Rafael and could tell by his eyes that Sister Lydia was lying. Tony was also on the edge of his seat, afraid I would mention Aunt Dot. Avory continued to seethe.

"Please forgive me for my previous callous comments," I said. "Someone is possessing Darth. I think it is Louis, the man with whom you fathered Luc."

When tears appeared in Sister Lydia's eyes, Avory said, "Shut the hell up, Wyatt Thomas!"

Avory wasn't the only one. Tony turned away when I looked at him, and Rafael wouldn't make eye contact with me.

"Someone may be plotting to blow up the Old Ursuline Convent. Is Louis in charge? I need help here."

"You have no idea who Louis is," Sister Lydia said.

"He's the grandson of the Sun King, a direct heir to the throne of France. It seems likely to me he was the first French vampire. Tell me, Sister Lydia, how did you fall in love with a vampire?"

"I think we've heard enough," Avory said. "Let me take you out of here."

Sister Lydia's head was buried in her arms. She didn't respond to Avory's offer, beginning instead with another confession.

"I was in my teens, working as an aide at the Old Ursuline Convent when I met Louis. I always found excuses to stay late. Louis appeared to me the first time in the library. He was the most handsome man I had ever met."

"Did you know he was a vampire?" I asked.

"I knew. It didn't matter. Something in his past had traumatized him. He said that meeting me was the only thing that had saved him."

"But you're not a vampire," I said.

"Louis never thirsted for my blood. We were best friends, and we shared everything. We fell in love."

"When did that happen?" I asked.

"The summer before my senior year in high school. I asked Louis if he would marry me. He said it was impossible. When I finally convinced him, we exchanged vows at the main altar in the convent. We are still married."

"Then Louis is alive?"

Avory clutched Sister Lydia's shoulders when her tears returned.

"This is so complicated. Louis, my love, isn't alive, he's undead."

"When was the last time you saw him?" I asked.

"I see him every day," she said.

Everyone at the table was uncomfortable with my questions. Sensing I was on to something, no one interrupted.

"This surely can't comport with your duties as a nun," I said.

"And that's where I've sinned," she said.

"Does Louis believe in Satan?" I asked.

"His thinking has been twisted."

"Who twisted it?"

"I can't tell you."

"Why not?"

"There are people in this city who are more powerful than the mayor, the city council, and the Greater Archdiocese of New Orleans," Sister Lydia said.

"How can that be?" I asked.

"They are businessmen, politicians, and even priests. They can't be stopped because no one knows for sure who they are," she said.

"The Order of the Blood?" I asked.

"The Order is powerful," Sister Lydia said. "Their tentacles extend far beyond this city and the state of Louisiana."

"We're not worried about the rest of the world," I said. "Tell me who we are dealing with here in New Orleans."

Sister Lydia's face was red, though her tears had dried. When she put her lips to her martini glass, she realized it was empty.

"I need a drink," she said.

Rafael waved for another libation. Bertram obliged, bringing everyone in the booth, except for me, a fresh drink.

Sister Lydia nodded when I asked, "Do you know who runs the secret society here in New Orleans?"

"Two brothers," she said. "Orson and Veston."

"What's their last name?" I asked.

"Montespan."

Rafael grew suddenly animated. "Are you kidding me?" he said. "Madam de Montespan was the mistress of Louis XIV. She had a Black Mass performed where she lay naked, a chalice on her bare stomach, on the altar. The Mass was meant to secure the Sun King's dying love. Are they heirs of Louis' mistress?"

"Direct heirs," Sister Lydia said. "If not for the French Revolution, Orson and Veston might be controlling a satanic France right now."

"How did their ancestors keep from losing their heads?" Rafael asked.

"They were spirited by stealth and subterfuge out of the country," Sister Lydia said. "They brought much of their wealth and influence with them to New Orleans. Some might even say they still command royalty."

"The vampire Malik told me horrible things about members of the Order of the Blood. He said they practice torture, and demonstrations which often end in death are part of their meetings," I said.

"Louis is a strong, brave man. He stops short of complaining about the Order. Still. . ."

"He's afraid of them?" I said.

Sister Lydia looked me in the eye. "I believe

he is."

Tony had his notepad out, writing down the names of Orson and Veston Montespan. Avory was no longer glaring at me. Rafael looked as if he were about to throw up.

"How can I find these people?" I asked.

"You don't," Sister Lydia said. "We could all be killed for even mentioning their names."

"That isn't the answer I want to hear," I said. "I'm on your side about your grandson Darth. One more thing; you had a son with a vampire. How is that even possible?"

"I don't know," Sister Lydia said. "What I do know is my grandson Darth has the power of a vampire, yet he is as human as you or I. My granddaughter Leia was a beautiful human being and didn't deserve to die. I've pledged my existence to protect her memory and Darth's life with whatever power I possess. I hope I hired the right person to help me."

"Then I'm still on the case?" I asked.

Sister Lydia kissed me on the cheek, downed the rest of her martini, and then scooted out of the booth.

"If Leia were still alive and you had married her, I would have been honored to accept you into my family."

Tony spoke as Sister Lydia left the booth. "You know, Cowboy, you still got lots of asshole attorney left in you."

Chapter 28

Sister Lydia had a word with Bertram before leaving the bar. He quickly arrived at the booth with a glass of lemonade for me.

"You off the hook, Cowboy. At least for now." Everyone at the table raised their hand when Bertram asked, "Anybody need a drink?"

"I think we could all use one," Rafael said. "Please bring us another round."

"Orson and Veston Montespan shouldn't be hard to locate," I said. "How many Montespans can there be in New Orleans?" I asked.

"Probably more than you think," Rafael said.

"Bertram," I said. "Can I borrow your phonebook?"

Lilly Bliss came out of the back as I was shouting to Bertram. Taking the phonebook from him, she brought it to me.

"How's the script coming along?" she asked.

"Crazier every minute," Avory said. "Since I'm doing all the legwork, you're going to have to write this one."

"Nothing I'd like better," Lilly said. "Bert has me working like a dog. We haven't done anything fun since I've been here. Well, except for a few things that doesn't involve money."

"I'll watch the bar tonight if Bertram promises

to take you someplace nice," I said.

"You mean it?" she asked.

"Absolutely," I said.

Lilly gave me a hug before returning to the bar. After a conversation with Bertram, she waved at me and smiled. Rafael closed the phonebook he'd been searching through.

"No Montespans in here," he said.

"Their numbers are probably unlisted," Tony said. Tommy has a book that lists every number. I'll call and ask him to check the name for me."

"Ask him in person," I said. "He and Marlon just walked through the door."

Tommy and Marlon joined us when Tony waved to get their attention. Lilly brought an Abita for Tommy and pineapple juice for Marlon.

They were both smiling when Avory said, "Hi, boys. Slumming again?"

"Looking for someone," Tommy said. "Sammy Ray Nations is now officially a missing person."

"Surely the N.O.P.D. has more important things to do than search for a missing ex-con," I said.

"Might be more to it than that," Tommy said. "Maybe a serial killer at work."

"What makes you think so?" I asked.

"You found the bill with Nation's blood at the Old Ursuline Convent. A man who works at the towboat company with Nations gave the convent as his address," Tommy said.

"No one lives there," I said. "It's a museum."

Tommy ignored me. "His name is Darth Heaney. His father Luc worked at the convent and has been missing for more than two years."

"What's the story on Luc Heaney?" I asked.

"Adopted as a baby by the Heaney family. In and out of trouble his whole life. Got religion and became a priest. He apparently had a relationship with a convent cleaning lady. She had twins by him. She's missing, her daughter's missing, Luc Heaney is missing, and now Sammy Ray Nations is missing. We need to question Darth Heaney."

"Doesn't Father Luc's family know where he is?" I asked.

"His adopted parents are deceased, and no one else in the family would have anything to do with him. Seems no one in the priesthood liked him either."

"You know what they say, Tommy; no body, no crime."

"Darth Heaney is the only one connected to all four missing persons. If we can find him, we might be able to break him down during interrogation. Have any idea where he is?"

"No clue," I said.

"How you doing, Tony?" Tommy asked.

"Passable. You?"

"Like a pig at a fresh trough of slop." Seeing Avory's expression, he said, "Sorry, Miss Avory, just cop talk, you know?"

"No problem, Tommy," she said. "I'll use that one in my next screenplay."

Tommy downed his Abita and slid out of the booth. Marlon followed. Tony handed Tommy a slip of paper.

"Can you run this name for me?"

"You bet," Tommy said. "Let me know if you hear where I can find Darth Heaney."

When the door closed behind them, Rafael said, "I'm not feeling very priestly right now."

"They'll find Darth soon enough without our help," I said.

Rafael cast me an introspective look. "Wyatt, you seem to be going out of your way to protect this man Darth. Is there something I'm missing?"

"I'm not protecting anyone," I said. "I've never met Darth and have no feelings for him one way or the other."

"You were rough on Sister Lydia," Avory said. "Even if everything turned out all right in the end, you could have handled things differently."

"Sorry you feel that way," I said. "Sister Lydia might take the fall for Leia, Mona Marie, and Father Luc. When it comes to Sammy Ray Nations, she won't be able to cover for Darth. I'm just trying to protect our best lead."

"Sure about that, Cowboy?" Tony said.

"You're not turning on me, are you?" I asked.

Arriving with fresh drinks, Bertram had caught most of the conversation concerning Darth.

"If he's guilty of murder, why not just tell Tommy where to find him?" he said.

"The only person I'm fairly sure he killed is his father, and it sounds to me like the bastard had it coming," I said.

"Assuming Sister Lydia doesn't try to take the rap, even a half-ass defense attorney could get Darth acquitted," Tony said. "If the cops can't find Sammy Ray Nation's body, they're gonna have a helluva time proving he's dead, much less convicting someone of his murder."

"And Darth is instrumental in the case we're working on," I said.

Though Bertram was still frowning at me, he let the matter pass. "You told Lilly you'd watch the bar for us tonight."

"Yes, I did," I said.

"She got a nine o'clock reservation at the most expensive restaurant in town."

"Clarabellas on Tchoupitoulas Street?" Rafael asked.

"That's it," Bertram said. "You gonna pay for dinner for me, Cowboy?"

"It won't hurt you to spend some of your dough," I said. "If I had your money, I'd burn mine. Have a ball and don't worry about it."

"Clarabellas is in a converted 19th-century tobacco warehouse that's all candles, antiques, and atmosphere," Rafael said. "The food is fabulous."

"I want to go," Avory said.

"Let us tag along, and I'll pick up the tab," Rafael said. "The dining experience is worth every penny of it."

Bertram's smile had returned when he said, "Can't beat a deal like that."

"Great, then we'll be here around eight to pick you up," Rafael said.

Our Cajun bartender was smiling as he returned to the bar.

"Bertram doesn't need anyone to pick up the tab for him. He has more money than all three of us put together."

"You wouldn't know it by those old clothes of his," Avory said.

"He'd better wear something nice tonight, or he'll stand out like a sore thumb," Rafael said.

"Bertram would make Scrooge look like a philanthropist," I said.

"Lilly won't put up with that for long," Avory said.

"Why do you think she left him the first time?" I asked.

Avory grabbed Rafael's hand. "Let's go shopping. Sounds like I need a new outfit for tonight."

"Let's," Rafael said.

After clearing the tab with Bertram, they hurried out the door. Tony signaled Bertram for another drink.

"Won't be seeing them for a while," he said.

"Doesn't look like it," I said.

"I'd help, but tonight Lil and I are eating out at our favorite Italian restaurant."

"No problem," I said. "It's mindless work, and

I'll have time to reflect on the case."

"Rafael and Avory are right, you know," Tony said.

"About what?"

"I don't understand why you're shielding Darth Heaney."

"I have reasons," I said.

"I've been investigating cases for more than twenty years. I've found myself in a few blind alleys and had to reverse course to get back on track."

Tony got off the stool, patted my shoulder, and started for the door.

"I'll bite, Lieutenant. What is the right track?"

"Sister Lydia. You were pretty rough on her, though not nearly enough to get her to tell us all she knows."

"I rarely disagree with you, Lieutenant," I said. "I think she told us everything we need to know."

"You might be right, Cowboy," he said, patting my shoulder and walking out the door.

Except for a couple of tourists drinking Abita, the bar was empty. I was suddenly dog-tired. Remembering I'd had no sleep the previous night, I went upstairs to check on Kisses and take a much-needed nap.

I found the door to my balcony open, Kisses sleeping in my favorite chair. She awoke and began purring when I rubbed her head. After giving her some treats, I stripped down to my boxer shorts and lay on the bed. It was the last thing I remembered before slipping into a vivid dream.

⚜

I was alone, somewhere in New Orleans, on a major street I vaguely recognized but couldn't quite place. The street was dark, and I could see why. Power lines were down, some touching the ground. The lamps that weren't laying flat were all dark. Traffic signs were down. The streetlights were out. It didn't matter because there were no cars in sight. Operational cars, that is.

Abandoned vehicles were everywhere, strewn in every direction. Doors splayed open as if their drivers and passengers had hurriedly abandoned them. They were all trashed out, their paint jobs dull and lusterless.

Roofs were missing on many of the houses and businesses lining the street. A stray dog came out of the shadows and ran away when he saw me. I had a sick feeling in the pit of my stomach that something terrible had occurred.

Water was pooled in the street and on the sidewalks. Not a breath of air was moving, my nose objecting to the under-stench of mold, mildew, and rot. I jumped when someone tapped my shoulder. It was Leia, dressed in her ghostly garb and smiling at me. When she offered her hand, I grasped it.

We began to levitate, rising upward above the ruined neighborhood. As we did, I saw the carcass of New Orleans below me. It was eerily dark in all directions, and the sick feeling in the pit of my gut returned. The city, it seemed, had died. There were no lights, no music, not even the whisper of a cockroach racing under a baseboard.

Shadows of the tall buildings down by Canal loomed in the distance. I closed my eyes, expecting when I opened them to see New Orleans again as I remembered it. Though I blinked several times, nothing changed. The city below me lay destroyed and deserted. Something apocalyptic had happened. I couldn't help but wonder if things would ever be the same again.

I had little time to reflect on my shock and sadness because we'd begun to descend. As we grew closer to the ground, I saw a roof I recognized. It was the Old Ursuline Convent. We entered the convent through the open shutters of a third-floor dormer.

"I have something to show you," Leia said.

I followed her into the attic, the radiant aura cast by her body lighting our way. She halted when we reached a stress beam. The beam was wrapped in white plastic cord that climbed into the rafters.

"What is it?" I asked.

"Detonation cord. The attic is laced with it. The cord is attached to explosives."

"Someone is planning to blow the roof off the convent?" I asked.

"Darth. He means to bring the entire building to the ground. You can't let him do it."

"But what can I do?"

"Only Darth has the power to cause the explosion. Stop the person who is controlling Darth's mind, and you'll prevent the convent's destruction."

"Who is that person?"

"Louis, my grandfather."

"Louis, the vampire?" I said.

"Yes."

"He's all-powerful. How can I stop him?"

"There is only one way," she said.

"Which is?"

"I can't tell you. You must find the answer on your own."

"When does Darth plan to blow up the building?" I asked.

"During the light of the full moon."

"That doesn't give me much time," I said.

"We don't have much time. There's something else you must do."

"Such as?"

"Put an end to the Order of the Blood forever. They are vile and evil. They control people and use them in the worst ways."

"How do you propose I do away with them?"

"By blowing them and their headquarters to Holy hell," she said.

"I know nothing about explosives."

"Darth does. There are enough explosives left-over from his work on the convent to accomplish the task. But first, this very night, you must kill my grandfather and free Darth from his machinations."

"He's undead. He can't be killed."

"I will help you all I can though only you have the power to accomplish this task," she said.

"And if I don't?"

"There is no don't. When the moon is full, you will find Louis where I am now standing."

When she started to fade away, I reached for her hand. "Wait," I said. "You are the most beautiful vision I've ever seen. I think we made love. Is it true?"

Leia grasped my head with her soft hands and planted a burning kiss on my lips.

"You are my one and only lover, and that is the last kiss I will ever give to anyone. Please don't fail me."

"Will I ever see you again?" I asked.

She had something in her hand: a single white rose which she gave to me.

"Take this. Next time you see a rose like this, you'll know I'm there with you."

As Leia faded into the darkness, I became aware I was pressed against a warm body. It was dark when I opened my eyes and found I wasn't alone in bed. It was Hope, her arms entangling me, her warm breath on my neck.

Chapter 29

My heart was beating so fast, I was afraid for a moment it would burst out of my chest. Hope was smiling and squeezing me tightly.

"Are you kidding? Of course, we made love," she said.

It took me a moment to understand Hope's confusion. I didn't understand my own. Unlike most waking dreams, the one I'd just had didn't fade away. It was indelibly imprinted on my brain. Though I didn't know it for sure, I sensed Leia had something to do with Hope's calming presence. We lay in each other's arms until Kisses jumped into the middle of us. Hope began to giggle.

"I think Kisses is jealous," she said.

"I believe you're right. What time is it?"

"No clue," she said.

I glanced at the alarm beside the bed. "I have to get downstairs," I said. "I promised Bertram I'd run the bar for him tonight. They'll be wondering where I am."

"This is my day off," Hope said. "I'll help you."

I kissed her and got out of bed. "You saved my life, you know?" I said.

"How's that?"

"There's something I have to do later on tonight, and frankly, I didn't think I was up to the task. You've restored my courage."

"How did I do that?"

"One of these days, if I'm still alive, I'll tell you," I said. "Why are you off tonight?"

"It's a full moon. I'm a vampire. The boss gave me the night off."

"Everyone at the Eden Club is a vampire," I said. "Why do you get special treatment?"

"I'm the boss's favorite bartender, and also his niece," she said.

"Nepotism, huh?"

"Call it what you like. When it comes to mixing drinks, I'm the best bartender in town," she said. "I know it, and so does my uncle."

"You haven't met Bertram yet. He may not be the best, though I haven't found many bartenders who can outdo him."

"Though I've been in here before and talked to him a number of times, he probably doesn't remember me."

"I find that hard to believe," I said.

"When we do meet, I'll challenge him to a cocktail-mixing contest."

"Dammit!" I said. "Too bad I'm a teetotaler. I'd love to participate in that one."

Hope pinched my cheek. "You weren't a teetotaler last night."

"No, and I have a feeling you're going to be bad for my sobriety," I said.

"Maybe I'll work on you again tonight."

"Like I told you, there's something I have to do. I need to be sober as a judge," I said.

"If you're talking about Orleans Parish judges, then it sounds like you're going to get toasted."

As an ex-attorney, I knew she was right about many of the judges on the bench. The thought made me laugh.

"Bertram's customers aren't used to having a pretty woman waiting on them. Bet we'll sell a bunch of booze tonight." I said.

"Flattery will get you everywhere," Hope said.

"Then I intend to flatter you every time we speak."

"Keep it up. I'll quit my job and move in with you," she said.

"Let's not be too hasty. When you get to know me, you'll find I'm a real rat."

"We'll see about that. All I have to wear are my khaki shorts and Eden tee-shirt," she said.

"I'm betting you'll get no complaints. If we do, I'll boot them out the door."

"You're a sweetie," she said.

"As much as I like ogling your gorgeous tush, we need to get dressed and go downstairs. Bertram doesn't like being left hanging."

Hope got out of bed and pulled on her shorts and tee shirt.

"Sounds like fun," she said.

We found Bertram, Lilly, Avory, and Rafael waiting for us at the bar.

"Where you been?" Bertram said. "We gonna be late."

"No, you aren't," I said. "The head chef of Clarabellas is one of Hope's uncles. She called ahead. You'll be first in line when you get there. This is Hope Bosh."

Avory gave me a confused look. "We're not playing house anymore?" she asked.

"You have a date," I said. "What's a man to do?"

"You could have waited on me," she said.

"I'll be here tomorrow. Have a wonderful time at Clarabellas."

Rafael was dressed like a GQ runway model, and the gold chain around his neck was expensive. Avory and Lilly were wearing matching gowns and looked as if they'd come straight out of the latest issue of Elle. Bertram didn't quite measure up, his striped burgundy suit at least twenty years old. Hope glanced at him and shook her head.

"You can't go to Clarabellas looking like that," Hope said. "You're about Wyatt's size. He has some classy clothes in his closet. I'll be right back."

Hope jogged up the stairs to my room, soon returning with an armload of clothes. Pulling Bertram behind the bar, she began undressing him. When she had him stripped down to his boxer shorts, she began helping him get dressed. Soon, Bertram looked resplendent in off-white linen slacks, a white silk shirt open to the waist, and a baby blue blazer complete with a red handkerchief in the top pocket. He was even wearing my favorite dress shoes.

Before Bertram could protest, Lilly said, "Bert, you look amazing. I'll have to fight off the women."

Hope bundled up Bertram's old suit. "What are doing with my clothes?" he asked.

"Tossing them into the nearest incinerator," Hope said.

Lilly waved her fist at him when he said, "Now wait just a minute."

Hope glanced at Lilly and said, "Well?"

"Toss them," she said. "Tomorrow, Bert and I are going on a shopping spree and buy him a new wardrobe."

"Here, here," Rafael said. "I'll tag along and provide my fashion expertise."

"There are already lots of customers tonight," Bertram said. "You up to the task, Cowboy?"

"Hope's the lead bartender at the Eden Club. She mixes the best drinks in town," I said.

"Unless I miss my guess, we'll set a sales record tonight."

"Want to try one of my martinis before you go?" Hope asked.

"If you can mix a martini as good as this old Cajun can, I'll kiss your ass."

"You're on," Hope said.

She went to work behind the bar and soon presented the four partiers with martinis.

"Cheers," Rafael said, hoisting his glass.

"Oh, my God!" Avory said after taking a sip. "I didn't think anyone could make a martini as good as Bertram's."

Lilly agreed. "Sorry, Bert. Your martini is good. This one is better."

"It is pretty damn tasty," he said.

"What now?" Rafael said.

Hope pulled down her shorts, directing her exposed rear toward Bertram.

"Pay up," she said.

Bertram's face had turned bright red, but he bent down and quickly kissed her bare derriere. He liked it, and it was apparent that Lilly noticed. Hope was mixing the second round of martinis when Bertram grabbed my arm and drew me to the side.

"Sister Lydia was here earlier," he said.

"Oh?"

"She had me open the safe and give her that cross. Can't say as I ain't glad it's gone. It kinda had me spooked out."

"It seemed like too much of a priceless artifact to keep in a bar, even if it was in your safe."

"Way too much responsibility, if you ask me. You sure about tonight?"

"I've subbed for you a hundred times," I said. "Why should this be any different? And I have someone to help me. Are you and Lilly having problems?"

"Is it that obvious?" he asked.

"It's all over your face and hers too," I said.

"Lilly's tired of waiting tables. She wants to see the town and have some fun," Bertram said. "I've already done all that."

"Can't you loosen up?"

"That's what I'm doing right now. I love her, and she loves me. Don't matter none because we're as different as dogs and cats."

"Doesn't sound good," I said.

"She even mentioned marriage. Scared the hell out of me."

"You could do a lot worse," I said.

"I'm not cut out for marriage," he said.

"Have you told Lilly?"

"I'm pretty sure she already knows it. Talk to you about it later. We gotta scoot."

Avory gave me a look as she walked out the door. I could tell she wasn't happy seeing me with Hope. Our association to that point had been almost nonexistent. Didn't matter. In her mind, I had betrayed our relationship. Since there was nothing I could do about it, I decided to do nothing.

Hope and I were both laughing when Bertram, Lilly, Avory, and Rafael left for Clarabellas with go cups in their hands. As Bertram had said, it was beginning to look like a banner night for liquor sales. Hope was up to the task, meting out drinks as fast as they were ordered.

"Sorry to make you work on your night off," I said.

"I love it. I'm doing what I've wanted to do my whole life," she said.

"You sound like Bertram."

"He's cute. I love his dog, Lady, and I love this bar. It's so old and has so much character," she said.

"But no vampires," I said.

She gave me a wink. "You might be surprised."

"Lots of things have surprised me lately," I said.

It was midnight before Bertram returned alone from Clarabellas.

"Where's Lilly?" Hope asked.

"Left me," he said.

"What the hell did you do?" I asked.

"Nothing I know of," he said. "We had a great time. The food and drinks were first class, and it turned out I know the owner. Every now and then, he comes drinking here in the bar. The waiters and waitresses treated us like royalty. Things started getting kind of crazy after that."

"Like what?"

"Quinlan Moore showed up with a flashy blond in a low-cut dress. He was already pretty drunk because when he saw Lilly and Avory, he busted over to our table."

"What happened?" I asked.

"He was fire-breathing mad and started calling Avory every dirty name in the book. Rafael asked him politely to leave our table. When he didn't, Rafael got up and gave him a shove. Moore went sailing into another table. Two waiters escorted him and his girlfriend out of the restaurant."

"Rafael shoved him?"

"Didn't take much. Like I said, Mr. Moore was pretty looped. When we left the restaurant, Avory had Rafael drop her at his hotel."

"What happened to Rafael?" I asked.

"He dropped me off."

"And Lilly went with him? Why did Lilly get mad at you?"

"Like I told you before we left, it's been building up for a while," he said. "She told me when we were in the car coming home she'd moved her stuff earlier today to a hotel."

"Why did she bother going to Clarabellas with you?"

"She didn't have an answer."

"Then it's over?" I said.

"I tell you, even though I love that woman, we don't see eye to eye," Bertram said. "She said I'd never change."

"What did you say to that?" I asked.

"I told her I thought the way I am is the reason she loved me in the first place," he said. "Didn't turn out that way."

Tears had begun streaming down Hope's cheek, and she embraced Bertram.

"I'm so sorry," she said. "You don't deserve being treated that way."

"Thanks, baby. I'm thinking I had it coming. Lady and this bar mean the world to me. It's all I ever wanted. It just ain't what Lilly wants."

"Nothing wrong with that," Hope said. "Since I was eighteen, I've saved every penny I've earned. A bar like this is my dream, and someday I'll have it."

"Yes, you will. You mix a mean martini. I didn't think anybody could make one as good as me."

"Ever had a Grim Reaper?" she asked.

"Can't say as I have. What's in it?"

"Kahlua, 151 proof rum, grenadine, and ice. Vampires love them," she said. "We sell hundreds at the Eden Club. Want me to make you one?"

"Won't turn me into a vampire, will it?" he asked.

"Maybe."

"Then mix me one up," he said. "Tonight, I'm fit to be tied."

Hope began searching the bar for the necessary ingredients. As she did, Bertram glanced in the cash register.

"Holy cow!" he said. "You must have been busy while we was gone."

"You kidding?" I said. "Hope's a drink magnet with that tight tee-shirt she's wearing. Your customers love her."

"She your girlfriend now?" Bertram asked.

"Thinking about stealing her from me?"

"I wouldn't do that," he said.

"Hope's a free spirit. I have no permanent ties on her. She just showed up at an important time for me. I don't have a clue what tomorrow will bring."

Hope tapped Bertram's shoulder and handed him the Grim Reaper.

"Tasty," he said.

"Let's do a special on them," Hope said. "See how many we can sell."

"How you gonna do that?"

"Watch me," she said. She stood on the bar and tapped a glass with a spoon. When everyone looked at her, she lifted her tee-shirt and flashed her tits. "Now that I have everyone's attention, we're having a two for one sale on Grim Reapers. Buy the first at the regular price and get the second one free."

Before long, the cash register was ringing, patrons getting drunk, as Hope continued flashing her tits. I had no idea what time it was though knew I'd have to leave soon for the Old Ursuline Convent. I grabbed Bertram's elbow and pulled him aside.

"There's something I have to do," I said. "Is it all right if I leave Hope here with you?"

"What the hell are you doing this time of night?"

I grasped his hand and shook it. "Can't tell you," I said. "I just want you to know you're the best friend I've ever had. I'm proud to have known you."

"Wait," he said as I started out the door. "What the hell do you mean by that?"

I didn't answer him as I hurried down the dark street toward the Old Ursuline Convent.

Chapter 30

I was questioning my sanity as I reached the back entrance to the Old Ursuline Convent. My brain was telling me to run the other direction. It also kept repeating Leia's words.

"This very night, you must kill my grandfather and free Darth from his machinations."

For whatever reason, I was powerless to do anything other than to comply with Leia's wishes. Maybe it was just a dream. It didn't feel like one. As I made my way to the stairs leading to the attic, I fully expected to encounter Louis, the vampire, and I had no idea how I was supposed to kill him.

When I reached the third floor of the convent, I had a surprise. The alarm was disabled, the door to the attic standing open. A dim light flickered through the gloom, the old wooden floors creaking. I started to call out though I quickly decided that tactic might be a bad idea. When I took a step through the door, it was if I had walked through a portal into another dimension.

Well after dark, the bats had already flown outside in search of flying insects. The rats and mice were still there, as were a few cockroaches. A big one raced past my foot as I crept closer to the light. I needed a weapon. I couldn't kill anyone with my bare hands. I found a piece of wood about the size and heft of a baseball bat on the attic floor. Picking it up, I stashed it behind my back.

As I grew closer to the light, I expected to see a giant vampire. Instead, I found a person diligently stringing detonation cord. The man working without a shirt was shorter than me. Even in the dim light of a single candle, I could see he had the upper body of a powerlifter. He turned when the old floor beneath my feet signaled my presence.

"Who are you?" he asked.

"Wyatt. Who are you?"

"Father Luc Heaney," he said.

"Father Luc is dead. You are his son, Darth."

My words brought a frown to his face. "What are you doing here?" he asked.

"Stopping you from destroying this convent. You're sister Leia sent me."

"It's Leia who is dead, and she's my daughter, not my sister."

"Doesn't matter," I said. "I can't let you blow up the convent."

"Go to hell! You can't stop me."

"You're not speaking for Darth. The words coming from your mouth are your grandfather's. He was a great man before he lost his mind. Please, stop what you're doing and think for yourself."

"And what'll you do if I don't?"

"If it means I have to use force to stop you, then that's what I'll do."

Father Luc snickered. "The only way to do that is to kill me."

"What you're doing is wrong," I said. "Mona Marie wouldn't have liked it. Leia doesn't like it."

"How dare you invoke Mona Marie's name."

"She was your mother," I said. "She loved and cared for you. You're father killed her, beat her to death, just as he did your sister Leia."

"Stop it," Father Luc said.

"A madman and a group of radicals who believe in something totally absurd are controlling your thoughts and actions."

"You don't have a clue," he said.

"Leia's here with us. I feel her presence. I think you do too. Resist your grandfather. Let Leia guide you."

Father Luc blinked and closed his eyes, a grimace immediately appearing on his face. Sinking to his knees, he emitted a plaintive wail that echoed through the attic of the Old Ursuline Convent.

"I can't take this much longer," he said. "Release me from the pain."

Bending forward, he began pounding his head on the floor and clawing gashes in his face with his fingernails. As I watched, a wisp of vapor appeared behind him. Someone dressed in black and bigger than the vampire Malik materialized.

"You are a dead man," he said. "You will die, but not until I drain every drop of blood from your body."

It was Louis, Le Petit Dauphin, the first vampire who'd ever come to America. His eyes grew red as he stared at me.

"Killing me will serve no purpose," I said. "Your enemies are the Order of the Blood. They've lied to you, used you, caused you to destroy your own family and the people who love you."

"What do you know about the Order of the Blood?"

"They've done nothing but manipulate you. When you differed from the Order's beliefs, they saw to it you spent decades in solitary confinement."

"That was my own doing," he said.

"Was it? My guess is the Order of the Blood orchestrated the whole affair. You were poisoned and in a weakened state when the police arrived."

"They wouldn't have had a chance against my strength except. . ."

"It was no ordinary priest who happened by on the sidewalk, was it? He knew where you'd be, and he had the means to control you," I said.

"He knew my weakness," Louis said.

"And employed it against you," I said. "The priest was a member of the Order of the Blood and used the Cross of Gilead on you. I think you know what that infers."

"Things have changed," he said. "I now see eye-to-eye with the council."

"Sister Lydia doesn't condone the destruction of the convent. She believes in you. You can't forsake her," I said.

"Keep her out of this."

"She loves you. If you have no compassion for the citizens of New Orleans, then think of Sister Lydia, the wife you accepted in holy matrimony."

"Lydia is but a part of my life. You know nothing about the rest of it and what drives my actions," Louis said.

"I know you are the grandson of Louis XIV. I know you were in line for the throne before you, your wife and sons contracted measles. I know your wife and one of your sons died of the disease. I know you became a vampire in an attempt to save them. I know you were the first of the twelve Disciples who originally arrived in New Orleans. Shall I go on?"

Louis' booming voice echoed through the attic when he said, "Who told you these things?"

"Malik, one of the Disciples."

"Malik is dead," Louis said.

"Undead, maybe. I assure you, he lives right

here in New Orleans."

"You are lying to buy time," he said.

"Release Darth from your possession. He's innocent and doesn't deserve to be involved in this madness."

"I'm not mad," Louis said. "Darth will finish wiring the attic."

"Over my dead body," I said.

"As you wish."

Louis showed me his fangs. When he moved toward me, I took a round-house swing at his big head and connected. It felt as if something popped. My blow staggered him for only a moment before he issued a banshee's scream and pounced on me.

Yanking the bat out of my hands, he tossed it aside. Grabbing my collar, he slammed me against the wall. I was trying to regain my breath when he piled on top of me, pummeling me with his fists and tearing my skin away with his inhuman fingernails. I had all but lost consciousness when someone else joined the fray.

It was Avory. Grabbing the giant vampire around his neck, she began pummeling him with her fists.

"Help us," she called. "He's killing Wyatt."

Not worrying about Avory, Louis had me by the throat. I couldn't breathe. I had all but lost consciousness when a wail issued from deep in the vampire's throat. I opened my eyes to see Sister Lydia holding the Cross of Gilead against her husband's heart. The next thing I knew, Avory was patting my cheek, trying to revive me.

"Wyatt, please open your eyes!"

Louis lay comatose beside me on the floor of the Old Ursuline Convent as Avory rocked me in her arms. Sister Lydia wasn't far away, sobbing as she tried to revive her grandson. As my mind began to clear, Darth opened his eyes.

"Who are you?" he asked.

"Your grandmother. I just killed your grandfather, my husband, and the love of my life."

"You can't kill a vampire," Darth said.

"Yes, you can," Sister Lydia said. "You must help me."

Blood oozed from my nose and the multiple cuts on my swollen face. My ribs hurt like hell. I was dizzy, and my eyes crossed when I tried to stand. Avory ripped away part of her dress and used it to staunch the blood flowing down my cheeks.

"You're a mess," she said.

"And my head is killing me," I said.

"Help us," Sister Lydia said. "We have to take Louis to the coffin."

Darth didn't need any help. Carrying a candle, Sister Lydia led the way as he dragged the body of his grandfather to a small room hidden in the attic. Flickering candlelight was all we needed to see the ancient coffin. Its lid was still open from where I'd used the crowbar on it. Darth loaded Louis' body atop the bones. Sister Lydia produced a wooden stake from her habit and handed it to Darth.

"Pierce his thigh with this stake," she said.

Darth complied, forcing the wooden stake through the fleshy part of his grandfather's thigh. A tear rolled down Sister Lydia's cheek as she opened the vampire's mouth and placed several pebbles in it. Once his lips were closed, Sister Lydia kissed him.

"Farewell, my lover. I'll never know another man like you. Rest in peace, forever."

My head was still banging, and I could barely think.

"I'm dying here," I said. "Anyone have an aspirin?"

"I didn't bring my purse," Avory said.

Sister Lydia handed me two aspirins. "Sorry I have nothing to wash them down with."

I tossed them into my mouth. "Thank you," I said. "What are you two doing here?"

"Saving your ass," Avory said. "After the debacle at Clarabellas, I had Rafael take me to Quin's hotel. He was stinking drunk, obnoxious, and belligerent. I could have forgiven him for all of that, except. . ."

"Except for what?" I said.

"He took a swing at me. He missed. I kicked him in the nuts, got the hell out of there and took a cab to Bertram's."

"I didn't tell Bertram where I was going. How did you know I'd be here?" I asked.

"You shook Bertram's hand and told him he was your best friend. He said it sounded as if you were giving him your final farewell.

"It almost was," I said.

"I figured you were coming here, so I called Sister Lydia to let me in. Thank God she brought the Cross of Gilead with her. Let's get the hell out of here."

"There's something more we have to do. Leia said there's a meeting tonight of the Order of the Blood."

"They are waiting on me," Darth said

"Leia told me you have leftover explosives," I said. "Is there a way to use them on the Order?"

Darth smirked. "We don't need them. The Order of the Blood has a warehouse on the river with enough weapons and explosives to destroy half the parish. All we need is a detonator and a timing device."

"Leia instructed me to accompany you."

"Because I can't do it alone and need someone's help," Darth said.

"I'm going," Avory said.

"I only need one of you," Darth said. "If I bring two extra people with me, it could get us all killed."

"Let me go instead of Wyatt," Avory said. "He can barely move, much less assist you."

"She's right, you know. You're shirt's a bloody mess," Sister Lydia said.

"I have no choice," I said. "I'm going with Darth."

"Not looking like that, you aren't," Avory said.

"Yes, he can," Darth said. "The members want no one, not even the other members, to know they belong to a subversive secret society. We all wear robes, our identities masked. We are allowed to don our robes in privacy. There's a back door. I'll let you in when I enter the room to put on my robe."

"Great," I said.

Avory and Sister Lydia cleaned the blood from my face and neck with water from a courtyard hose. When they finished, Darth squeezed Sister Lydia's hand.

"Are you truly my grandmother?"

"I am," she said. "My granddaughter is dead." She hugged him to her breast. "I don't want to lose my only grandson."

"Three days ago I had no one," Darth said. "I now have a grandmother and a woman in my life."

"Who is the woman?" Sister Lydia asked.

"Her name is Maeve. I'm crazy about her," he said.

Chapter 31

There are many dark alleyways in New Orleans. I thought I knew all of them. I learned differently as Darth led us on a circuitous route to the river. Fog was rolling in off the Mississippi, though we could still see the running lights of several boats plying the Big Muddy. Darth pointed to a large warehouse on the bank of the river.

"That's it," he said. "Members are arriving, and the meeting will start shortly. There are things I must tell you before you enter the building."

"We're listening," I said.

"The meeting is in the main chapel. It looks a lot like the main chapel of the Old Ursuline Convent. That is by design. These people have a religion, and it's called Satanism."

"Please go on," Avory said when Darth hesitated.

"There's a central stage. At some point during the ceremony, the horrible torture of a person will take place on that stage. The members of this order are more bloodthirsty than any vampire. The demonstration will sicken you to witness it."

"Who will they torture?" Avory asked.

"Usually a woman or a child," Darth said. "More often than not, it is someone related to one of the members who has incurred the ire of the Elder Council."

"Tell us about the Elder Council," I said.

"Orson and Veston Montespan and six others. They always sit on stage to conduct the Black Mass, which includes the torture ceremony."

"Who are the other six?" I asked.

"No one knows their exact identities. It's rumored they are judges, important bankers, and even high-ranking officials in the local police department."

"And they all participate in the torture?"

When Darth nodded, Avory said, "Wyatt, I don't think I can bear seeing someone being tortured without trying to help."

"What can we do?" I asked.

Avory was fuming. "Something, anything."

"We're already risking our lives," Darth said. "The Order, much like the Swiss Army guards maintained by the Vatican, has their own police. They are trained to kill first and ask questions later."

"I think I'd rather die than witness the torture death of some innocent person," Avory said.

"Then maybe you'd better wait outside," I said.

Avory grabbed my hand and Darth's. "Pledge to me that part of our mission is to save the person from being tortured. There must be a way."

"No guarantees but I'll try to come up with something," Darth said.

Avory kissed his forehead. "Thank you, Darth."

"Wait here for me," he said. "When it's safe, I'll open the door and motion you to come inside."

Darth left us hidden in the bushes and went

in the front door. Avory was fidgeting.

"I'm scared, Wyatt," she said. "I've never dealt with pure evil, and I think that's what these people are."

"I'm scared, too," I said.

Avory squeezed my hand. "What are we going to do?"

"Darth doesn't need you. Wait here for me."

"That's a coward's way out. You're not a coward. Neither am I."

"I promised Leia I would help Darth do this."

"Leia is real?" Avory asked.

"She is to me," I said.

Twenty long minutes passed before a door in the back opened a crack. Darth stuck his head out and waved for us to join him. We entered a dimly lit dressing room with brown robes hanging from pegs on the wall.

"Hurry," he said. "I've already been in here too long. The Blood Police will be looking for me soon."

"What about the explosion?" I asked.

"After you're seated in the chapel, I'll slip away for a moment and set the detonation device."

"You have access to the arsenal?" I said.

"I know the passcode because of the work I've done at the convent. I'm scheduled to speak before the congregation and announce that the destruction of the Roof of Lucifer is imminent."

"What then?" Avory said.

"They'll probably try to kill me," he said.

"For what reason?" she asked.

"I'm not a real member of the Order of the Blood, and I'm considered dangerous."

"How can they get away with that?" I asked.

"The police are looking for me for the murder of a deckhand on the Emma Lou. If they kill me, the police will say tomorrow I died while resisting arrest."

"Jesus!" I said.

"Not Jesus, Satan," Darth said. "It's why I needed you here with me. Though the explosion isn't yet set, I'm giving you the detonation device. If I die, you must blow this building to hell."

Darth handed me the detonator.

"How does this thing work?" I asked.

"Radio signal," he said. "Just pull the trigger."

Once we were clad in the brown robes, Avory said, "Now what?"

"You're on your own," he said. "The meeting is over when the service ends. Walk out the front door like you own the place, and then disappear into the darkness."

"What about you?" Avory asked.

"If I can, I'll get away," he said. "Whatever you do, don't be afraid to use the detonator. Now, give me five minutes before coming out and then make your way to the chapel."

Someone in a Mardi Gras mask was waiting at the door to enter the room as Avory and I exited. The man looked vaguely familiar, though I couldn't be sure.

"Let's follow the flow of people," I said.

Darth had been correct. The auditorium looked like the main chapel at the Old Ursuline Convent. The only difference was the numerology signs placed among the holy Catholic statuary. We found two empty seats at the end of a pew.

As Darth had said, there was a stage in front of the altar. On the stage were twelve coffins fronted by eight high-backed chairs. Ten minutes passed as robed members filed into the chapel and seated themselves. Finally, the lights dimmed, and an organ began to play, its music sounding more like the theme song from a horror movie than a Catholic hymn. As we watched, the Elder Council filed on stage and took their places in the chairs. Each of them was carrying an unlit black candle.

The council was followed by two men dressed as priests. The first man's clerical garb was white, the second man's black. The two men hadn't bothered covering their faces, and I took it to mean they were Orson and Veston Montespan. The priest in white took a chair; the priest dressed in black remained standing.

"I am Father Orson," the priest in black said. "Before the Mass begins, I have an announcement to make. The Old Ursuline Convent has been wired with explosives. Tomorrow, the Roof of Lucifer will fall and the Dark Lord, our prince, will once again be free to walk the earth."

A subdued round of applause spread through the congregation. Orson began the Black Mass, for the most part, a parody of Catholic Mass. As the ceremony continued, a black goat trotted on to the stage. The goat had a lighted black candle between its horns. Orson, Veston and the Council of Elders lighted their candles from the one between the goat's horns.

The ancient pipe organ began playing again, reverberating through the room. The lights dimmed even further. Three people in brown robes appeared from behind a curtain. They pushed a portable altar to the center of the stage. A naked woman was spread-eagled on the altar, a silver chalice balanced precariously on her bare stomach.

Orson took the chalice and appeared to fill it from the urinating goat. He had something else in his hand: a bright red fleshy object that looked like a heart. Veston and all the members of the Elder Council took communion from the chalice and the false heart.

Avory's fingernails were clawing into my hand as she whispered in my ear.

"That's Maeve."

I did a double-take. It was Maeve. She was apparently drugged because her mouth was open, her eyes rolling in their sockets. Though I didn't know the name of the medieval device Orson had in his hand, I knew it was meant for torture.

The congregation murmured when Orson said, "One of our members has been duplicitous. Because of his backstabbing behavior, he must take part in the sacrifice to the Dark Prince of a person he loves."

As we watched, two of the Order's Blood Police escorted a robed man to the stage. Two more soldiers armed with swords followed them. The captive man's hands were cuffed behind his back. When Orson removed the cowl, I saw it was Darth. Avory squeezed my hand even harder.

"This device I'm holding is called a breast ripper," Orson said. "It was specifically designed to punish women. In the hands of a master torturer, the device exacts exquisite pain. Darth Heaney will soon witness the torture first hand."

Darth was yanking on his cuffs, trying to get loose from his captors. Orson had a dagger, and he showed it to Darth.

"Before I use the breast ripper, the woman's skin must be lacerated."

Blood oozed as Orson made a cut from Maeve's collarbone all the way to her pubic hair. Another murmur of approval spread through the congregation. When I started to rise, Avory yanked my hand.

"What are you doing?" she asked.

"We have to do something," I said.

Before she could reply, a large man came out of the congregation and began walking up the aisle to the stage. When he reached Darth, he smacked one of the guards in the face. Before either of the remaining guards or the Blood Police could react, he dispatched them as well. Grabbing Darth's cuffs, he pulled until they broke. Turning toward the crowd, he removed his cowl.

"I am Malik, last of the Disciples. I'm here to avenge their deaths, something I should have done decades ago."

"Armed men began pouring up the aisle from rooms in the back of the warehouse. Darth didn't notice because he had grabbed Orson by the head. After forcing him to drop the dagger, he lifted him by the neck, shaking him until we heard a sickening pop. Not checking to see if he were dead, he grabbed Veston and killed him in the same gruesome manner. Malik was in a life-or-death fight with the guards when he tossed Darth a sword.

"We have to free Maeve," Avory said.

Grabbing her hand, I pulled her up an aisle to the stage. Darth saw us, stopped what he was doing, and started in our direction. After yanking off my cowl, I did the same to Avory's.

"Darth, it's Wyatt and Avory. Throw me a sword."

With a nod, he tossed his weapon to me and grabbed another from one of the Blood Police.

Because of the close quarters, the guards couldn't use their firearms for fear of killing members of the Order who were trapped in their seats. Their only access to the stage was the aisle. Darth and Malik, using swords from guards they had killed, were blocking the entrance. After I'd used the sword to sever Maeve's bonds, Avory covered her with her robe.

The Elder Council had disappeared through a door in the back of the stage. It was only a matter of time before the guards would come charging in from behind us. Malik turned for a moment when he saw me.

"We've got to get out of here," I said.

Malik stepped down off the stage and began chopping his way forward.

"Follow me," he said.

Avory, Maeve and I were sandwiched between Malik and Darth as we fought our way to the front door. When we got there, Malik pushed us outside.

"I'll hold them off until you get away," he said.

"Come with us. The warehouse is wired to blow," I said. "You'll never survive."

"Get the hell out of here," he shouted. "I'm going nowhere."

"Then I'm staying with you," Darth said.

Malik stopped fighting long enough to put his hand on Darth's shoulder.

"You're the closest person to a son I'll ever have. I'm three-hundred years old. If I die, then so be it. Go now, have a child with your woman and name it after me."

"If you can, try to buy us ten minutes," Darth said. "And then save yourself."

Darth had dropped his sword, Maeve in his arms as we raced away from the warehouse. Soon, the sound of the battle behind us had died into darkness. Darth stopped and turned around.

"Blow the building," he said.

"What about Malik? I said.

"Do it now," he said.

Chapter 32

We were at least a mile from the warehouse when I detonated the building. The blast was like nothing I'd ever seen or heard. Flames rose hundreds of feet above the river. The ground beneath us shook. Maeve was growing coherent.

"Darth," she said. "Is it really you?"

"Are you okay?" he asked.

"I had the worst dream," she said.

"You're awake now," he said. "And you're safe with me."

"Let's go to Bertram's," I said. "You and Maeve are both injured. He'll clean and dress your wounds."

The door to Bertram's was locked, the lights dim. When we got inside, we found Bertram and Hope drinking at the bar. Hope's face lit up when she saw Darth and Maeve. She ran to them when she noticed the blood on Darth's clothes and Maeve's robe.

"Oh my God!" she said. "What happened?"

"Long story," I said.

"We heard a blast," Hope said. "The building shook. It felt like we were having an earthquake."

"An explosion at a warehouse on the river," I said.

Bertram went behind the bar, returning with a pail of hot water and an armload of bandages.

"You three could use some cleaning up," he said.

Hope wasn't waiting for Bertram. After stripping away Maeve's robe, she undressed Darth. She soon had Darth and Maeve's wounds cleaned and bandaged. Bertram worked on my wounds, cleaning me up as best he could. When he finished, Avory and I took stools at the bar.

Bertram mixed a martini for Avory. He gave me a glance after handing me a glass of lemonade.

"You don't look so good," he said. "Your nose is broke. I popped it back in place. You'll be fine until you can get to a doctor, though it's probably gonna mess up that pretty face of yours."

"Thanks," I said. "That's the least of my worries."

"Got a headache?" he asked.

"Headache, body ache, you name it," I said. "Got a couple of aspirins?"

Bertram handed me a tin container from behind the bar.

"Better keep them all," he said. "You're gonna need them. What happened?"

"Got into a wrestling match with a vampire. I'd be dead right now if it weren't for Avory and Sister Lydia," I said. "Did Lilly ever return?"

Bertram glanced up at one of his slow-moving ceiling fans.

"I been wishing all night she'd walk through the door. This old Cajun's heart tells him she ain't coming back anytime soon. Hope's been keeping me company. What about you, Miss Avory? You didn't say much before you went running out of here."

"I broke up with Quin," she said.

"So it's a done deal?" Bertram asked.

"Done with, over, finished." She smiled. "He didn't like it when I told him he needed counseling. I got my story. All I have to do now is put it on paper."

"How long will that take?" Bertram asked.

"I'll have a first draft before the week is over," she said.

"That fast?" I said.

She nodded. "I'm going to miss your martinis, Bertram."

"I ain't going nowhere," he said.

"I am. My home is in Los Angeles. Without Quin, I'll need to find a place for my new script."

"They have phones and computers in L.A.," he said.

"They have everything in L.A.," Avory said.

"They ain't got the French Quarter," Bertram said, "Once it gets in your blood, it's impossible to ever get it out."

"You may be right," she said.

Bertram began mixing Avory another martini.

"What about Rafael? It looked like you had a thing going with him," he said.

"He's a wonderful man," she said. "We had a fun couple of days playing house."

"Is that all there was to it?" he asked.

"Sometimes, it's all there is," she said.

"What about Lilly? Will you be talking to her?"

Avory grasped Bertram's hand. "I'm so sorry, Bertram. Lilly's done with you. I'm pretty sure she went home with Rafael."

"He always did have the hots for her," Bertram said.

"You're not angry?" Avory asked.

"More relieved than anything, I think," he said. "I loved Lilly, and she loved me, but the only real thing we had in common was the bedroom. That don't get you very far in life."

"Guess not," Avory said.

"Ain't nothing left to do down here, Cowboy," Bertram said. "Why don't you go lay down?"

I took two of the aspirins from the tin and washed them down with my lemonade.

"Good idea. I'm calling it a night," I said. "At least what's left of it."

My muscles were sore as I climbed the stairs to my apartment. The door to my balcony was ajar, a refreshing breeze blowing into the room. Since Kisses was off tomcatting, I filled her food bowl and checked on her water. After undressing, I fell sound asleep until a warm body pressing against my chest awakened me. It was Avory.

"We have unfinished business," she said.

⁘

Light shining through the open door to my balcony, awoke me. Kisses was kneading dough on my chest, and Avory was gone. When I got out of bed, my aching body reminded me of the recent beating I had taken. After thirty minutes beneath a hot shower, I got dressed and went downstairs. Rafael, Tony, and Sister Lydia were waiting at the bar. Tony glanced at his watch.

"It's almost noon," he said. "I was about to come check on you."

"You look like hell," Rafael said.

"I feel even worse," I said. Bertram didn't

279

say anything as he set a steaming cup of Cajun coffee in front of me. "Where's Darth, Maeve, and Hope?"

"Went home. Hope went with them," he said.

"Will they be all right?" I asked.

"They didn't look half as bad as you do," he said. "Sister Lydia told us what happened at the convent."

"We all want to know about the warehouse," Rafael said. "Let's go to your booth, and you can tell us.

Once we were all seated and had fresh drinks, I recounted the story for them.

"Orson and Veston Montespan are both dead. We would be dead if it weren't for the vampire Malik. He held off the Order's police force until we could escape. I have no idea if he survived the blast."

"Then it's over," Rafael said.

"Not quite. Lots of influential local people were at the meeting. The police have apparently tied Darth to a missing deckhand on the towboat Emma Lou. I have a feeling after last night's explosion he'll be on their radar."

"Oh, no!" Sister Lydia said.

As I was speaking, Tommy O'Rear and Marlon Bando came through the door. They headed over to the booth after seeing us.

"Looks like we're about to find out," Tony said.

Both Tommy and Marlon were smiling as they scooted in beside us.

"Where's Lilly and Avory?" Tommy asked.

"On their way back to Hollywood," Bertram said as he brought their Abita and pineapple juice. "You two boys slumming again?"

"Exactly what we're doing," Tommy said. "It's a slow day, so we dropped by for a drink."

"You're not looking for Darth Heaney?" I asked.

"Not after the explosion down by the docks last night," Tommy said. "The Chief told us to can the investigation and move on to something else."

"Did he now?" I said. "What happened?"

"Me and Marlon were wondering the same thing ourselves," Tommy said.

"Departmental politics," Marlon said.

"More like departmental bullshit," Tommy said. "Whatever, as long as Darth Heaney keeps his nose clean, he's off the hook with us."

"Anything else?" Rafael asked.

"Yeah," Tommy said. "The mayor, two prominent business owners, a judge, and a couple of bankers are missing. Thinking is they were somehow involved in last night's explosion."

"That's going to shake up the local power structure," Rafael said. He glanced at his watch. "I hate to drink and run, but my ship is sailing today. See you when I return."

"I'll walk out with you," Tony said.

"Us too," Tommy said.

Sister Lydia moved closer to me. "You did a wonderful job," she said. "I can't thank you enough."

"What's the Greater Archdiocese of New Orleans intend to do with the satanic altar?" I asked.

"Just like any other place that's more than two hundred years old, the Old Ursuline Convent has had a checkered past. It's now a museum. The Archdiocese intends to open up the altar to the public and highlight it's historical significance."

Sister Lydia grinned when I asked, "What will the Vatican think about the smear on the church's reputation?"

"Protestants once called the Pope the Antichrist. The church survived that crisis and many more since then. Trust me when I tell you we'll still be around two hundred years from now."

After Sister Lydia had departed, I returned to the bar. The day was warmer, the outside temperature limiting the number of tourists on the street. Bertram topped up my lemonade.

"What did Avory tell you?" he asked.

"Not much. She didn't even say goodbye," I said.

"She'll be back," he said.

"How do you know?"

"For one thing, she rented a house in the Quarter. She and Lilly have decided to write and produce the movie themselves. She told me she'd be putting you on retainer when she returns to film the movie. How do you feel about that?"

I smiled. "She's a lot of trouble, but if you had to share a foxhole with someone, you couldn't pick a better person to do it with than her. What else?"

Bertram placed a single white rose on the bar in front of me.

"She told me to give you this. She said you'd know what it means."

End

Book Notes

Though *New Orleans Dangerous* is fictional, most of the historical details in it are real. The Old Ursuline Convent on Chartres Street exists. The little room where the satanic ceremony was performed is real, as is the inscription on the chalice.

Most of the French history in the book is correctly represented. Madam de Montespan was actually the mistress of Louis XIV. She did pay to have a Black Mass performed while she lay naked on a satanic altar, a chalice on her bare stomach and black candles in her hand.

The Kolly House plaque at the corner of Chartres and Bienville is really there, and it was the first location for the Ursuline Convent. The maze Avory, Wyatt and Rafael were looking for was actually near the intersection of Chartres and Bienville in 1727. While I don't know if Jean-Daniel Kolly was a Satanist, he probably was a Freemason.

The attic of the Old Ursuline Convent is definitely off-limits from public viewing. If it's empty then why is it protected by a modern alarm system? Yes, the Casket Girls were real. Some say they carried their worldly goods in a small overnight case called a casquette and thus the name. To me, traveling thousands of miles with nothing more than an overnight case seems implausible. If you check the historical dates closely, you'll see the timeline of events don't correlate with the timeline of the Old Ursuline Convent. I think it suggests manipulation by someone trying to find plausibility for an alternate history of what really happened.

I hope you enjoyed reading *New Orleans Dangerous* as much as I enjoyed writing it, and that you liked Wyatt Thomas, my moody private investigator. If you did, please consider leaving a review, and reading the other seven books in the French Quarter Mystery Series. You may also like my Paranormal Cowboy Series which includes Ghost of a Chance, Bones of Skeleton Creek and Blink of an Eye. Please watch for the upcoming French Quarter Mystery #9 coming in 2020.

Thanks for being a fan. Without wonderful readers like you, my stories would be little more than morning fog wafting across a forgotten lawn before disappearing forever into the Great Unknown.

About the Author

Born on a sleepy bayou, Louisiana Mystery Writer Eric Wilder grew up listening to his grandmothers' tales of ghosts, magic, and voodoo. He's the author of thirteen novels, four cookbooks, many short stories, and Murder Etouffee, a book that defies classification. His two series feature P.I.s adept in the investigation of the paranormal. He lives in Oklahoma near historic Route 66 with wife Marilyn, three wonderful dogs, and one great cat. Follow Eric on Facebook at Louisiana Mystery Writer.